Skip,

I truly be_____,
us together for this!

Thank you for being
willing to take the risk!

Will

John 5:24

Will

Riley

Hinton

Lonely are the Hunted

Book one in the Rocky Mountain Odyssey adventure series.

Published by White Feather Press. (www.whitefeatherpress.com)

ISBN   978-0-9766083-5-6

Printed in the United States of America

Interior photo by Jeff Campbell, courtesy of Byron and Sandra Sadler of Two Dot Ranch - Texas

Exterior cover photo ©iStockphoto.com/Cynthia Baldauf

White Feather Press

Reaffirming Faith in God, Family, and Country!

I would like to dedicate this book to my mother, Hazel, who taught me to think as adventurously as possible and to Riley "Gramps" Davis, who was my male role model regarding horses as well as my mentor for everyday life.

ONE

The hot, early fall sun felt good on Dan Kade's back as he crossed the Metzal Valley at an angle that would intercept the road running down the other side. Being fairly new to the area, he was still spending a lot of time learning the lay of the land.

Six feet of slender, rawboned youth, he was the fifth son of John and Suzan Kade; and the only one who remained with them at home. Of the other four brothers, only two had been heard of since the war between the states, and they had chosen to forsake the life of the horse rancher for lives spent in the settlements; drinking and carousing away what money they didn't lose gambling.

Art, the oldest, was a huge man who earned what he could as a blacksmith, when he worked at all; and Martin, just one year older than Dan, hunted meat for the townsfolk.

They were both outgoing, gregarious, and quite lovable; but with no sense of purpose in their lives. This had long been a source of grief and sorrow to John and Sue, and they spent long hours on their knees on the boys' behalf.

Dan had been different from his first breath. A sensitive, caring person, he was too young for the war and had grown to manhood astride a horse. His temperament made him a natural at breaking horses, and there had been few horses that he couldn't gentle. As a result, he was held in high esteem as a wrangler in spite of his youth, and at 24 years of age, was much in demand for his services.

But the shame of Art and Martin's activities had told its tale on the lives of their folks and when the opportunity to purchase a ranch a hundred miles to the west arose, it was too good to pass up. They'd been on the new place just a month, with two hundred head of horses for a start , and had quickly grown to love the valley.

During that time Dan and his folks had been to the town of Metzal only twice for supplies, and were still unfamiliar with most of the people of the area. It was on the first of those trips that Dan met Ira Nelson. He was instantly drawn to the kindly old rancher and as they visited, Dan learned of the area, the ranchers, and Mr. Nelson's love for beautiful horses. They spent more than an hour talking horses and growing a friendship that both felt would become a focal point in their lives. It wasn't a spoken feeling, just something that each felt and sensed was mutual.

That first trip was also the time that John was questioned in a rude, crude, and very rough manner by the local sheriff and his deputy, Max and Jules Chelsea. They were nothing more than elected ruffians who had fooled the county at election time and now ruled with gun and fist as though they enjoyed inflicting pain on those unfortunate people they chose to hassle.

At that point they had deliberately killed three men in less than two years, men who had tried to surrender. The last one had, in fact, done so right in the middle of town before half the townsfolk. He was taken into custody, safe and sound, only to be found beaten to death in his cell the next morning. Strangely, neither sheriff nor chief deputy "could imagine" how it happened.

There had been a general outcry from the townspeople, but it soon died out under the scathing stares and comments from the Chelsea brothers.

It was for this reason Dan was riding the ten miles to town. He had fretted and stewed for days over the mistreatment of his father; a quiet, gentle man. The memory of Max Chelsea pulling his father from the seat of their spring wagon and shaking him roughly as he questioned him of his business and his former home.

The memory continually goaded him day and night until it grew into a hate and he had never hated a man before. That roused him to hate even more because Max Chelsea had opened him up to a weakness he had never before experienced. It became a vicious circle.

Finally, he saddled a young gelding that needed work to overcome a skittishness and headed for Metzal. It proved to be a very fateful decision, though he couldn't know it now.

Dan had no idea what he was going to do or say to Sheriff Chelsea. He only knew they had to reach the understanding that his dad was not to be touched or subjected to such roughness again. He was not a gunman, though he wore a Colt and was accurate with it. There had been only one fight in his life, that in third grade, and he had lived peacefully since. The tough life so often found in the western ranges had escaped the K-D Ranch and his brothers were the closest thing to ruffians he had ever known.

Whatever ensued when he met up with the Chelsea brothers, he was a very determined young man; not to be pushed from his chosen course.

The quick raising of the gelding's head and the sideways dance he hoped to work out of the young mount broke into his thoughts and brought him back to the present with a start.

There were two riders on the road who were about to intercept his course and as he fought to rein in the skittish bronc, they didn't help any by yelling "Howdy!" and waving.

The gelding was settling down as he drew alongside the two. "Good mornin'," he drawled as he looked the pair over.

"Howdy," replied the larger of the two. "I'm Tom Seever and this homely gent is Candy Johnston."

"Pleased to meet you, I'm Dan Kade," he answered, "You fellas from around here?"

"Heck no," was Johnston's reply, "We're just passin' through; headed south outta here. I want to get away from anything that even remotely resembles Arizona!"

"You gotta' overlook him, Dan, he's got a bad case of the Ari-

zona blues," was Tom's comment, "he really don't mean nothin'
against your beautiful country here."

"Say," Dan told them, "that's okay, I'm new around here
myself and so far I'm not all that familiar with things. I've come
to love this range, though. It's all the people that sold it to us said
it would be. Besides, the only thing south of here is desert and
Mexico."

"I really don't care which it is, as long as it don't have bars
on it!" said Candy.

"He got railroaded into prison up Flagstaff way. Wasn't none
of his doin', but it cost him three years that wasn't any fun. I
spent that time workin' close by waitin' for him to get out so I
could keep him from turnin' loose on those crooked hellions that
framed him. Didn't want to see him right back in, or worse,"
Tom told Dan.

"Tom Seever, how's come ya gotta always be answerin' for
me?" Candy asked, feigning anger, "Cain't I talk fer m'self?"

The closeness and camaraderie of the two had become very
obvious to Dan and he smiled at the gentle bantering that continued on. He could also see that the prison term had certainly
taken its toll on the otherwise seemingly carefree Candy Johnston.

He seemed to Dan to be a very confused mixture of former
jokester turned present angry young man. The bitterness he
harbored was obvious.

Within a few miles, however, as the three bantered back and
forth, he became quite enthralled with meeting these two. They
were the typical young cowboy of the west's ranges; fun-loving,
carefree, but willing to work themselves to death for someone
they respected. It didn't take long to feel an established friendship with them. Much like he felt towards the horse loving
rancher, Mr. Nelson.

By the time they reached town he had shared with them the
valley's beauty, and the town's shortcomings; mostly the Chelseas. Candy, in particular, seemed rather alarmed at that, and
even suggested to Tom that they ride around the county seat and
avoid any possible contact with the ilk of the Chelsea brothers.

"Now, Candy, you've paid your debt, and you've got your

papers to prove it, so there's nothing to worry about. We'll just pick up some grub to pack on with and move out,"

It was then that Dan's breath was taken away. He spotted the most beautiful sorrel mare he'd ever seen in his life. A tall, rangy, firm-limbed creature with flowing mane and tail all decked out in a saddle that was trimmed for show and had never seen or felt the burn of a dallied rope on the silver crested saddle horn. This had to be Sheba, the wonderful mare Mr. Nelson had spent a full twenty minutes talking about.

She stood hip shot at the hitching rail in front of the general store on the left, with a bridle rein simply laid over the rail; an indication of her temperament and training.

Only two months shy of her third birthday, Dan could see how the kindly rancher could be thrilled at the thought of producing a great strain of horses through her.

It was then that he was snatched from his revelry by the harsh voice from the right side of the street.

"Hey, you three there, hold up!"

Tom Seever quickly hauled in and said, "Yes sir, what can we do for you?"

Dan's heart leapt to his throat and beat so hard it hurt. It was the Chelseas', and Max was the one who had hailed them!

"Lemme have a look at you three!", he growled, "Down off them horses, and keep yore hands high!"

"But, sheriff", began Candy. He got no further. Jules Chelsea, standing off to the right on the board sidewalk with rifle in hand, cut him off.

"Max, I've seen that fella up at the prison when I delivered a prisoner, he must have escaped! Look how pale he is."

Max Chelsea was in the middle of the street now, and had grabbed the bridle of Tom's horse. The animal was very nervous over this and danced sideways, pulling and jerking against the strong, hairy arm that gripped it.

Max yelled, "Hold that nag in check you, and all three of ya, drop them guns, easy like."

But Candy tried reasoning with the two ignorant, kill-minded brothers.

"No, you're all wrong. I've served my time and have my

6

release papers! They're right here."

"NO!", yelled Tom, "don't reach for 'em!"

But it was too late. Candy, in his fear and frustration, darted his hand to his shirt pocket under his vest.

The shout, "Look Out!," from Max and the roar of Jules' rifle were simultaneous. In his lust to conquer, Jules had seen his chance to cry self defense and fired.

All was bedlam instantly. Dan's young gelding literally exploded into the air at the sound; Seever's mount reared so hard that Max Chelsea was lifted from the street. As he fought to keep his seat and wits at the same time, Dan saw, as though through a fog, the lifeless body of Candy, half his face shot away, falling under Dan's own pitching mount.

In seemingly slow motion, and very far away, he heard more shots, both rifle and handgun, and felt a sudden shock go through his mount, seeing at the same time the horrible hole from the forty four-forty rifle slug appear in the sleek neck. Then he was pitching forward from the falling horse. As he smashed into the street he saw Seever trying to crawl to the sidewalk, streaming blood from seemingly all over.

Then he was vaguely aware of leaping, stamping horse's hooves near his head; and as he instinctively rolled over on to his feet and leaped erect; a silver crested saddle horn flashed almost into his face. His next move was purely instinctive. The horn was there, within reach, and he just grabbed it!

His arms were instantly jerked nearly from his shoulders as the totally panicked horse leaped forward into a full gallop within three jumps. Dan pulled himself up onto the horse, executed a pony express mount, and no sooner hit the saddle than he heard strange buzzing sounds go by.

The reality of those sounds struck him like a train. Bullets! They were firing at him!

Dan Kade had never even been close to a gun battle in his life, but he could ride. As few others in fact, and he instantly rolled to the right side of the horse, hooking a spur behind the cantle and a hand in the fork.

He felt a tremendous shock on that left hand, and a horrible numbing. Looking up as he hung on the side of the speeding horse, he saw the fancy silver saddle horn was nearly shredded by a bullet.

Then it dawned on him, he was riding Sheba, Ira Nelson's beloved mare! The main street was slightly curved in Metzal and Dan pulled the mare to the right side of the street to put buildings between himself, the mare, and those horrible men as quickly as possible.

Then it happened, as he started to pull himself up to the saddle the mare screamed and leaped frantically sideways as a slug buzzed by. He could tell she'd been hit, and his pounding heart nearly broke.

Yet, the wonderful stride returned, and in fact, lengthened, as the game animal stretched out to a steady run that brought her to where it seemed as though her belly was at sage grass level. Dan had ridden few horses her equal in speed, and his eyes fairly watered at the whipping of the wind in his face.

A mile out of town he turned in the saddle to look back and see two riders hard on his trail already. He saw something else, too. Blood! Then he breathed easier. The slug had dug a furrow along the mare's rump, but no more blood seemed to flow from it. She wasn't hit hard, and that meant he might still escape. Indeed the sorrel was easily outdistancing the pursuers.

He pulled her down from an all-out run to conserve her wind and set course to the east side of the valley and the many canyons and draws it afforded for cover. They were going to make it, he and this marvelous steed. They would escape!

Two

Ira Nelson was a very steady individual, having been tempered into a tough, but resilient steel sort of man by the hardships of being one of the first settlers and ranchers in this area of Arizona. Four things in his life guided his decisions and actions, and these four governing factors entered into his thoughts nearly every waking moment.

All four were based on love. The first was his faith in an Almighty and Supreme being. The second was his love for his wife that still consumed him years after the harsh frontier had become too much for her frailty, claiming her life at a very youthful forty years. That was twenty years ago. The third was the close family ties with his sister and her husband, also horse ranchers, several hundred miles to the north in Idaho, and the fourth was his love for horses and people in general. Sometimes he was accused of placing the horses before people and he reckoned maybe at times that was sure enough right. But he could usually tell what a horse was going to do, not so with people!

For whatever reason he felt compelled to step outside for some fresh air even though the smells in Figy's General Store were always a pleasure to him. Art Figy also owned the livery stable and feed store, with the latter right next door, allowing smells of the freshly ground corn, oats and wheat to filter into the general store. Mingle those with the pickle barrel, the wonderful smell of leather goods and many other things and it was a nice place to be, but he needed air.

Being a man of years, with instincts developed by dealing with man and beast in nearly every type of situation, the hair on the back of Ira's neck tingled and his skin crawled at the sound of Max Chelsea's voice as he challenged the three horsemen. He knew instantly that trouble was inevitable. He quickly moved to his left to get out of the line of fire from Jules' rifle. Oh, how he hated it that he hadn't worn a side arm today. If he had, he'd have drawn it instantly and fired into the air to get the Chelsea's attention in an attempt to avert tragedy.

But all he could do was yell at Jules to lower his rifle, only to realize no one heard him above the stamping of three nervous and nickering horses.

He plainly heard Candy though, as he informed all of his release. Ira also saw with near panic that the young man was going to reach for the paper and knew that such a move was all the Chelseas needed.

With old eyes that had seen Indians fall from his own guns, had learned to discern details in the heat of battle, both with red men and Mexican, as well as with white marauders, he determined his best course was to see all the details he could in order to once and for all rid the county of these two paid killers.

He saw Candy die instantly from Jules' rifle, and Tom Seever claw for his gun as Max poured shot after shot point blank into him while the elder Chelsea still gripped the rearing horse's bridle. Ira noted this about the two strangers and then was totally taken aback. A cold feeling that completely gripped him as he recognized young Dan Kade!

By then, Jules' rifle had spoken twice more; missing Dan, but taking his horse from under him. The cold increased in Ira Nelson's stomach as he saw Sheba tear by the falling gelding in fear and Dan's hands grab the saddle horn of the leaping mare as he vaulted astride, only to roll to the right side away from Jules as the speeding sorrel was at top speed instantly.

He watched helplessly as bullet after bullet went down the street and when the horse screamed and leaped sideways at full speed his heart nearly stopped.

But after the one break in stride, she pounded out of sight

around the buildings and suddenly Ira Nelson became furious. One man was needlessly dead for sure, another was trying to crawl away, and one of the finest young men he'd ever met was running for his life. Worse yet, Ira's 44-40 was in the scabbard on a saddle that was a quarter mile away by now! He tore into the street, around the dead horse and ran up to Max Chelsea, who was walking calmly up to Tom Seever's blood soaked body.

As Chelsea deliberately raised his pistol to finish the job, the range-toughened old man hit him full force in the ear with an iron fist, followed by his running body smashing Max to the ground.

Slightly stunned, the huge man bounded quickly to his feet; raising his hand to Ira, then realized he'd dropped the Colt when the old fellow clubbed him. That same .45 was only an inch from his nose at full cock, and steady as a rock. Behind that prospect of death were two of the coldest blue eyes Max Chelsea had ever stared into.

"Chelsea, if you even blink, I'm gonna kill you like a dog. You got that?"

"Listen you, you're interfering with the law and I'll lock you up for that old man, and we'll see how you hold up in a cell!" Max spat at him.

"Max, you are exactly one finger twitch from losing what few brains you ever had, and your brother is about to make me pull this trigger. As to you ever locking anyone up again, forget it; plenty of people just watched you murder one innocent boy, maybe two. I aim to see to it that you're hung for it. Now, tell Jules to lay that rifle down. Now!"

Something in the old man's voice warned the Chelseas' that it was not going to be a good day from that point on. But though they were unscrupulous, they were also smart, and both realized the town was afraid to cross them, Ira Nelson or no Ira Nelson.

Jules simply climbed astride the nearest horse, which happened to be Seever's, and tore off down the street in the direction Dan Kade had ridden. When Ira wheeled to take him down with the Colt, Max grabbed his arm and forced the gun from his hand. Then, in a typical act of brutality, he kicked the old rancher in the stomach, grabbed another horse, and yelled down as he mounted:

"We'll be back old man, and if you're still around, you're not gonna like what happens."

The savage kick had doubled the old fellow over, and he wavered there on his knees in the dust. As Max and horse disappeared, people ran up to both he and Tom Seever, now laying there in the blood-soaked dirt, seemingly dead.

Bill Curry, the saloon owner, called out from beside Johnson, "This young feller's gone, half his head shot away!"

Art Figy ran from the general store to examine Ira but, when growled at, went as directed to Tom Seever. "He's still alive, Ira, but he ain't gonna make it. Cain't have any blood left in him; he's got lead in him in at least four places, all in really bad spots but the one in his arm."

Ira had regained enough breath to bark at them, "Get him up to Doc Pritchart's, if he's got just one breath left there's hope. And I want a town meeting in the saloon in ten minutes, and you all better be there or you'll answer to me. Now get!"

Few men in this part of Arizona had spawned the respect this lean old rancher commanded; even fewer did it in as quiet a way and when people heard Ira Nelson bark out in this totally uncharacteristic manner, they jumped to comply.

The young body, "shot to rags," as one fellow put it, was loaded on a cot and carried to Doc Pritchart's where the good doctor immediately began to care for the bleeding.

Then word was passed about town for the meeting. They all knew that Ira had picked the saloon simply because it held more people than any other building in town, so no one had an excuse to not show up.

So it was, that when the Chelseas' returned a couple of hours later, they found all the townsfolk gathered in their "watering hole." They also discovered "that confounded old rancher" hadn't run; but was conducting a meeting designed to first oust the Chelseas from office, and next, to charge them with murder.

Tension was very high and the brothers made some threats then backed off just enough to let the threats sink in as the people cooled off. Thus it was that the meeting broke up with nothing yet resolved.

THREE

The late afternoon sun found Dan Kade and Sheba in the high country on the East rim of Metzal Valley. Dan had headed directly for the canyon area two miles from the K-D Ranch in an effort to disappear. It had proven to be a good choice.

The east side of Metzal Valley is an array of rough, furrow-like canyons; cut into the mountain range by years of run-off. They stretched from the high bluff that marked the cessation of valley and beginning of mountains like the fingers of some giant hand that had wanted to wander, but couldn't decide where. They crisscrossed one another, ended in box canyons, or just petered out into steep ascents far too treacherous to climb, but still covered with pinions and cedars. They had all the appearance of a hat full of giant stones dumped into the middle of a cedar lawn and left where they had landed.

The cedar growth was augmented in places by pinions and aspen alike, with spots between that appeared as small parks. These were areas that were void of trees but teeming with belly-high grass and wildflowers. Each of these parks seemed as magnets to deer and other wild animals, for bounding figures seemed present in each such area that Dan passed through. "Martin would love this," was a thought that passed through his mind time and time again as though attempting to push out the troubled thoughts that continuously assailed him.

Though Dan had not been raised in the mountains, he was smart enough to take note of his trails and the various landmarks so as to be able to either back-track, or to find this same way up to the rim once again.

It seemed that blind luck had caused him to stumble onto the crevice. He and Sheba had just entered one of the small parks when they spooked a small band of wild horses. The mare's whinny set the group to flight instantly and they tore off to the north through some junipers and simply disappeared into the side of a cliff!

"Hey girl, let's have a look at that," Dan said to the excited mare. He galloped her in that direction. It seemed as if the five wild horses must have just melted until he found the outcropping stone that appeared to be the marker for an entrance to yet another narrow canyon. And indeed, if one went to the left past the huge rock at least three stories high, he found himself in a very narrow canyon with room for maybe three horses abreast. But the bottom was sandy for a short stretch, and there were no horse tracks.

Now really curious, Dan eyed an extremely narrow crack by the back of the high outcropping and upon dismounting, he led Sheba to it and found that they could fit through. As a precaution, he tied the mare and loosened the cinch, deciding to first check things out alone. He drew the old rancher's well worn rifle from the scabbard and checked the loads. Then, after removing his spurs he slipped into the narrow opening and found he was facing a crevice that led upward in a curving path to the right, back towards the face of the cliff that rose above him. It remained narrow, and Dan realized the mare wouldn't fit through with him in the saddle; it was that close.

As he climbed laboriously upward, the crack appeared to dead end. But when he reached that point, he found that it veered sharply to the left. It was just around the sharp corner that he spotted the still-steaming droppings of one of the wild horses. That was enough to convince him that Sheba could make it. He returned and untied the mare and pulled the stirrups of the ornate saddle up over the seat and tied them together. Even in this time of great stress he thought of old Ira Nelson and didn't want this passage to scratch up the finely tooled leather if he could help it.

It took absolutely no coaxing at all to get Sheba to follow him and he got the feeling that he could just loop the reins over the saddle horn and the obedient and faithful horse would tag along. This was, indeed, what he ended up doing once around the sharp left turn, as the ascent became much steeper with several more abrupt direction changes on the way.

Over an hour later, sweating profusely and limping on feet that were sore from the rock-strewn passage, they finally broke out on top after a final ten to fifteen feet of very steep and dangerous climbing.

As he pulled to help the struggling mare up the final climb, he looked back and realized that the trail appeared to be nothing more than a crack in the rock, falling rapidly and ending quickly against one of those abrupt turns. The top was as well hidden as the bottom.

He very carefully surveyed the area; taking special note of all possible landmarks so he could find the trail again should he need it.

"Good land, Sheba! Here I am, already thinking like a criminal," he spoke to the mare, who cocked her ears forward in apparent interest at what he had to say.

Dan led off through the forest, still walking to both give his legs some time to loosen up and to rest the faithful horse. My, but she was impressing him more with each step. He was sure going to hate to return her to Ira. He could see why the old fella went on so about her.

After half an hour of moving back south he mounted up and put another mile behind them at a brisk walk. Then, on impulse, he turned towards where he thought the rim should be. Another fifteen minutes and the pair of them broke suddenly out of the forest to gasp in wonderment at the stunning panorama that spread out before them!

They were on the rim that looked down on Metzal Valley, and the entire valley spread out before them as if drawn on paper. As Dan surveyed the beauty with awestruck eyes he realized he was only two miles from the K-D Ranch! He could see the buildings about a mile to the left and a mile out from the base of the huge promontory. They looked tiny and unreal from so high and lofty a perch.

With further scrutiny, he realized he was on the highest point of the rim on the east side of the valley. He had known the Metzal Valley was an exceptionally beautiful place; but this view told him all he had heard was not even close to doing the area justice. Why, he could even make out the town nearly fifteen miles from his perch; almost in a straight line from the ranch to the point where he sat.

The valley, all of ten miles wide and nearly fifty long, curved gently as it meandered from near the Tonto basin to the south where it then spread wide into first an area of sparsely vegetated plains and then desert. As it made its way south, cutting a green, flat swath in the rich forests and rocky mountains that bordered it as guardians of a fortress might stand at attention around its walls, it gleaned its nutrients from a stream that flowed continuously over rocks and sand; never more than four feet deep anywhere, but never drying up. This was Ice Creek, actually nearer to being a river than a creek.

An increasing chill in the air stirred him from his tranquility, and he realized that the shadows of the far wall, nearly unbroken, were stealing nearer, and dusk was about to make its way into the light, to turn it rapidly away and separate it quickly from the darkness known as night, as if to prevent the two from ever meeting.

"Old horse, I'd say you and me are in for a bad time up here. We're out here with no food and probably no heat. I have no blankets, and you have no warm stall with straw in it!" Dan spoke softly to his companion.

She answered him with the same cocked-forward ears as before, turning to look at him as if to size up his real feelings. Dan turned her back into the forest of tall oaks and began searching for a protected area. He soon found what he was looking for and dismounted.

After stripping the saddle, he laid it down and searched the saddle bags for hobbles, which he doubted he would need, but he intended to take no chances. All intentions aside, he had no choice, as there were none.

He found matches, however, and was beside himself with the

joy of the prospect of a fire. There were also the necessary trappings for fishing, a rather powerful looking telescope, a box of 44-40 ammunition, as yet unopened, and some salt in an oilskin pouch.

The other saddle bag offered up a very small frying pan, sugar cubes, probably intended for Sheba, some beef jerky, and a small bag of flour. It looked like old Ira Nelson loved the taste of fresh trout from Ice Creek and kept himself prepared to enjoy such a fair at any time. Dan figured he might just owe his new friend a lot for that taste.

He had no recourse for Sheba but to slip her bridle and allow her to graze in the tiny glade that his little nook in the rocks overlooked. He surely hoped that morning wouldn't find him on foot. If only the old fella would have carried a rope on his saddle.

"What kinda horse rancher is your boss, that he doesn't carry a rope, anyway, Sheba?" he queried the now munching horse. He laughed aloud as those ears went forward and he found himself looking square into the two huge, soft brown eyes of the horse.

"You're sure something, lady," he chuckled, "Nearly human, I'd say."

Her only answer was to return to her grazing and select another mouthful of the rich grass from the floor of the open glade.

Hoping to find some small game, Dan took up the Winchester and trudged off into the rapidly darkening forest, only to come up empty handed. He'd missed meals before, but seldom two in a row. Breakfast tomorrow would make it three!

"Oh well," he thought. He built a fire in the nook, took the saddle blanket for warmth, and attempted to rest, comforting himself with the knowledge that the fire was completely hidden from the valley.

As night fell and tiredness set in with a vengeance, he attempted to sleep, but sleep came hard to a man who had seen his two young companions shot to death for no reason other than man's desire to conquer fellow man. When he did sleep, on those rare and brief occasions, the horrible sight of Candy's face haunted his dreams, and the sight of young and carefree Tom

Seever crawling with his last strength ebbing into the dust, still trying to survive when it was already too late.

Twice he arose to restock the fire, as the saddle blanket just wouldn't cover much of him at a time, and the parts left uncovered rapidly chilled through and through. It gets absolutely bone-chattering cold at the higher elevations and fall was fast approaching.

The last time he stoked the fire, he built a second, just four feet from the first. He piled on the deadwood and lay between them. It was in this manner that he finally fell into an exhausted sleep for the last two hours before first light.

Dan awakened with a start, grabbed for his sidearm as he did so, and realized that the faithful mare was nuzzling his cheek and softly "whuff, whuffing" as she awakened him.

Dan was instantly aware of two overwhelming thoughts. The first was his continually growing astonishment at this wonderful horse who seemed to be nearly human. The second was hunger.

The hunger was so intense that it actually hurt. He slipped off into the underbrush in hopes of shooting some small game, and was able to do so when a hapless squirrel sat scolding him. He knocked it down with his Colt and hurried back to his fire to feast on it. After dressing it out, he cooked it on a green branch for all of five minutes before he tore into the hot but nearly raw little rodent. For whatever reason, and in some mysterious, not yet understood manner, the body has a way of blocking out the negatives such as this when hunger becomes pain, and Dan Kade's was no exception for he devoured the whole thing.

With his hunger pangs quickly becoming memories, he saddled up and rode the short distance to the rim in a matter of five minutes. It was his intention to scope out the valley and see if there were hunting parties out looking for him.

He had already decided that to ride in and surrender would mean certain death. The Chelseas had demonstrated that all too well. Thus it was that his fears steadily built upon themselves.

Dan had just spent a night in physical misery, emotional hell, and with building fear, so when the round revealing circle of his telescope settled on two riders approaching the K-D ranch from separate directions, and in obvious stealth, his whole nervous system jumped. Instantly he was completely overwhelmed with a cold, gnawing fear that seemed to pump through his veins.

The glass of Ira Nelson's was indeed a powerful one, and with the ranch being two miles away and fifteen hundred feet below it still brought the riders close enough to plainly recognize the Chelseas! His chest instantly heaved with a terrible pounding and shortness of breath. A dread for his folks nearly sent him reeling. And, as the tableau unfolded, a distinctly changed Dan Kade began to emerge.

The K-D ranch house faced south, just on the edge of a grove of oak trees to the north and west of it, with the barn, corrals, and bunk house to the east. At this time, there were no hired hands at the ranch, as Dan and his dad had been doing everything themselves. Two hired hands were in the plans, but this task had not yet been taken care of.

Dan could see his dad forking hay over the corral fence into a bunch of yearlings that John and Dan had been working with. Dan felt a sudden pang of regret that his dad had to do his chores. He should be there! This was quickly replaced with the returning dread.

He was frozen to the spot as Max rounded the corner of the barn from the east, gun in hand, and accosted John Kade. He watched as the two exchanged heated words, with the exchange ending abruptly when Chelsea grabbed John and pushed him towards the ranch house. He marched him to the front door as Jules came into view around the west end of the house; his ever present rifle in hand.

Dan's heart beat so hard and fast that his head swam with dizziness. It got worse when he saw the Chelseas emerge alone and head for the barn, splitting up with one entering the front and one going into the rear. Shortly thereafter Suzan Kade came out of the house with a rifle and let fly into the air with two shots. Dan could hear them moments after he saw the puff of smoke. They seemed flat and far away, but still quite distinct.

The Chelseas backed out of the barn, only to be driven back by two more shots aimed in their direction. Sue Kade was fightin' mad, and ready to go the full distance! That full distance didn't take long. Shortly after those shots, the brothers drove the stabled horses from the barn in a bunch while running alongside them in the process to get close to Sue Kade and her rifle.

It was Jules who got the job done. When Max tripped and fell, Sue's attention quickly focused on him and that allowed Jules to get by her, then leap out of the quickly moving mass of horseflesh to club her down. She lay there motionless.

Dan was rooted to the spot as he saw them drag his mother into the house, only to emerge a short time later to head for the barn. As they emerged from the barn rather quickly, Dan focused back on the house in desperation, only to see instead of a sign of human life, wisps of smoke starting to rise from the open windows. They had fired the house!

He quickly looked back to the barn to see a repeat of the smoke there! For what ever reason, the bunkhouse was ignored. The Chelseas mounted up, sat for a few minutes to watch their handiwork on the house, and then rode away at a gallop.

Dan was physically sick, and the violence towards his beloved parents was so shocking that he spent several minutes losing the squirrel. He knelt weakly in the grass, alternately catching his breath and sobbing out his grief. He knew that the hidden trail was several minutes away, and probably as long to descend in time as it had taken to climb. There was nothing he could immediately do to rescue them.

He finally got hold of himself, and as he began to do so, the gentleness of his nature slipped into hiding as a lust to kill began to emerge. He vaulted into the saddle and spurred the mare north towards the trail down.

It was two hours later when the lathered mare pounded into the ranch yard, and by then both buildings were nearly gone. The roofs on both buildings had collapsed while the walls were merely low vertical sections of charred and still-burning wood. Dan loosened the cinch to allow the horse to blow, pulled the bit from her mouth so she could graze, and went to the bunkhouse.

There he retrieved a rope some long gone cowboy had forgotten along with a few canned peaches that had been overlooked. There was also a packsaddle in the tack room at the back of the bunkhouse, so he grabbed it and headed for the corrals.

There he opened the gates to the yearlings and drove them out, suddenly thankful that no horses had perished in the barn. Small comfort, but sometimes a little comfort goes a long way.

He then stepped into the corral with the older riding stock and quickly roped a small, sturdy bay gelding he knew would easily submit to a pack saddle but would have lots of stamina.

When he had the bay saddled he coiled the rope and tied it onto the ornate saddle of Ira Nelson's beloved Sheba. He knew then there was every possibility that neither he nor Sheba would ever see Ira again. He hated taking her, but the bay was the only horse at the ranch with any staying power, for the good stock had run off when the Chelseas drove them from the barn.

Slipping the bit back in the mare's mouth, he tightened the cinch, mounted and headed for Metzal. This trip was different, he sensed, for this time it was he who had killing on his mind. It didn't feel good.

FOUR

Several hours later, Dan tied the now-laden pack horse to one of several trees in a small grove halfway to the ranch. He had slipped into town from the east, not using the road and arrived at the back of Figy's store. He wasn't sure how he'd handle any questions, but found the concern was all for nothing as the store was unlocked and deserted.

This seemed strange to Dan, but he availed himself of the opportunity and gathered supplies for a long trip, trying to think of everything but knowing he'd miss something important. After he had the bay packed, he returned and left a list of his purchases on the counter, along with all the money in his pockets, and a voucher for Art Figy to select enough horses to pay for everything not covered.

He then left a letter to Ira Nelson asking him to oversee the ranch and notify his brothers of the travesty. He also promised to return Sheba at the earliest opportunity; and finally, apologized for all wrongdoing and grief he was about to cause. Then he'd ridden out the same way he came in and secured the pack animal in the grove.

Thus it was that at eleven o'clock he rode into town via the main street with a double barreled ten gauge shotgun he'd "purchased" at Figy's in his hand, hammers already eared back and ready to fire. The thong was off of the hammer on his Colt, and to any who would have seen him, he would have appeared to have been a fighting man for most of his life, such was his demeanor.

Even though his fury burned deep and hot because of the terrible events of the last twenty four hours, his stomach was in knots and his nerves were as taut and barbed as a newly strung fence wire.

Questions and doubts assailed him in unending streams. What if the Chelseas saw him first? What if he couldn't pull the triggers? What if he missed? And also, the burden of knowing that what he was doing was wrong weighed heavily.

Approaching the saloon where he figured to find the brothers, he stopped two doors down and dismounted, reining the mare to the hitch rail. The street was so deserted that it was eerie, and this nerved him up even more. He could hear a rousing commotion in the saloon, but before he had time to think about its meaning the Chelseas burst onto the walk from the saloon's swinging doors, guns already in hand!

Max hauled up short, his gun hand starting up at the same time, only to go slack as nine double ought buckshot tore his chest to pieces. Dan simply dropped the ten gauge level and jerked the front trigger all in one motion. Max never knew what hit him. He was dead before he even hit the walk.

The recoil of a ten gauge fired off-hand is rather harsh, to say the least, and Jules was well on his way to leveling that deadly rifle before Dan got the double barrel level again. Dan leaped to the left and yanked the second trigger, the boom of the deadly ten sounding simultaneously with the rifle's sharp report. He saw Jules smashed backwards into the windows of the saloon, crashing out of sight through it, and was not even aware of the whip of the lead slug that tore his sleeve on its errant way past him.

He ran quickly to the nervously dancing Sheba, and for the second time in twenty four hours, sent her flying north out of town, dimly aware of the shouts from behind him. He slung the ten gauge over his back on the small rope sling he'd prepared for such a task, and allowed the magnificent horse to have her head for fully five miles. At that point, he hauled her in a bit and turned off to pick up the pack horse. The mare caught her breath quickly as he untied the bay, and when he rode off leading him, it was at a rapid run with the east rim in mind.

With hard riding, he made the canyon country in a couple of hours, and spent another hour winding in and out of the various canyons to cover his trail, finally reaching the tall outcropping rock that hid his escape route at mid afternoon.

As he tied the stirrups up on Mr. Nelson's saddle, a sudden shock assailed him. The pack saddle! It would never fit up the crevice! He would have to make a couple of trips to get it all through! With his heart once again thundering in his chest, he slapped the mare to start her up the trail, confident she would go on alone.

It was only after she had disappeared around the first turn that the realization struck him that he could have put some things on the riding saddle.

"You're sure thinking clear, Dan Kade," he muttered to himself. He unpacked a large portion of the supplies, shouldered what he could, and struck off up the trail leading the pack animal with its now lightened load.

An hour later, after a tremendous struggle to get the bay up the last steep incline, he rested, tethering the heaving animal to an oak tree and throwing the saddles from both broncs. He had already decided it would be easier to return alone and pack what he could on his own back than fight that bay to get him down there again. Sheba would have easily done it, but he just couldn't bring himself to put a lowly pack saddle on this beautiful animal that was stealing his heart. He glanced her direction, only to find those incredibly intelligent eyes staring at him from below those forward pointing ears.

"Girl, I swear you're human," he said to her. "You almost talk when I see you looking like that, and somehow I get the idea you want to go back down there with me to get everything."

With that soliloquy, he decided to rest for an hour, then he and the mare would go for the rest of the supplies, hoping to avoid detection.

The passage was made as planned, and three hours later as dusk once again began its duties of blending light with dark, he trudged wearily into his previous camp with two tired animals in tow. This time was different, however, as he was equipped for the night and for many nights to come. Yes indeed, this night he would be warm and he would sleep.

He hobbled the bay, leaving a halter on him as well, and let the two horses into the glade to graze. After building a fire, he fixed a very quick and meager meal, not being the least bit hungry, but knowing his body required nourishment. Then he rolled into his bedroll intending to literally die to the world in exhaustion for both his emotions and his body were completely drained.

But such was not to be, for the sudden impact of stopping all physical activity caught up with him and allowed his thoughts to activate. The grief of watching two killers deliberately fire the house with his folks in it wrenched him into agony, and fast on the heels of that shock came the vision of Max Chelsea's shocked look and then blanked eyes as he died on his feet.

Uncontrollable sobs wracked his body, and he was again physically sick. It seemed like days before he stopped trembling, and by the time it happened, he was so weak and wet with sweat that he literally and mercifully passed out. Sleep became his ally from that point, and not even the faithful mare could awaken him until late the next morning.

His fire was out, the sun was already up, and he realized that he needed to be heading back into the mountains post haste. He also realized he had to eat, for he was very weak. He therefore prepared a meal and forced it down, then packed the animals and mounted up. He thought of riding the short distance to the rim for a final look, but couldn't stand the thought of seeing the smoldering ruins that marked his parents' final resting place. So, with the thought of being a hunted man wanted for the murders of two lawmen, the lonely young man rode away with blinding tears streaming down his face.

FIVE

Early October found Dan Kade in the high country north of Flagstaff, very worried about his circumstances with winter at hand. In the distance from Flagstaff to the Grand Canyon, winter hits really early at the higher elevations and he feared for the future of himself and the horses. He knew that if he spent too much time in the high country they could easily be snowed in, and that would spell the end. It was for this reason he pushed north as fast as the animals could take it, realizing the limitations they had because of the thinner air.

Up until now he had carefully avoided all but the smallest settlements and at this point, he'd not seen another man for two weeks. Thus it was that when he awoke one morning he was startled to discover a form sitting by his fire. In fact, how was the fire still going? He eased his hand towards his Colt silently, for the man's back was to him. As his fingers slowly coiled around the handle, the form spoke.

"You don't need that. Ain't loaded anyway."

Dan tensed, then opened the loading gate to see only empty chambers staring back at him. He slipped from his blankets and jerked on his boots, then quickly went to the fire for warmth. Once he was across from his intruder he could see by the fire light that his stealthy camp mate was unmistakably Indian. As the many questions were ready to burst forth the fellow spoke.

"Before you ask, at the mission school near Yuma is your

first answer. The second is Red Elk in your language, you'd never be able to learn how to say it in mine without embarrassing both of us. The third answer is that you young guys are all the same. You sleep like you're dead, and it was easy to unload that Colt so you wouldn't be jumping to any wrong conclusions that could prove costly to a marauding renegade redskin like me."

"The fourth answer is, I got this food from your pack to go with the venison I carried in with me, and the fifth answer is quit asking so many dumb questions and eat before your breakfast gets cold. And have some coffee, just don't take too durned long at it, cause we got to be haulin' our hindsides outta here; snow's on its way in a couple of days, and it'll take us that long to make it down into the canyon."

Dan sat in amazement at this rendition of answers and instructions, and was totally speechless.

"C'mon paleface, eat up; since ya got your mouth open wide enough to swallow a whole prairie chicken you might as well not waste the chance to put something in it."

As Dan calmed himself he observed that a bountiful meal was indeed at his fire. The frying pan held strips of meat and several tiny eggs! Where'd this self proclaimed renegade redskin get eggs?

In a Dutch oven he found sourdough biscuits and with the strong, scalding hot coffee, began to make himself into quite a pig. As he did so, he studied his benefactor closely.

The man appeared to be in his mid 30's, dressed in a combination of "white man" clothes and native; and, obviously, enjoying Dan's plight with lots of joy. Dan stopped eating just long enough to ask, "How do you know snow's coming in two days? Why not three or one?"

"It's called many things by many people," the Indian replied, "but mostly the right word would be, in your language, experience. And to answer the last two questions you get before we move out at sunup, I traded for the Dutch oven with an old prospector, and they're from a prairie hen's nest."

"What is?" Dan asked.

"The eggs, paleface, the eggs. You see, those stupid birds don't lay only in the spring, like most, they lay just like a regular old chicken. Year round. By the way, what's your name? Pale-face seems sort of awkward, cause you're darker than I am. You ain't part Indian are ya?" was his reply.

At this Dan could no longer contain himself and the tension of lonely weeks on a fearful trail suddenly gave way to a spell of uproarious laughter which he didn't even try to suppress.

"My name is Dan Kade," he forced out, "and you are absolutely crazy! I don't even know what my questions were that you 'answered'. And, how come you speak cowboy English betterin' I do, anyway? What kind of school was that?"

"Well," came the reply as he feigned deep hurt, "I worked for a very long time for a cattle ranch as their main wrangler. I was pretty young. Just a kid, really, when I hired on, and just left five "white man" years ago. As to the questions you wanted to know; where I learned English, my name, how'd I get your gun and your food; the last question you get today is, I got tired of one place for so long, so I just lit out. Been ridin' grubstake ever since."

"So you're a wrangler?" Dan replied, "I'm a horse rancher myself. Or rather, was."

"Why you way up here in the high country this time of year? Don't you know the dangers?"

"Well, I sort of do, but I'm hoping to get somewhere soon where I can hole up for the winter," Dan answered.

The Indian's reply came after a thoughtful pause, "If I get you down in that canyon tomorrow that's just about it 'til spring. At least where I'm goin'. But I gotta warn you, if'n you want to hang on to those two horses of yours, you're gonna have to learn to sleep a lot lighter and keep better track o' that hog leg than you did last night. I coulda taken everything but your pants and hightailed it if I'd a wanted to. They's men what use those canyons for wintering that'll cut your throat in your sleep for horseflesh like that. Especially that mare. The bay is a keeper, but that mare is like few I've ever seen before."

Dan's flesh crawled at his new companion's words, for he grasped the truth of them. Yet, he felt he needed to follow this strange and windy mix of cowboy and red man, for he felt a strange sense of protectiveness coming from him. With little more thought than that, his decision was made.

"I know, and she's not really mine, but I plan to hang on to her 'til spring and then ship her to her rightful owner," Dan said.

"Have you ever killed a man?" the Indian suddenly asked. Dan was so startled that his mouth dropped open, and he froze at the task of packing he had applied himself to.

"Wh … Why do you ask?"

"Cause if you haven't, you're gonna have to, to keep those horses and your own life," Red Elk told him. "Can ya do that?"

"I don't know," was Dan's truthful reply, "I just don't know. A life isn't something to be taken by others, and I've seen enough of that to last me a life time."

He knew Red Elk sensed his dilemma, and the wisdom and sensitivity in those sloe brown eyes beneath the long straight black hair and above the hawk-like facial features had an unsettling effect on him. He felt as though the red man could look right in to his inner self and read him like he could read the weather. He returned to his packing and soon had the bay under the load of supplies.

"Let's get on with it," the Indian said, "we're 'bout sixteen hours from the canyon, and another six from the bottom. But do us both a favor before we ride out."

"What's that?" Dan asked.

"Reload that hogleg," said Red Elk as he handed him the .45 cartridges.

"Oh, yeah," Dan murmured as he dropped his head to avoid the Indian's eyes.

"Hey, don't feel too bad about it," his jovial companion offered, "I once slipped into the Army fort at Yuma and stole the commanding officer's britches right off of his bed post just to prove I could do it to a bunch of liquored-up cowpokes as what wanted to lose a lot of their money on foolish bets. Then I run 'em, them britches that is, up the flag pole right under the guards' noses just to show off a little." He chuckled at the memory, and Dan just shook his head at this enigma before him. He'd come to think, through limited experience, that the red man was a very sober and serious breed by nature, and here was a seemingly delightful man who appeared to be bent on a life of lighthearted enjoyment mixed with just the right amount of wisdom and seriousness.

I'm going to have to do a lot of watching and learning about this 'red man' I seem to have been adopted by, he thought.

They mounted up and rode out, spending the next ten hours in the saddle, stopping only to allow the animals to rest a bit. As they loosened the cinches each time to allow the horses relief, Dan could sense the urgency in his companion's face.

It was growing dusk when they rode out from a meal stop, which had consisted of only some cold meat and canned peaches. Thus, meagerly fed and with ten hard hours behind them, they rode off once again.

"If'n I hit the trail I'm looking for right, we'll be able to go a couple of more hours yet, so just give that mare her head and let her follow me," Red Elk instructed.

A half an hour later he called back to Dan, "We've got her, we'll put in some good miles yet!"

The miles didn't seem so good to Dan, as he was exhausted and could feel the fatigue in the mare beneath him. It felt like being delivered from some evil thing when they finally halted two and a half hours later, and he just sort of went through the motions as they set up camp.

The Indian was a different matter. He bantered about, issuing forth anecdotes of this and that, and Dan could see nothing of the rigors of the thirteen hours of hard trail behind them showing in the man's demeanor. He commented on the fact, to be received with yet another jest.

"Wal, ya see, yore a paleface and I'm a renegade redskin. Ever'one knows we injuns is trail hardened. Why, we kin set fer days in the hot sun and never move if need be. I could ride another twenty miles, but these here hosses cain't see as good as I kin, so I had to stop."

Dan shook his weary head in mild amusement and discovered that he half believed this character he'd taken up with. Then, without a bite of food or a word of goodnight, the "renegade redskin" rolled into his blankets and was out almost immediately. Dan soon joined him, taking only a couple of moments to wonder about the next day's journey. He spent the night in an exhausted sleep, escaping for once from the haunting nightmares that he'd failed to elude for weeks. Exhaustion can sometimes be a soothing companion.

Six

When the two weary and cold travelers awakened the next morning it was not yet daybreak. A light snow had fallen and they had to shake the silvery mantle from their blankets.

Dan started a fire quickly, then headed out of camp to track down the horses.

"Wait, don't go that way!" Red Elk snapped out in mild alarm. "At least, not 'til daybreak."

"Why not?" Dan asked him.

"You'll see later on," was the red man's reply, and with that, he stalked off in the opposite direction.

Dan could tell that it would be of no use to pump the Indian further, and trooped off after him. They soon had all four horses by the fire, then had a quick and cold meal of biscuits, purposely left from the night meal for just this time, some beef jerky, and scalding coffee. By the time this meager fair had been consumed and the horses packed and saddled, the sun was coming up.

"Well, Dan, it's time you stepped through that little grove of trees there and took a look, but step slow and easy," Red Elk told him.

With his curiosity growing, Dan did just that, and when he stepped from the thick underbrush, he gasped inwardly and took an involuntary step backwards. He was immediately totally frightened and awestruck, both hitting him like an avalanche, for there before him, not ten feet away, was the largest abyss one could ever imagine.

Gaping at him like some huge monster attempting to swallow all before it was the famous subject of many campfire talks during his childhood. The Grand Canyon! He knew it without asking.

As he swiveled his head left and right, at first quickly and then more deliberately, he stayed firmly rooted to his tracks, as though a movement might pull him to the rim. He noted the various colors on the opposite wall miles away, the dark reds, giving way to the yellow and tans, with outcroppings here, overhangs there, all with scrub oak clinging precariously to their scant footholds.

Below him, maybe halfway down, was a shelf, extending out at least a mile or two, and fully twenty miles long. He could see that it sloped a bit more gently to the bottom, which seemed to be near the very center of the earth itself.

At the bottom, nearly against the opposite wall, and at least twenty miles away, ran an ugly reddish brown streak. The Colorado! He knew of the mighty river's appetite for horses, men, and any living creature that was impertinent enough to venture into its swift waters in an attempt to cross it. He experienced an involuntary shudder at the thought.

His revelry was interrupted by the arrival of Red Elk. "Well, we gonna stay here all day and gaze at the sights, or are we gonna get movin' and get down there afore the snow flies some more?"

"You mean … this … this is the canyon you said we were going into?" asked Dan incredulously.

"Don't see another one close by, do ya?" replied the Indian.

Dan detected a bit of a mischievous twinkle in those dark eyes, so he said nothing in reply. If this crazy half cowboy, half Indian, half jokester, half philosopher said he was going down there, Dan believed it! In the short time they'd spent together, he had come to the point of putting his complete trust in the man, for he was surely the most unique individual Dan had yet encountered.

He evoked from one the quick trust and friendship that Ira Nelson brought forth, but was a completely different type of individual. Or was he? The thought of Ira brought forth an immense burden of sadness and guilt as he sensed the smooth stride of the mare beneath him. How the old man had loved this horse!

The coldness in his veins continued, driving him to the decision that he must, at all costs, get another horse and try to ship this marvelous creature back to Ira by train. The matter became a true resolution that would build in the weeks to come. And responsibility for the well being of Sheba became a burden he could not, nor did he desire to shake.

His thoughts were again interrupted by his companion. "Just another hour, and we hit the trail down!" he called back. "If'n you're scared o' high places, ya better be gettin' your mind set on whippin' the thing, for we've six hours of the most gut challengin' trail ahead anyone's ever seen. Just remember, you got great horseflesh there, and both o' those animals will do just fine if'n you let 'em just have their heads. If they balk, get down and lead 'em, and they'll go on."

"I don't know if I'm scared of heights or not," Dan spoke truthfully, "but coming out on that rim like that back there sure set me to breathing hard!"

"Aw, that was just the high country air," the red man replied graciously. Dan could sense that his companion wished to comfort and reassure him.

Just a few minutes less than an hour later they angled sharply towards the rim, and Dan could see the definite break in the wall that signified a probable trail. As Red Elk reached it, he dismounted and loosened the cinch on his saddle. Dan echoed the action on his own horse.

"We'll let our horses rest here for a bit. They need to be fresh when we start down. Mules would be better, but we have what we have, and if we take our time, these mounts'll do just fine."

Dan didn't know if his friend was reassuring Dan Kade or Red Elk, but either way, he thought, they must be in for a rough ride. He spent the next several minutes rubbing and petting both Sheba and the bay, and they both responded with playful nuzzles and pushes with their soft noses. Dan had come to appreciate the bay nearly as much as Sheba, for he was a very complacent but hard working animal with a lot of stamina. He decided the horse needed a name, and decided that Bay was as good as any.

Shortly he saw the Indian arise from his place of rest and start tightening cinches on his mount and pack animal. The time had come!

Dan's nervousness over this descent wouldn't allow him to remain silent, so he approached his affable companion.

"Say, Reddy, you haven't been spoofin' me about this trip have you?" he asked.

Red Elk turned to him with sober countenance and only a ghost of a smile. "No pard, I don't reckon I have. I wish I could say yes to that, but I can't. All I can tell you is hundreds of Comanches have made this trip down, an' who knows how many white outlaws, so it can be done, it just requires your full attention ever' blessed minute. Now stop frettin'. We'll do fine."

Then, allowing a hidden softness to show through, he continued, "And if'n you're gonna call me Reddy, ya gotta be my pard, pard."

Dan grinned his reply and attended to his cinches. It didn't take long for Dan to see that Reddy's instructions were quite accurate. Fifteen minutes after the two mounted and started down the trail, they were on foot, leading the animals, for the ledge had become too narrow for a mounted rider's knee to fit between horse and canyon wall. It was now that Dan realized that if he didn't have a fear of heights before, he did now! As he looked down from the trail, he estimated the initial drop to be at least a hundred feet. Then, he mused, after the first bounce, one would go another fifty or sixty feet before coming to a halt on jagged rocks.

As he gazed out ahead, he could see places where the trail widened to where a buggy would fit, then it wound out of sight around a point that jutted out to block his view. He estimated that point to be three miles away.

It was fully half an hour later when the point was reached, and the last twenty minutes had been really restful as they were able to mount, and even jogged the horses for a stretch.

Upon arrival at the point, Reddy dismounted and again let the horses rest a bit.

"Next hour's the worst, Dan, and I reckon 'afore it's over,

you're gonna hate me, and maybe even take my scalp," he declared.

"What makes it so bad?" was Dan's query.

"Well, we gotta make three different drops that are nearly straight down and full of rocks the size of your head. It's tough on horses more than on men, and there's every chance to have a horse fall and either break a leg or worse yet, land on one of us. I'll go first, and you watch close the route I take and how fast I go. Just pile right into it after I'm down, and keep ahead of the horses."

With that, he picked up his reins and disappeared around the point. When Dan started around, he gasped and stopped dead. He wasn't sure a man could successfully make this turn, let alone a horse, and instead of seeing the wall slope out from the canyon wall, it cut back in under it! It was at least three hundred feet straight down if he slipped.

As he began to tremble, he looked ahead and saw that Reddy and both of his horses were several yards ahead, not even looking back, and he knew he had to go on.

Keeping as close to the wall as he could, he pulled Sheba along gently. She very calmly strode to the point, inched her way around it, and made a deep chuckling sound in her throat, as if to inform him that "this was nothing".

Bay negotiated the turn just as well, with seemingly no reluctance, and Dan once again gazed upon this gorgeous sorrel mare with tremendous admiration.

"Horse," he said, "you're sure gonna make it tough for me to send you back to old Ira, you keep this sorta' thing up."

And, of course, he received the cocked forward ears and deep look as always when he talked to her. He chuckled, shook his head slowly and continued on.

He caught up to Reddy a couple of hundred yards later. He was standing between his two horses looking down a near vertical precipice strewn with small rocks. The incline ended several hundred feet below on a shelf, and Dan could see the semblance of a trail leaving the shelf and going back to the left in the direction from which they had just come. Except, of course, it was still descending.

"Well, Dan, here we are. If we get by this one okay, the rest is a cake-walk by comparison. Now, watch me, and don't start down 'til I'm clear down and out of your way. Also, go down between your horses, that way, if one of them falls, you won't lose them both because the back one rolled down across ya. And whatever you do, try, try, try, to keep 'em going' slow. They'll likely wanna get to hopping, that's their nature, but if they lose their footing in this loose stuff, they'll likely not get stopped on the shelf, and it's a pretty bad drop off of it. Okay? Good, here I go."

And with not another word or even a deep breath before starting, he stepped off the trail, pulling his horses with him.

Sure enough, the mounts began to make little hops with their hind legs tucked under them to keep from speeding up, but Reddy kept talking and holding back until he was at a crawl, and his horses were obedient. They settled down and returned to the practice of putting one foot forward at a time, keeping their pace to match that of Reddy.

The trio was two thirds of the way down when near tragedy struck. The pack horse lost his footing and began to slide, with his hind legs slipping completely from under him. Reddy hauled on the halter rope and the frightened animal got stopped. But now, it was facing back up the incline and snorting out its fear.

Reddy, rather than trying to turn the animal, began to very gently back it down the slope. For fully two-hundred feet this little drama took place, ever so slowly, seemingly inch by inch. Then they were down!

Reddy stood for a long time, stroking the animal's head and neck, pulling its ears, and just talking to it gently. Dan couldn't hear him talking, but he knew from experience what was taking place. Shortly, he looked up at Dan, waved, and moved on down the trail.

Dan began to breathe deeply and slowly to calm his trip-hammer heartbeat; then, with soft words to Sheba and Bay, he stepped off into the nightmare. Both horses resisted mildly at first, but as soon as he pulled a little harder and spoke to them a little more firmly, the two stepped off and began to plunge on down the slope, crow hopping with Dan holding back and hollering "Whoa."

He got them slowed to a crawl, and the rest of the slope was negotiated without incident. At the bottom, he caught Reddy and they talked briefly, as much for themselves as for the horses.

"Well, Dan, I thought this old redskin had lost a pack horse up there, but the worst is over. From here on we have two much smaller, and not so steep, places like that and we're down. How you holdin' up?"

"I'll do," Dan told him, "but I hope I never see that place again. How in the world do you get back up it?"

"I don't know if it's ever been done," Reddy replied, "it's mostly a down trail as near as I can tell. I'd sure hate to try it."

"I presume, since you're here, that you have another, and I hope, better way out?" Dan asked.

"Oh my yes! There's probably a couple hundred of them. I just came this way cause it was gettin' close to too late on top! I mis-calkilated my time and headed this was way too late to hit a better trail," Reddy replied. "Now, let's get on with this, we've three or four hours left 'afore we get down."

It was actually five hours later that they made camp at the trail's base. There was no shelter, no nothing. Just desert. Dan understood completely why Reddy had insisted that all four huge deerskin water bags be full before beginning the descent. One had been used up just on the trail down, and the horses certainly showed signs of needing much more.

"We'll be leaving here in about four hours." Reddy told him, "Our destination is two day's ride, and the sooner we get there, the better I'll feel."

SEVEN

Twilight the following day found Reddy beside himself with excitement, for they had made great time in their travels, having gone upriver several miles, crossing the Little Colorado twice in the process. Both times were terrifying experiences for Dan, and he had been very relieved when Reddy turned them up a side canyon to the North, away from the horrible river.

That had been early morning and they were now in their fourth canyon which spread itself out to be more of a valley for about ten miles. It was at the other end of this that Reddy declared he intended to winter. He seemed to take it for granted that Dan would stay.

"Listen Pard," he said around a biscuit, "it's time we had a serious talk."

"So talk," Dan replied, "but somehow I can't picture you as ever being serious."

"Well, I am now. I don't know what your plans are, or even if you have any. I also don't know where you've come from, or why, but I don't care. It ain't healthy to ask too many personal questions around these parts, so I won't. But you've proven yourself to be dependable, and with a lot of grit, so I'm gonna make you an offer."

"Some friends of mine and I have a deal goin' here. It involves catching 'n tamin'' wild horses, startin' soon, 'n then takin' em outta here to the north into Utah where we've got a market for 'em."

"We'll be able to trap a few 'afore the snow gets us too bad here in this valley, 'n we'll have all winter to gentle 'em, then come spring we'll hit it hard and by July we should be able to make a small killin'.""

"Now, we've talked horseflesh, an' I've watched ya with those two of yourn, an it's plain ya know your way around, so what say, wanna throw in with us?"

"That sounds great to me," Dan replied, "but how will we do anything in the snow all winter. And, how do we know we can trust these others? After all, you said that only outlaws headed down in this canyon. And does that mean … ?" He left off the sentence, realizing he was intruding.

Reddy laughed aloud, poured another slug of coffee, and leaned back on his saddle blanket.

"Now, my cousin Joe, he's comin' in from the other end, an' he may have some fellas with him as you'll not wanta ask that. As to the snow, you'll see that the area is very sheltered to begin with, and we'll not get the depth down here that they get on top. Oh, it'll be a long, lonely, desolate winter, but one I calkilate will set us up for a long time."

"Ya see, I been plannin' this for a couple of years now, an' Joe and I, we built the camp last spring an' scouted all the area over fer the best trappin' places where the hosses wintered. We're gonna do great, providin' Joe gets good help. He's supposed to bring four guys with him."

"Your cousin's name is Joe, is he Comanche too?" asked Dan.

"Yeah, he is, but he took on Joe as a name when some white squaw started calling him that 'stead o' Five Ponies. You'll like him fine. His only weakness is gals, an' white ones at that, which gits him in a lot of trouble. He moves around a lot, as a result. You fellers don't take kindly to some low-life redskin courtin' those rancher's daughters." With that, he chuckled deeply and tossed the remainder of his coffee out.

"I'm turnin' in soon's we finish cleaning up, I want to start real early tomorrow," he said.

At that, Dan wondered what this character called "real

early". He'd been in the saddle before daybreak for five days now, and was ready to sleep in. But, without a word, he turned his attention to the chores of camp life with a strange sense of eager anticipation mixed with a foreboding fear coursing through his mind.

He then double checked the hobbles on Bay and Reddy's two mounts, petted the curious nose of Sheba as he rubbed her neck, and then rolled up in his blankets.

Reddy observed this from afar, and said to himself under his breath, "You'll do, Dan Kade. You'll do."

Another's love for horses never failed to touch him.

An hour after daybreak the next morning found them mounted and following a small icy stream as it bubbled and burbled its winding way down the valley. They watched it grow gradually in size as other small tributaries joined it in its meandering, until it seemed content to remain a shallow stream averaging twenty feet in width and a couple feet in depth. There were pools, however, that looked to reach as deep as six feet. These would provide water at the downstream end where wildlife would drink after most everything else was frozen over.

The little valley never reached more than a mile wide, and looked even narrower because of the three thousand foot sides that loomed above, looking down upon the lush grass and small pinion groves as if to insure that peace and solitude remained undisturbed.

Mid morning found them approaching a grove of oak trees set back on a shelf like rise on the west side of the stream. It was in this grove that Dan spied the small, rough cabin built by Reddy and cousin Joe in the spring.

A simple one room affair, with bunks two high against two of the walls, with a stone fireplace at the end opposite the door and a rough hewn table between the two rows of bunks. Dan looked around, seeing that there were eight bunks, four to a side, but no place for personal effects. So, he simply dumped his warbag and saddlebags on the right hand lower bunk nearest the fireplace and went out to look around.

He was looking for corrals, but finding none, when Reddy

came silently up beside him.

"Well, Pard, whatdaya think?"

"It's beautiful," Dan replied, "but we're going to need a couple of corrals if we do anything during the winter."

"Yeah, I know, but Joe and I thought we could fence the mouths of two draws just back of this grove. They open up into small little areas, with the smaller of the two being about the right size to rope in, and just twenty foot of fence each will close both of them off just fine. We should be able to do it in half a day, with help and a pair of post hole diggers. Joe and I didn't bring any with us last spring."

"Sounds good, Reddy, but how about food?"

"After dinner, we'll go huntin', jerk out what we kill, and just keep at that 'til Joe gets here. He's packin' in the staples and such."

"I sure saw a lot of tracks on the way," Dan said. "Shouldn't be too tough to bag deer and such in here. You've picked a great spot providing there are horses."

"Trust me, Dan, you'll see wild horses 'afore this day is out, if'n you keep quiet," Reddy replied. "Now, lets go eat."

It seemed a true luxury to sit at a table for a meal and the two new friends lingered long at their food and conversation. It had been but a few days since their meeting, but their shared trials and dangers had already drawn them close.

It was mid afternoon, with a well deserved nap behind them, when they separated and trudged off in search of game. By evening, there were three deer and a large turkey gobbler hanging from a low tree limb for skinning. Game was very plentiful.

It was a week later, and Dan Kade had regained most of the weight he'd lost on the trail. The time spent jerking out venison, hunting the valley through, and generally preparing for winter was just what he'd needed for a healing time. He lost the eerie feeling of someone on his trail, so he slept wonderfully sound at night, and the resulting gain in energy was much in evidence when one looked at the tremendous pile of wood neatly cut and stacked beside the cabin.

It was with a sudden shock that fairly made his blood go cold that he heard a distant "Helloo the camp," during the noon lunch. His hand found the handle of his Colt before he even realized it, and he found Reddy's piercing dark eyes on his when he looked up.

They looked down canyon to see a line of horses winding down a distant slope on the far side of the stream.

"It's Joe!" Reddy exclaimed. "Hellooo the food!" he returned at the party.

Dan finally counted four men and sixteen horses in the party, with each man leading three heavily laden pack animals. They picked up speed as the leader spurred his mount to an easy trot, and pounded into camp fifteen minutes later.

The lead rider proved to be a lean, dark young man of Dan's age, who measured at least up to Dan's six feet of height, if not a couple of inches more. His visage would have been quite fierce had he not broken into a huge grin at the sight of Red Elk, and he leaped from his horse to clasp hands with his cousin.

Dan noted that the two spoke briefly, but rapidly in Comanche for a moment, and then the rest of the party was dismounting and approaching the cabin.

"Joe, I want you to meet my new pard, Dan Kade. And Dan, this is my cousin Joe. He's a true injun 'cept when it comes to women."

Dan clasped a hand of steel that fairly trembled with energy. The black eyes pierced his own and he knew he was meeting a person that expected honesty and who would return the same.

The voice that spoke shocked Dan. Not only was it deep and resonant, but the English that issued forth was finishing school perfect. The contrast with Red Elk's cowboy jargon was actually humorous to Dan.

"How do you do, Dan, I am very glad to meet you," Joe said. His voice rolled out like a low rumble of thunder.

"And I'm glad to meet you, Joe," Dan replied. "This crazy cousin of yours saved my bacon by getting me off the top. Or so he says."

"Well, we are four days later than planned because of the first snow. There's three feet on top, and more on the way," Joe told them. "So maybe he did. But I wouldn't let him think that if I were you, or he'll take advantage of you."

Further talk was halted by the arrival of the other three to the cabin porch. Joe quickly introduced them. "Cousin Red Elk, Dan Kade, please meet "Bear" Rollins, Jack Varley, and Johnson," he said, pointing to each as he did so.

Bear Rollins met both with a huge paw that left their hands crushed from the handshake. He was a true mountain man dressed in dirty buckskins and hair that appeared to explode from his head in a tangle of auburn red. A fur cap of some sort made a futile attempt to hold the hair in place. He grinned and spat a tobacco wad out, and simply thundered "Howdy!" from atop his six foot, four inch frame of 230 pounds.

Jack Varley was younger than Dan's twenty four years by far. Dan guessed him to be around twenty, and he only nodded self consciously as he offered a limp handshake, which Dan likened to a handful of limp carrots.

Johnson was a short, burly, unkempt man of mean visage, a powerfully built individual who appeared to be mad at the world. Dan noted the well worn six gun strapped to his hip and tied down. He neither offered his hand or a nod, only growled something unintelligible.

Reddy, however, stuck his hand towards him and said, "Glad to have you on our crew, Johnson. You got a first name ya go by?"

"If I had one, you'da heard it by now, so don't get nosy, awright?" was the surly reply, followed by a reluctant half hearted handshake.

He then turned on his heel and stalked to the pack horses and began to offload the nearest one. Following Johnson's example, the rest of them set upon the animals with a vigor that soon had the heavier coats coming off. Even with the winter chill in the air, the amount of work to be done had them all sweating with the exertion.

Dan had already noted that the valley chosen by Red Elk was much lower than he'd first thought, and he figured it to be roughly the same altitude here as was Mescal Valley. Otherwise, they'd be experiencing even colder air by now.

It took several hours for them to off load and unpack the

goods, then store them in the lean-to in back of the cabin. By the time they were done with this, Reddy had gone into the cabin and started the evening meal. It was, therefore, a pleasant odor of venison stew and sourdough bread that greeted them as they trooped into the cabin.

EIGHT

As the crew sat around the table after the evening meal was finished and the cleanup completed, Reddy laid out his plan to them.

"Well fellas, I guess I'd better lay this thing out for you, so we'll all know what we're in for this winter. This here valley is one that I stumbled on to a couple of years ago in the late fall. I stuck around long enough that I nearly didn't get out 'afore winter caught me and closed me in. The reason for that was that I saw several good-sized bands of wild hosses migratin' this way, and I got this idea to make a sweep of the valley to catch enough for a good stake. The more I watched them the more I realized this was a natural made trap for them in the winter.

"We'll get snow a plenty, but not so much that they won't get down to the graze for food, and they cain't go out either way. There's two major draws off in the west side that they'll be easy to drive into to work as traps. All we gotta do is cover the fronts with fence that don't look like fence, and the rest is done for us. That'll be tomorrow's job, buildin' fence.

"When spring comes, we'll have a good-sized string gentled and driveable, each man'll have the chance to choose a string of four or five for himself, an' the rest we'll be able to sell fer a really good price up at the fort in Oxbow.

"Now, I know myself, Joe, and Dan here are all wranglers, so we'll do the gentlin', if'n any of you other fellas wan to join us, you're welcome to, an' those that ain't gentlin' will be doin' the wood cuttin', cookin', an' other chores an' the such. Any questions?"

Johnson quickly growled out, "I don't build fences 'n I don't chop wood, so ya can just forget about that!"

"Then leave right now!" Reddy barked out so quickly that the rest jumped.

There was a stillness that stretched for what seemed to be several minutes, though Dan knew it wasn't. It was broken by Johnson's growl.

"Look, I'll leave when 'n if I'm ready, 'n no redskin tells me otherwise. You gotta problem with that, let's take care of it right now," he said.

Then as if some unforeseen thing touched his heart, he stiffened quite visibly, his eyes bulging and his breath stopping. As Dan watched this sudden transformation of the stocky man, he sat fascinated, glued to his seat to Johnson's left.

The man began to very slowly arise, maintaining his stiff posture, his hands strangely suspended in the air in front of him as though they were still on the table.

No one else moved, for a few seconds, that is. Then Dan began to ease away from Johnson's left side, as all the others but Reddy and Bear also started to separate themselves from the table.

As Dan eased away, he could see the reason for Johnson's strange posture. The huge mountain man was still seated at Johnson's right, but his left arm was extended upward towards the smaller man's head. At the end of that arm, a huge hand grasped an even larger knife with a blade at least a foot long, the point of which was pricking the skin just where the square jawbone met the throat. A tiny trickle of blood showed by the tip.

"Now mister," came the strangely softened voice of the big man, "you need to understand somethin' hyar. My mother was half Kiowa, and I don't take kindly to them as looks down on injuns. Also, I just happened to be there when you signed on fer this trip, and I recollect you agreein' to what Joe thar called hard work, long hours, cold bunks, an' little else.

"Now, let's you and me git two things straight hyar. One,

if'n you ever talk down to or bad about an injun agin, yore gonna hurt fer a real long time, an' two, if'n you go back on yore word an' don't carry yore share of the load hyar 'bouts, you ain't eatin'. That's simple truth, mister.

"Now, should you care to argue the point, we kin do this several different ways. I think you fancy yerself somethin' of a gun man, and I also happen to think that you only signed on to get someplace outa reach o' the law for a few months. So, we kin go outside 'n face each other, you with yore hogleg, 'n me with my sharps. I'll give you my word to only use one hand on it, 'n I'll hang it down by my side uncorked 'til you make yore play.

"Or, I'll give yer another knife 'n we kin do it thataway. Or, we kin jist go at each other with our hands, but that ain't hardly fair to you, since yore sech a runt.

"Or, one other way. Yer kin jist set back dare, shet yore big mouth, 'n git ready to dig post holes 'n split wood tomorrow. Now which will it be, little man?"

Johnson's face was terribly contorted with anger. That there was no fear in him was obvious, but his common sense told him there'd be more advantageous times to pursue this. Dan realized that if Johnson had his way, the mountain man had just signed his own death warrant.

"I'll pull my load," he said, "but yore better pull yours, or I'll be on you like a bee on honey."

"Wal, now I reckon you won't have no reason to be buzzin' round my flower bed, Johnson, cause I aim to pull more'n my load," Bear replied. "Now supposin' you jist sit back down 'n we'll drink some coffee on that."

There was a sort of collective sigh of relief among the other four men, and they all returned to the table.

At that point, Reddy spoke out again. "I want all of us to understand something. I came up with this plan, I found the hosses, I brought Joe in here and built this cabin, so I'm runnin' this outfit. Now, we'll split the profits equal, and we'll get a way set up fer a fair way to choose our personal strings, so I get no more money or hosses than any one else. But, hear me well, I'm runnin' the show!

"Any of you object to that, an' don't plan to foller my orders, get out now, while ya can. If'n you stay in this here cabin tonight, yore workin' fer me tomorrow. Any objections?" With that, he leaned back and surveyed them all closely, one at a time. As his eyes met each of theirs, all but Johnson nodded their agreement. Johnson only scowled and grunted his assent.

"Okay," Reddy went on, "we're up at dawn, we'll build a fence that funnels down to each draw from a ways out away from the mouth, with a narrow gate we can close when they're driven in. Dan, you and Johnson are workin' with me diggin' post holes. Joe, you take Bear an' Jack and start cuttin' posts. I'll work breakfast. Jack, you come in an' fix dinner. Dan, you'll come in early an' get supper. Any questions? If not, I suggest we turn in, cause tomorrow's gonna be a rough one.

With that, they all selected the bunk that was to be theirs for the next few months, and soon were rolled in blankets and drifting off. Dan's last thought before he fell off to oblivion was that even Johnson's snores sounded insolent, and he felt a profound dislike for the man forming within him. Johnson reminded him all too much of the Chelsea brothers, and that brought on anew the terrible loneliness that had haunted him until just recently. Red Elk's friendship had dampened that feeling, and Dan resented the intruding of the outlaw into his life to stir up the feelings once again.

Dawn broke the next day to the smells of venison frying, and true to his promise, Reddy had them all up by first light.

The meal was wolfed down, and the little valley was soon to have its serene tranquility disrupted by the ringing of steel on wood as the axes began their work. And while post hole diggers make very little sound, the topsoil was being wounded time and time again, as the three laborers silently attacked the despicable job.

Dan marveled at the way Johnson worked at a job he had disclaimed, and decided that Reddy's choosing to include himself had been a stroke of genius. Johnson was a strong hulk of a man, and obviously felt as though the Indian had challenged him. As a result, the dirt fairly flew, and by noon one complete side was ready for posts. They stopped only when they heard Jack's

distant call to dinner. Dan, for one, had decided that the call
would never come, as he was really exhausted and hungry.

When they arrived at the cabin, they were greeted by a
rather dreadful looking Jack. He was dirty all over, his hands
were red and raw with blisters, and even his face was scratched
up. Bear and Joe had set a terrific pace, and the youngster had
tried valiantly to keep up. When those two showed up, they still
looked rather fresh, and made an obvious attempt to cheer up
and encourage young Jack. It appeared that he was too tired to
respond. It was also very apparent that his hands needed doctoring.

"Say, Reddy," Dan offered, "you know I'm not much of a
cook, and this stew is pretty fair stuff. What would you say to
Jack taking my place for supper, and if need be, I'll go over and
help out later on?"

"Well, Dan," Reddy replied, "I was just thinkin' that very
same thing, 'specially since I ate some of yore cookin' on the
trail in. But to be fair to Jack, I don't think we kin do that to
him. Right, Jack?"

"Oh, no, it's O.K. I wouldn't mind at all!" Jack eagerly
spoke out. "I sorta like cookin'."

"Seems to me yore lettin' him off without carrin' his share o'
the load," Johnson growled. "Wonder what happened to the big
speech 'bout that?"

"So, you want yore turn at cookin', too, huh? O.K., we'll
forget about it. Johnson's right," Reddy said.

Dan could actually see the thought process going on in the
man's head as he mulled that clever approach over, and it became his conviction that the outlaw wasn't any too bright.

"Well now, I ain't much of a cook, always figgered it to be
woman's work," Johnson said, with a mean glance at Jack," so
if'n ya want the sissy to do it, I got no objections." He then
added a sneering chuckle to the statement.

The effervescent and clever spirit of Reddy immediately
jumped in and glossed over the nasty slur with the comment, "Ya
know, I think we'll be lots more efficient if'n we have Jack do
the splittin' of the firewood fer the first couple o' weeks here, an'
that way he'll be right close to take care o' all the meals. That

O.K. with you, Jack. Then when we git some broomtails cor-ralled you kin help with the ropin' and sech."

Jack, though stung by Johnson's verbal slap, quickly agreed to the deal, and this clever Indian friend of Dan's had shown again his prowess to lead and avert trouble in doing so.

They finished their meal and the five of them left quickly, with Dan holding back just long enough to assure Jack that there was enough wood ready to last for the two weeks, and to just soak the hands and heal them for a couple of days. He parted with this comment, "Look Jack, don't take anything that grub-worm says to heart. If you were any less than a real man, you wouldn't have been willing to work like you did to get your hands in that shape in the first place. The only mistake you've made was in not wearing gloves.

"You take care now, and I'll see ya at supper."

With that, he strode off towards his appointed duties of punching holes in the ground.

NINE

Two weeks of backbreaking toil later, the fences were done. They were six to seven feet high and well camoflaged with brush, funneling down from a hundred yards apart to a mere ten feet in about an eighth of a mile.

During the second week Jack had insisted upon joining the rest for a couple of hours between meals, and this had helped a lot. It did, however, cause him to be near enough to Johnson to endure unmerciful harrassment from that individual. Dan could see that Jack was beginning to falter under the cruel man's attacks, and had taken about all he could handle of the calculated mistreatment. It all came to a head the night before the first drive.

All had taken the afternoon off to rest and gather sore muscles back together again, and were sitting at the table awaiting supper as Reddy laid out the plans.

"Now here's the plan for tomorrow. There's a bunch of about thirty-some four miles up the canyon that's got some real good stock in it. We'll station Johnson, Bear, an' Jack at hundred yard intervals across the canyon over here across the crick. You'll each have a white gunny sack to wave to turn 'em towards the chute back here behind us.

"Joe, you'll be just on this side of the crick in those junipers, so that after they get by you and the others turn 'em, you kin ride out hollerin' an' wavin' a sack to head 'em right past the cabin.

"By then, Dan and I kin be up tight behind 'em to keep 'em goin'. I'd say it won't take us more 'n an hour to get the job done.

"Dan, you'll take that greased lightnin' mare o' yourn an' go upstream on this side, get by 'em 'n spook 'em this way. I'll stay just by the middle of the valley to sorta add insurance that they come this way an' not swing around past yer. Any one have any questions?"

"No, but I'd like to take that mare an' do the chase job, 'steada Dan there," Johnson growled.

"Listen, absolutely NO one rides Sheba but me," Dan spoke softly.

"Oh yeah, bet I own 'er afore the winter's out," Johnson replied.

"Never," was Dan's curt reply, and dropped the conversation.

They were interupted shortly after by Jack setting the tin pans used for eating in front of them.

"I'll serve you guys tonight instead of you coming over for it. Real restaurant style," he said as he was doing so. With that he brought biscuits, coffee, and some venison hash to the table. As he served the hash, heavily laden with potatoes, he reached over Johnson's shoulder to do so, and the man reached up and deliberately bumped Jack's arm. A little of the hash missed the plate.

"Hey, sissy boy, watch it!" No one spills food on ME without payin' for it!" Johnson barked.

This deliberate attack on Jack was finally more than even the mild mannered Dan could take. Johnson had stirred up the old hurts, fears, guilt, and especially the loneliness of feeling alone and hunted, and it was too much. He was sitting directly across the table so he just calmly reached out his left hand, took hold of the tin plate, and turned it upside down in Johnson's lap, hot hash and all.

All sound other than Johnson's sputtering stopped, and Dan looked him straight on and said, "Is that a fact, outlaw? I guess you better try and collect then."

Johnson leaped to his feet with a mighty heave.

The unexpected move so unbalanced the outlaw that he fell

heavily backwards, his head hitting the dirt floor with a sudden thud.

Dan's fury was now unleashed, and by the time Johnson tried to get up, the younger man was astride his chest beating his face with both fists. It became quickly evident that the stocky man was used to brawling, though, for his superior strength and experience soon overpowered Dan and ended up astride HIS chest.

The advantage was short lived, for Dan's youthful body was strong and wiry, and he flung his right leg up over Johnson's shoulder from behind him, hooking that same spur on the man's face and flipping him backwards.

A scream of agony burst from the heavier man as the spur ripped a gash from his chin to his ear, and in a second Dan was on him choking him.

It all happened so quickly, and yet seemed so far away to Dan, and he wondered vaguely why Johnson didn't hit him to try and get away, for he certainly intended to choke the man until he stopped breathing. Didn't Johnson realize that?

Then, as the sturdy body of the outlaw began to sink to the floor, Dan slowly became aware of someone, or rather, several someones, shouting in his ear. He also realized that his arms felt terribly heavy. As he slowly came out of the mental haze, he realized that the heaviness was Bear and Joe clasping his arms to his sides.

Reddy was now in front of him shaking him by the shoulders. "Come out of it," he yelled, "it's over!"

"Yeah, yeah, O.K.," Dan mumbled, having trouble with the words coming out intelligibly. "Why do you suppose he didn't fight back much, Reddy? Why'd he just let me do that to him?"

"Ha! Listen pard, you jist can't see yore face now. If you could, you'd see that he pounded you to a pulp. Ya jist didn't feel anythin'.

"I'll tell ya, I hope I never rile that slow movin' temper of yoren, cause yore nothin' short of a buffler stampede when ya get goin'! We almost didn't git ya off'n him in time. I thot ya killed 'em!"

"Is he … is he alive?" Dan asked.

"Oh yeah, he's alive," Bear answered him, "but he ain't gonna talk right or look right fer a while. His neck's turnin' blue now, and fer a couple o' days it's gonna swell up terrible bad. But it serves him right, ya shoulda' jist shot 'im."

"Listen Dan," Joe spoke up, "you're going to have to watch your back from now on. He'll be out to kill ya for sure."

Reddy added, "From now on, you spend an hour a day practicin' with that side arm o' yours, cause he's gonna force the issue sooner or later."

"O.K. Reddy, O.K., but I think he'll leave us alone now," Dan said.

"Listen fellows, I really must apologize for bringing him in here. I had no idea he was like this. I should have listened to you, Bear. You were against him from the start." Joe offered this apology, then went to Johnson, who was regaining consciousness.

Joe pulled that worthy to his knees, and as he did so, pulled Johnson's pistol from its holster. The others thought he simply intended to disarm the man, but Joe had other ideas.

As the outlaw looked up at him, rubbing his throat with both hands, Joe cocked the weapon and shoved the barrel against Johnson's nose, right between his eyes. It made a little tudy when he did so, as he was anything but gentle about it.

"Now listen very closely to me, white man," Joe began in his perfect English. "I'm the one responsible for bringing you in here. That makes me responsible for the discord you've brought unto us. Therefore, my friend, I intend to be responsible for taking that discord out of here. I am going to tell you just this one time: if you cause any more strife here, you are a dead man. I will kill you myself, pack your ugly body in snow until spring, and then pack you out of here to the nearest law man to see if there's a reward for your slimy skin. Do you have any comments?"

Johnson had turned white at the mention of a reward, and could tell that this indian meant exactly what he said. He glanced furtively around at the others, seeing in every face but Jack's the agreement to do exactly as Joe promised if Joe himself didn't carry through. He lowered his head a beaten man, and without so much as a sound, staggered from the cabin on unsteady feet, yearning to get more cool mountain air into his tortured lungs.

Dan went to the water bucket and washed his face and hands thoroughly, and was now aware of the tremendous pain that was making its way into his consciousness. Jack came to him and offered to doctor him up.

At Dan's refusal Bear stepped in and said, "I think you better let 'im Dan'l, you got some nasty cuts there that might infect."

So, reluctantly, Dan allowed himself to be doctored, and then hastened on to his bunk. That seemed a signal to the others, as they all followed suit. It was much later, however, before Johnson entered and did likewise.

Red Elk deviated from his usual habit of arising before daybreak, and allowed all to sleep in until later. When Dan awoke, it was a relief, for he'd spent a torturous night in nightmares and pain, not all of which was physical.

The things that had haunted the night for him were strangely not concerning the tragic death of Candy or his parents, but rather, the sight of Max Chelsea's blank face as his chest caved in from the shotgun blast. That was added to by the vision of Johnson turning blue under his hands, and of Jules Chelsea plummeting backwards through the saloon window.

Dan had no explanation as to why these memories wouldn't go away and stay away. He only knew that he'd never been a violent man before this, and he hated the gnawing feeling that refused to leave for good. He felt so terribly alone, in spite of Reddy, Joe, Bear, and Jack. So terribly alone.

Bear rousted him out with a lively, thunderous "Chow's on! Let's eat, 'n then hit them saddles! Time's a wastin', men!"

Joe clumped in stamping some of the four inches of fresh snow from his feet, and declared that he had all the horses saddled an' fed their morning grain. Dan's heart rose a few feet at the thought of riding Sheba again, and at the anticipation of breaking some wild horses.

The crew ate silently, and were soon donning their coats and gloves and heading out the door.

Reddy briefly recapped their plans, and all soon rode off to their appointed stations. Dan noted as he rode by Johnson that the outlaw's neck was all black and blue and that it was swollen terribly. The gash of the spur stood out as an ugly red scab, and Dan's bouyant spirit disappeared with a thump. He found it depressing that he was capable of doing that to a fellow human being.

Sheba must have sensed someting, for she began to prance sideways and get very frisky with him. It had been two weeks since she'd worn a saddle, and she had fattened up on the sweet, tall grass and the daily feed bag of oats. Her coat was shaggy with its winter growth and she really needed a good workout. Her eagerness soon bouyed Dan up, and he let her lope up the canyon just enough to loosen up and warm those magnificent muscles. She was hard to hold in, and soon he allowed her to have her head for a half a mile, relishing the biting cold wind on his swollen face.

He pulled the excited mare down to a slow lope, and began to look for the target herd. With the snow, it should be easy to track them if necessary. He wasn't three miles from camp when he ran across fresh tracks coming down to the stream, then leaving back in the same direction.

There appeared to be several youngsters by the smaller tracks, and he noticed one set of absolutely huge hoof tracks.

They appeared to be those of a work horse, and he wondered if the herd leader had stolen some rancher's plow mare. Dan circled upstream another quarter mile and then swung back down and over to the opposite side of the canyon.

He broke out of a thicket and was nearly in the herd as soon as he did so. He whipped out his Colt and fired a shot into the air to both start the group in the desired direction and to let the others know that the drive had started.

Almost as one the wild horses launched into a dead run down the valley at top speed, with Dan yelling behind them as Sheba easily kept pace. Dan could soon see the others waving their white sacks as they rode back and forth across the canyon at their appointed places, and, true to Reddy's plan, the herd swerved to the left, thundered past the cabin, and into the mouth of the chute.

By now all the riders were in a line behind them forcing them on, and in no time at all Jack was frantically pulling poles across the gate opening to slave the captives.

The small herd milled in a circle for a few minutes, panic stricken, until Reddy pulled everyone out of sight for a while.

The men returned to the gate an hour later, and found most of the horses pawing snow aside to get at the grass, a good sign that they were fairly well calmed down. It was then that Dan saw the source of the large hoof prints. It wasn't a plow horse at all, but the biggest, ugliest horse he'd ever seen.

The brute stood easily seventeen or eighteen hands high, was a dull blue roan in color, with winter hair at least three inches long. The chest was wide and could almost be referred to as massive, while his barrel was long, with hindquarters that shouted "power!"

While his legs were quite long, they were deceptively large. They reminded Dan of thoroughbred racing stock in shape, but half again in size. When at last he let his gaze rest on the long, brutish looking head, he discovered a pair of unusually intelligent looking eyes staring back at him from beneath appropriately large ears, disproportionate even for this sized head. He'd found Sheba's replacement.

"How soon can we claim horses for our personal string, Reddy?" he asked.

"Right now, far as I'm concerned, what say, men?" Reddy replied.

"Sounds good to me," Bear said. "What're we gonna do, draw straws to see who goes first?"

"Naw, jist start pickin', an' if'n any o' you want the same hoss, then we'll have them draw straws."

"Then I want that big blue roan over there," Dan spoke up quickly.

"Haw! haw! You sure can have him!" Johnson howled. "That's the absolute dumbest choice I ever seed!"

Bear, however looked a little more pleased, and nodded slightly to Dan.

"Did you want him, too, Bear?" Dan asked.

"Wal, Dannyboy, I reckon I'da chose 'im, all right. But I don't wanna draw for him. You go ahead 'n take 'im. I got my eye on a grulla dun back thar that's purty good size, 'n looks purty smart.

"But I tell ya, Dan, you got a eye fer great hoss flesh. That brute'll beat the tar outta any hoss hyar but that sorrel mare o' yoren, 'n I'll bet he'll give her all she cain handle fer speed. But, he'll give it out fer a lot longer 'n any hoss we ever saw, too. I tell ya boy, he's got stayin' power."

With that, Dan knew the rest would pass up drawing for the big beast. He stood staring at the animal receiving the same look back, almost as if there were communications between them.

Reddy spoke up, "Well men, I just counted thirty three head. We'll let 'em calm down today and get used to their surroundins', but tomorrow we start hit 'em hard come first light.

"An' I been thinkin'. The three of us, Joe, Dan, an' I will start gentlin', while Bear 'n Johnson start scoutin' fer other bunches. You two kin study a couple o' bunches fer a few days, then Bear'll need to hunt up some meat fer us. After that, he'll start workin' with us whilst Johnson keeps an eye on the other herds and gets what game he sees when ever he ain't too close to the hosses. We don't wanna get 'em spooked afore we make room fer 'em in this natural corral."

So with excitement in the air, the six went each his own way, to spend a lazy afternoon once more, the last any of them would see for quite some time.

TEN

Christmas was just approaching Metzal valley, and the early morning sun glinted brightly on the pristine crystals of new-fallen snow. The brilliance was such that the pale young man seated on Nelson's front porch had to squint hard against the glare in order to view the scene before him.

He was seated in a chair on wheels, clasping a robe tightly about his shoulders, while a lap robe of bear skin covered him completely to the waist. This was his first venture out of the large ranch house into the late December chill, and the cool, dry Arizona air felt wonderful to his lungs in spite of the bite that it caused.

The porch on which he sat was a wide one that stretched completely across the front of the white frame house, then turned to cover each end as well. The scene from the porch was magnificent, as the house was built on a normally grassy ledge that reached out from the front of the house some fifty yards before sloping quickly away towards the valley some three hundred feet lower. The slope was like a funnel in a sense, as to both the right and left it sloped upwards instead of down, and it narrowed to a break in the sheer west wall of the Metzal valley that was a mere quarter of a mile wide.

It was here that old Ira had chosen to place his ranch years ago, for it held a commanding view of the area around it, and could not be easily attacked. Behind the rambling house were three barns, corrals, and a long bunkhouse, with groves of pinion and aspen covering much of the area. The back of this land was situated against a hundred foot wall of rock, and it stretched several miles in either direction before sloping down to meet the walls of Metzal valley. All in all, there were several thousand acres of this grazing land that had positioned itself on a sort of middle ground between Metzal valley and the mountains to the west.

The young man was lost in the panorama before him when a musical, feminine voice broke into his thoughts.

"Well, Tom Seever, that's about all of the time you get outside for THIS morning. It's back inside for you, young fella."

He turned his head to smile at the owner of the voice, a lovely young lady who fairly bounced along the porch with a brisk step. She was neither tall nor short, but that was where mediocrity stopped for her, as her face was a vision of radiant beauty with full, red lips showing straight, white teeth through the smile that seemed to take permanent residence beneath her finely chiseled nose. The twinkling, sparkling eyes were a dark green hue, and seemed always to show lights of mischief and gayety. Her dark auburn hair was somewhat hidden beneath a scarf of green, but the few rebellious strands that escaped shone brightly in the morning sun. A rancher's sheepskin jacket and overalls tried unsuccessfully to hide the rounded figure that refused to be disguised by male garb.

"Allison McCord , you just leave me out here a while longer, or I'll take you down and rub your pretty little nose in the snow, you hear me?" Tom replied.

"Hey, that'll be the day, MR. Seever," she sparkled. "You'll not be able to accomplish that task even after you're completely well."

With that guantlet thrown out, she grasped the wheel chair and trundled the pale young cowboy to the open door of the ranch house.

Allison McCord was the only niece of Ira Nelson, and had been sent for to help nurse Tom Seever back to health. Her father Paul had married Ira's sister Ida, and had moved her into central Idaho to his own horse ranch. Thus it was that Ira saw very little of his sister or his niece. It was a natural thought that struck him, therefore, to send for Allison when he determined to take this young, unfortunate cowboy in to nurse back to health.

Young Seever had lain for three weeks hovering between life and death from the bullets of Max Chelsea. The first had nicked a lung, the second was a mere fraction of an inch from his heart, the third hit his arm, with the fourth doing the worst damage, having torn through his midsection.

It was two weeks before old Doc Pritchard would even try to remove that fourth bullet, although the first two had been taken out right away. It was during those two weeks that Ira stayed night and day with the youngster, deciding then and there to take him in and try to make up for the terrible wrong that had been done to him.

When it began to look like living was a possibility for Tom, Ira telegraphed his sister, asking for help, and Allison quickly responded. It was two more weeks, however, before her arrival, making it a full month since the tragedy had occurred.

During that time Ira and several town leaders were successful in getting a federal marshall sent in, who promptly launched his own investigation. It took him no less than a day to walk into Doc Pritchard's and arrest Jules Chelsea, who lay there with his left arm and part of his shoulder missing as a result of the shotgun blast.

Jules had been lucky, for the nine double ought buck shot had been fired from such close range that they hadn't scattered much when they smashed him backwards through the saloon window, and all missed any vital organs. Saving his life had required amputation though, and old Doc swore he'd live long enough to hang, even if it meant working miracles.

The next few weeks had been hectic, what with the trial, burying Max Chelsea and Candy Johnston, and trying desperately to find Dan Kade to let him know he wasn't a wanted man.

Two witnesses had seen the Chelsea brothers level their guns at Dan, and in spite of the fact that it had been his intention to kill anyway, no one but him knew that, so the circuit judge had ruled self defense.

As soon as he was able, Jules Chelsea had been sent to

prison, sentenced to fifty years hard labor. Many were very upset that he wasn't hanged, but were willing to settle for the imprisonment.

Had it not been for the confusion during the shooting and the survival of John and Suzan Kade, he surely would have hanged. His only good fortune through the entire thing was the fact that John Kade had regained consciousness enough to drag himself and Suzan into a root cellar that was entered through the back entrance of the kitchen. There he had pulled his wife into a corner beneath some shelving and covered them with an old burlap sack from over the sauerkraut crocks. Breathing had gotten very difficult, but never impossible, and the two emerged nearly twenty hours later with minor burns and some respiratory infection. Within a month they would both be as good as new.

Except for missing Dan. Both knew that for their mild mannered son to blow the life out of two law men with a shotgun meant that he was convinced that they were dead, and their hearts ached continuously for Dan to return to them to start fresh.

Allison closed the door against the chill and pushed Tom's wheelchair over close to the huge, roaring fireplace. The large living room ran across the full length of the front of the house, with a large couch and several overstuffed chairs placed in a semi-circle facing the fireplace that punctuated the long back wall. On the floor were several various rugs of bearskin, elk, and Indian design.

At the end of the the room on the right was a small spinet piano that Ira himself had freighted in for his then young wife, and he never tired of asking Allison to play for them, for it brought back wonderful memories of when his life was complete, having his bride with him for all those years.

The two young people were still bantering at one another when Ira strode into the room from his office.

"Say, you two wildcats, how am I supposed to get my paperwork done with the two o' ya squabbling so?"

"Oh uncle, you know we're not squabbling. It's just that this young whiporsnapper thinks he's ready to take on the world already."

"Hey, no such thing," Tom interjected. "I didn't say a thing about the world, just one smart alecky nurse IN the world!"

It was plain to Ira that these two had grown very fond of each other in the period of time spent together, but he had the feeling that Tom's fondness was based on romantic intentions, while Allison's was based more on a sister-brother type feeling. He would not have minded one bit if she would have felt otherwise, for he had grown to love this weak youngster as his own, and would have been very happy to pay for a wedding.

"Well, I think you'd better hold off on that, Tom, for I've plenty for her to do in preparation for our Christmas party first. Then you can straighten her out. Or … at least try!"

"Hey, you two, before you go ganging up on a lady, just remember who does the cooking and cleaning for you," Allison said.

"Ha! Now we've got you," Ira replied. "Mrs. Garrison and Julie do, not you, miss smarty pants. You forget you're not in Idaho now, but down here living a life of leisure, not cooking, not cleaning, just loafing."

"Why, uncle, you traitorous old rat. You think keeping this, this hombre in line isn't work!? Maybe I'd better go back to Idaho and rest up!"

"Hey,,, whoa you two," Tom interrupted. "Before this gets out of hand, I think we'd better call a truce. And who are you calling an hombre, madam?"

Allison only gave him a petulant look as she circled her arm around Ira's waist, and, wrinkling her nose up at him, stood on tiptoe and kissed the leathery old cheek. She then sped away to the kitchen, where her gay laughter could be heard as she informed Mrs. Garrison, the cook, of the utter hopelessness of men in general.

Tom became serious as he spoke to the older rancher in a lowered voice.

"Ira, you've been so good, and kind, and generous to me that I hate to ask this of you, but I really need a special favor."

"You name it son, it's yours if it's within my power to make it so. I sure want this to be your best Christmas for many a year," replied the kindly old fellow.

"Well, I know I can't think about going into town yet, but Julie Garrison said she'd do some shopping for me for everyone, and I thought if I could get an advance on wages … " and his voice trailed off with a swelling in his throat. It wasn't easy for Tom to ask for more after all this man had done for him, including the promise of a job when he was well again.

"Sure son, I'll be happy to. I'll tell Julie to just run up an account and we can settle up later. You don't worry none about it, hear?"

"Thanks Ira. Thanks," was all Tom Seever could say. He would talk to Julie at the first opportunity, knowing he could rely upon her silence.

The Garrisons had been with the Slash N ranch for a long time, as Ira had hired Dick as a wild young rider. He was the first of the present hands to sign on, and with Ira's steadying hand had become not just a mature rider, but the foreman as well. He had married a Metzal valley girl named Mary, and Julie, at seventeen, was their only child. Ira and Dick had built another house themselves while leaving the crew to run the ranch. It set clear back against the bluff, nearly a quarter of a mile to the south.

Mary Garrison had simply taken over as cook soon after that, trying to do so without wages. She lost the battle, as Ira insisted on paying her quite well, and over the years had begun to include the Garrisons as partners in the ranch as reward for their undaunted and energetic efforts towards a successful operation. Julie had been hired to help as soon as she was old enough, and was nearly a daughter to Ira.

Since this Tom Seever was a young, handsome, and for the moment, helpless fellow, it hadn't taken the teenager long to totally fall in love with him. That was exactly what Ira had expected, and was one of the reasons he'd sent for Allison This niece was older, more stable, and therefore more reliable as a nurse. Julie could be trusted in every way, but lacked the maturity needed for this ever so serious a job.

So it was that Julie was eager to do anything and everything that Tom requested of her. She was off for Metzal early the next morning with Tom's carefully thought out list. It was the day for Mary Garrison's normal weekly trip after the staples needed to feed a crew of fifteen people, so the three-hour drive to town was a normal part of the Saturday routine.

Usually, a hand was assigned the task of driving the spring wagon for the gals, but on this day Dick himself did the honors. He had in his pocket a number of telegrams to send out for Ira. They were part of another attempt to find Dan Kade and Sheba. Dan's folks had been trying since the black day of his "escape" to get the word to him that he was a free man and also not an orphan. It was as though he'd dropped off the face of the earth, and they had finally given up. Ira would not. Even though Dan was not his son, he could not get the terrible bloody scene out of his mind that had sent Dan rocketing down Main Street on a sorrel lightening bolt. It was all too unfair, and the tough old rancher had no quit in him. He was determined to succeed.

They tied the team to the post at the rear loading dock of Art Figy's general store and entered through the back door. Once inside they parted company in three directions, with Dick going out towards the telegraph office, Mary handing Art her list of needs, and Julie going into the mercantile section to begin her quest for Tom Seever's requested items.

She spent more time than usual selecting the gifts, more than she would have were they for herself. It was during this time that she ran into Suzan Kade, and the two stopped to chat.

"Why Julie, how good to see you!" Suzan exclaimed. "I'll bet you're doing your Christmas shopping."

"Yes, Mrs. Kade, well, not really. These are for Tom Seever. He asked me to do his for him."

"How nice. I feel so hurt for that young man. At least our Dan wasn't hit that terrible day. But young Tom is recovering well, isn't he?"

"Yes, he'll probably be able to walk around some by the first of year, according to Doc, and he sleeps a lot less then he was. Oh! And Allison let him be outside for awhile yesterday morning! He was so excited about that!" With her own excitement being so obvious she suddenly blushed and went silent.

Suzan laughed, and put her arm around Julie's shoulders as

she admonished her gently.

"Now you look here, Julie Garrison, don't you go getting flushed just because a nice, handsome young cowboy pays you a little attention. You're a very pretty young lady, and I'm surprised you're still single. So don't be getting all flustered when he pays attention to you."

"Oh. Oh … It's not really that. He doesn't even know I exist as a girl. Maybe his little sister or something. He's so taken in with Allison that no other girl would ever stand a chance!" With that impassioned outburst over, she blushed even more and was immediately sorry for being so open.

"Don't you bet on that, young lady. A horse isn't pulling a wagon until it's hitched up to it, and you dasn't give up hope. Does Allison feel that way for him?"

"No, I don't think so. I mean she's wonderful to him, and so gentle when she changes his dressings, but I think it's just because she cares for everyone. She's so much like Ira that it's hard to believe she's not his daughter. But poor Tom's going to be hurt by her if she isn't careful!"

Julie said the last with strong, nearly resentful, feelings, and became silent. Her task was suddenly becoming a burden she no longer wanted. But Suzan Kade's wisdom and discernment soon put her back on a bouyant path more suitable for an effervescent seventeen year old.

"Listen, it's only natural for a young man like Tom to fall in love with his nurse. But, that love is born out of a feeling of being taken care of, and may or may not last. You just be Julie, and if he should come to his senses and fall for you, you'll know that it's really love, and not just infatuation. Do you see what I'm getting at?"

"Yes, Mrs. Kade, but I don't have a lot of hope. But … if you really think … " and she faded off, beginning to smile again at the thought.

"Well," Suzan said, "I'd better be off to meet John or he's going to be getting impatient. You remember what I said, and I'll keep your secret safe."

The last was said with a big smile and a hug and she moved on. Julie then went about her tasks with a renewed vigor, the possibilities of romance once again spurring her on.

An hour later Julie was finished with her shopping chores, having found every single item on Tom's list. She stepped out of the final store just in time to hear Suzan Kade let out a loud cry that was a mixture of gladness and fear. Julie looked quickly in the direction that Suzan was running to see a huge man on a small mustang haul the creature to a halt and fairly leap off to meet Sue in the middle of the street. For a moment Julie was startled to see the rough looking stranger suddenly grab Suzan and lift her bodily from the ground in a vise-like bear hug.

Then she realized that Sue was reciprocating with her arms around his thick neck. Julie could hear the woman's gentle sobbing mingled with words that were unintelligible from her sidewalk vantage point.

Then a man's shout of "Art!" enchoed from behind her and rapidly running feet passed her by as John Kade went pell mell towards the couple. Upon his arrival, the scene quickly became a three-way hug.

Several onlookers stopped their passage and sort of mingled around to see what was going on. When the three finally disengaged themselves, Julie could hear the big fellow well enough to know what he said.

"Mother, I got your letter, and I just had to come. And I got word to Martin, he's on his way here as well. We plan to set out and find our little brother, one way or another. Martin can track a rattlesnake over a flat rock, and I figure to do what I can to help him.

"There's more, Mother and Dad. Martin and me, we talked it over a couple of weeks before your letter came, and we realized that we've shamed you. I haven't had a drink or a wom--- I mean, I haven't been on the town since then, and I aim to try my best to stay this way. I just hope you can find it in your hearts to forgive me!"

A poignant cry escaped the lips of Suzan Kade as she once again threw her arms around the neck of this giant. It struck Julie as nearly being funny; this six foot five ox, weighing nearly two hundred and sixty pounds, asking this little woman's forgiveness in a very soft, rather high-pitched voice. But at the same time, a lump came to her throat that she had to swallow hard to disperse, for she sensed a very wonderful thing was taking place in these lives before her. It was something that the young lady's strong Christian beliefs in reconciliation could reach out to and grasp firmly, and she felt so very good inside.

As she stood watching the three walk towards the Kade's buckboard, the giant in the middle and a teary-eyed parent on either side, she sensed the closeness of one standing beside her. She turned to find Mary standing at her side, gazing after the Kades.

"Oh Mother!" Julie exclaimed, "did you hear?"

"No dear, but I saw," Mary replied. "Who is that big fellow with John and Suzan?"

"He called them Mother and Dad, and said he was here to find their other son, Dan. Oh, isn't it like some story in a book, Mother?"

"Let's wait and see what the ending is, dear, but yes, it is exciting to see families reunited. Come on, your Dad is ready to go back. Here, I'll help you with those parcels." And with that, the pair trod off to meet Dick, and the return trip to the Slash N was soon underway.

ELEVEN

The sleigh, laden with four people, sounded its nearly silent whisper through the moonlit snow in tune to the twinkling bells on the two K bar D horses as they pranced along at a brisk trot. John, Suzan, Art, and Martin Kade were on their four-hour journey home from Ira Nelson's Slash N ranch, full of rich food and relishing the evening of warm fellowship, a nearly perfect Christmas eve. They would be home just before midnight, and, with the two somewhat wayward sons back with them for Christmas, all that could have made it better would have been Dan's presence.

Tom Seever leaned his head and shoulder against the post beside his wheelchair watching the black dot fade from sight. Allison stood beside him, her hand on his shoulder.

"Wasn't this a perfectly wonderful party, Tom?" she asked.

"Sure was. But I can't help feeling pretty sad for John and Sue. It's obvious they miss Dan and worry about him so very much," he answered.;

"Yes, they surely do. But it's so nice for them to have their other two sons back. Maybe they'll be able to find their brother. It's so sad that he's gone away like that when he doesn't need to be gone at all. If only he knew!

"I wonder what he's like? That big mountain called Art is so soft spoken, yet so outgoing too. And Martin hardly said a word all night! Do you suppose he's like one of them?"

Tom's reply surprised her.

"In a sense, yes. But for the most part, no. You see, we rode together for quite a ways, and I got to know Dan well enough to know I'd like him real well as a friend. Why, he was even trying to talk Candy and I into working for his dad.

"In fact, I just can't picture him as the type of guy to gun down the Chelseas. 'Course, he thought his folks were dead."

"Yes," she replied, "but it was still a horrible thing to do. Yet, I understand they did try to shoot first. Oh Tom, I do hope for Suzan's sake that he's O.K.!"

The poignancy of that last cry caused Tom to turn his head and gaze up at her lovely face. The moonlight glimmering off the snow made the late hour nearly as bright as day, yet with a tinge of romance added. He was trembling inside as he reached up and clasped her hand, holding it gently between his own as he watched her closely. It was becoming harder than ever to refrain from telling her how he felt, but for now Tom just basked in the warmth of her touch and the fact that she hadn't yet withdrawn her hand as she had before when he'd gotten brave enough to try holding it.

Finally she spoke, as if returning from someplace far away. "Listen, young man, if we don't get you back inside you're likely to become an icicle. Here, let me push you."

Tom offered no resistance, leaning forward and opening the big door when they reached it. The warmth from the roaring fireplace felt good, yet the cold crisp air on the moonlit porch had become a wonderfully rejuvenating medicine for him lately.

Ira was sitting on the huge sofa, his long bowlegs thrust straight out before him, stocking feet soaking up the heat as he sipped his coffee. Dick and Mary Garrison sat beside him, with Mary's head laying on her husband's shoulder. Julie was nowhere in sight, but the sounds of silverware in the kitchen suggested a presence there.

"Say, Allison, wheel that fellow over her," called Ira. "I think it's time we opened some presents!"

Allie did as requested, placing Tom in a position facing the couch. She then plopped on the floor by the old rancher's feet. It was shortly after that Julie came in carrying hot cocoa for all, a treat that had been sent for "back east" in anticipation of this night.

As soon as all were served and Julie was seated, Allison began distributing the gifts. There were the usual necessities and the unusual luxuries to be handed out. A pair of ornate Spanish silver spurs for Dick, bolts of dry goods for Mary, boxes of candy for each of the ladies, and so on from Ira. Gifts for every one from the Garrisons were passed out, and Tom was handed one from Julie as well. Upon opening it, he found a leather vest with Indian beads and fancy stitching all over the front in beautiful mosaic patterns. He was quite taken aback at such an expensive gift from the young girl.

"Julie!" You shouldn't have done this! It's much too nice and expensive!" he blurted out.

"Not for someone as special as Tom Seever," she answered, blushing immediately afterwards. It was obvious to all in the room but Tom that this young lady was in love.

"But, but, I don't have anything nearly as nice for you!"

At this, he quickly reached into the box beside his wheel chair and frantically searched until he found the small box for Julie. He'd had her mother select it for her, with some very specific guidelines he'd expressed.

Julie squealed with delight and snatched the offering from his hand. Her nimble fingers quickly laid to waste the green paper and ribbon, and she soon was opening the box held within, to find a golden locket inset with small stones gleaming back at her.

"Ohhhh! Tom Seever, you liar! This is beautiful! It cost way more than you should spend! Look at the diamonds!" she cried out, nearly in tears.

"Wait a minute you, those aren't diamonds, they're fake! So don't go ..." His protest was cut off by a kiss placed resoundingly on his lips, followed by Julie bounding embarrassed from the room. Tom could only stare after her for a moment, then he quickly glanced at Allison. Her amused smile and those beautiful eyes were shining back at his in quiet appreciation.

To cover his own embarrassment, he quickly began handing out the rest of his gifts. Leather gloves for Ira and Dick, more candy for Mary, Allie, and Julie, and a special package for Allie with locket, gloves, and silver mounted hand mirror inside.

As Allison opened her treasure and gazed upon the contents, her heart fell a notch for she suddenly realized that she meant too much to her charge. Julie's love was so obvious to her, Tom's for her should have been also. With beating, heavy heart, she walked over to him and kissed his cheek, whispering, "Thank you," as she quickly stepped behind him to mask the tumult of feelings she was experiencing. Julie loved Tom, Tom loved her, and she loved no one. At least not yet.

Her mind raced with the thoughts. After all, she was in her mid twenties already, and not married. Out here, that was unusual, with most young ladies marrying well before their twentieth birthday. And, she could do worse than Tom Seever. He was a very nice young man, intelligent, good looking. The moment was nearly too much for her, and she needed to step outside for fresh air, but to do so would raise questions she couldn't answer right now.

As if this latest realization wasn't enough, Allison had been wrestling with the fantasies all too common to the young and romantic. Since she'd come here a few months hence, she'd heard the story of Dan Kade's exciting escape on Sheba, and of his subsequent downing of the evil Chelseas and another flight to freedom.

She had pictured the young man alone by his campfires, grieving for his parents and suffering the loneliness of the hunted, while being cleared by the law all of this time! She had conjured up a sort of Romeo and Juliet outlook towards this young, gentle stranger upon whom she had never gazed.

The many talks with Suzan Kade hadn't helped, as Sue treasured her youngest, and when the huge Art had spoken so softly to his mother this evening, to be compared with Dan's mannerisms, she knew she had fantasized herself into loving Dan Kade. A man she'd never met! Yet, she could not shake the feeling.

Her love for John and Suzan had come so quickly, they were that kind of people. Ira's telling of his meeting Dan, of the instant rapport between them, and his later account of the tragedy, embellished somewhat because of Sheba's part in it, had served to start these thoughts. Hearing the accounts over and over, added to Tom Seever's opinion of Dan, had finished the process off for her.

Was there no hope of common sense taking over? Did she have to struggle thusly for the rest of her life? Allie struggled her way through these emotions in the matter of a few seconds, after which she busied herself with little tasks for the others. She picked up the empty cups, took them to the kitchen, hugged the still-blushing Julie, and returned to plop herself down onto Ira's lap.

"Now listen you," he said. "Just 'cause I pretend to be your favorite uncle doesn't mean you get more presents from me. You got that?"

"Yes, dear, dear, uncle Ira. You've given us all too much already. We'll probably have to sell out just to pay your bills," she replied.

"Well, it's not that bad. "Course, I do have three presents I haven't given out yet. But ... I think I'll wait 'til morning. You young folks can just sleep on it," and with that, Ira clammed up, and no amount of begging and coercing by the two young ladies could get him to even hint of the remaining gifts.

So it was that they soon tired of the game, and soon all were drifting to their respective beds.

As the six drifted off to sleep, vastly different, yet amazingly similar thoughts gently pushed each to the fuzzy edge of sleep.

Dick and Mary held each other tightly as they talked of their daughter's growing up. Ira smiled with the pleasant anticipation of the morning's pleasure, with the picture of his beautiful Sheba and Dan Kade slipping in at the last moment before sleep took over.

Julie's heart and lips burned with the memory of Tom Seever's actual touch, Tom's heart was aching with love for Allison, but was stirred in a strange way by Julie's kiss. Could a young, wayward cowboy love two women?

And Allison. Her very soul now cried out to Dan Kade, somewhere back in the canyon country, now that the full truth had finally forced itself upon her; stirred to the top by the realization that another man loved her. And what of him? Though her body lay still beneath the quilts, the soul within was in a turmoil that defied sleep. Yet, sleep did come, only to bring with it the romantic dreams of the youthful.

Morning dawned cold and crisp on the bench high above Metzal valley. The inhabitants of the Slash N awakened in a festive mood. The cowboys and other hired hands, except for one, knew the whole day was theirs. Many would be riding off to see family, or girlfriends, while others would remain, knowing that a feast would welcome them all at the main ranchhouse.

Ira Nelson was a strict rancher, he expected a day's work for a day's pay, but he was also a fair man, and expected no less of himself. He also considered those who worked for him to be family. If you worked hard enough to be kept on at the Slash N, you were respected and held up to the same level of consideration that any professional man was given, whether doctor or lawyer.

So it was that Ira's hands were loyal to a fault. And it was the reason that one hand didn't have the whole day off. Shorty Eber had volunteered to do all the necessary chores around the barns and corrals as his Christmas gift to his cronies. It was an appreciated one, for sure, as the men knew that old Shorty would spend at least two hours in the morning and half again that long in the evening just taking care of the livestock. Except for milking the six dairy cows that supplied all of the milk and cheese for the ranch. Shorty was a wrangler, and he was one who hated cows, especially milking!

"So who milks the cows, Shorty?" Ira had asked.

"I guess you do, boss," the diminutive little wrangler said as he drew all of his five foot six frame to its full height.

So Ira milked, but he gave Shorty a very special task to do. One that was extra; but after all, he couldn't very well do it himself if he did the milking, now could he?

At breakfast, which everyone went to the main house for as well as the noon meal, Shorty excused himself quite early, something no one ever did around there, and disappeared. As he did so, it just so happened that the two young ladies of the house remembered Ira's promise of the evening before. With that knowledge reappearing, they both assailed him with their demands to see what was to be forthcoming to them.

While they pestered Ira, Dick slipped out and went off in the same direction Shorty had taken, to reappear just minutes later with that worthy by his side. They both nodded to Ira, who promptly stood to his feet.

"I want each of you here to listen," he started. "I have something very special for each of you.

"This year has been the most prosperous year in the history of the Slash N. We've sold more riding stock to the Army than all the other area ranches put together as well as the horses we've shipped to the Eastern buyers.

"This wouldn't be happening without top hands who are not only faithful, hard workers, but who also know their business better than any other wranglers around. So, I'm giving each of you an envelope with an extra month's pay, as well as a ten dollar raise!"

Everyone stared for an instant, then Pandemonium broke out as the hands began to cheer, whistle, beat each other on the back, and just generally raise cain. As Ira passed out the envelopes, he also gave one to Tom, Allie, and Julie.

"But Uncle, I'm not a wrangler, just a nurse to one of your future wranglers," protested Allie.

"Sir, I'm not a wrangler here yet, just the object of wrath for your nurse there," added Tom.

Julie said nothing, being dumbfounded.

"Well now, before you get all over my case, you'd better just open those to see what's in them," Ira replied.

They eagerly did so, noting the sudden quiet that had engulfed the hands, who stood around in interested silence. All three contained the same thing, a note that said, "Go to the front porch and see your gift."

They hesitated just long enough to cast confused looks at each other, then tore for the door, both girls leaving poor Tom to fend for himself.

The crew was but a split second behind, one of them rescuing Tom's wheelchair to push him outside. Everyone stood in rapt silence at the sight at the hitching rail in front of the house.

Standing with heads up, ears forward, and curious eyes suspiciously moving from person to person stood three of Ira's finest horses. There were two smallish mares with black, silver mounted saddles, each with a name tag hanging from the silver studded martiingale, and a gorgeous sorrel gelding that could have been born to only one horse, Sheba!

He, too, sported a beautiful silver mounted saddle, this one in brown, complete with tapedaros, martingale, bridle, and a new rifle in the saddle sheath.

The sign hanging around his neck said, "To Tom."

Tom Seever's chest fairly heaved with the pressure from within as he fought to keep his emotions in check. After swallowing several times and blinking to clear his eyes, he spoke, his voice choked with feeling. "Ira, you just can't do this. You've doctored me, fed me, no doubt you've saved my life. I just can't take a gift like this on top of all that."

"Now you youngsters just listen to me," the old fellow answered. "I'm old enough to spend my evenings TRYING to remember my youth. Tom, you've become like the son we never had. Allison and Julie, you've become like the daughters we never had. These last few months have been the happiest I've had since my Sarah died.

"To see your exuberance and jesting, your practical jokes on each other, and your, your love for each other has meant more than any of you could imagine.

"So there's my thanks. It'll be time for you to be riding before you know it, Tom, and when that time is here, there's your mount. No arguments, no discussion. You want to work here for Dick and I, you better learn to take orders, and we ORDER you to take that horse."

Ira found himself in the middle of a crowd of three; himself and the two girls hugging him, dragging him over to Tom, where they clasped hands in a very emotional moment, both looking into the others tear-dimmed eyes. It was a great Christmas day.

TWELVE

Spring was gently pushing its way into Wild Horse Canyon, so aptly named by Five Ponies during the winter's tenure. The mild-mannered stream had experienced a change in temperament and was running over its banks in an angry rush of crystal-clear melting snow water.

As it roared its way around each curve it pummeled the cutbanks with a vicious rush, and as each succeeding bank added part of its soil to the rush, the water grew more and more clouded with the muddy tint until it was passing the wrangler's cabin in a wild transit of seemingly liquid earth.

There were small bands of wild horses spotting the valley, usually eight to twelve in a bunch, and they remained dressed in their three-inch-long, shaggy winter coats, reluctant to accept the gradual warming as a sign of impending spring.

On the high plains and canyon tops, three feet of snow remained, but it was porous from the combination of melting and sublimation until it seemed a coarse honeycomb of white ice. In a short few days, it too would join the creek in its mad rush to the valleys.

In the two fenced canyons behind the camp was a total of one hundred head of mustangs, all gentled enough to saddle and ride, as long as one didn't relax too much in the doing of it. Some, of course, were further along than others, for like men and dogs, the rippling, muscle-bound bodies of horses encased a being that geneology dictated would have different temperaments and personalities. Therefore, some accepted their new places in life in a more docile way than others. These had quickly been detected and singled out for Dan Kade to spend all of his time with, for he exhibited that rare natural affinity for horses that drew from them their best.

No animal in the herd had exhibited more willingness than the big ugly brute that had by now been named Blue. The intelligence Dan and Bear had seen in those eyes right away had certainly manifested itself, and Dan now had the finest overall mount he had ever ridden.

Huge, powerful, intelligent, and nearly as fast as Sheba, Blue had endeared himself to all save Johnson, whom he hated. The man had gotten too close once, and spent three weeks healing from the terrible bruises and contusions the powerful teeth had left on his shoulder. The beast had grabbed him and lifted him from the ground as though he were a rag doll! Had he not been tied at the time, the outlaw would probably have died a terrible death, but he was fortunate and fell just out of reach of the big hooves when Blue tossed him away. He never went near the horse again, and thereafter the hatred was mutual.

As a result of Dan's constant work with the more teachable stock, there were forty-three head of excellent riding stock, all broken to herding and roping. After all, it had been a long winter.

Of these, each man was allowed to pick three for himself as well as two others, for his personal remuda. The rest would be sold and the profits split evenly. With twenty-five head of top horses left, and forty-five that were at least average riding stock, they figured to rake in a really fair profit for their winter's work.

Dan was taking an afternoon off when Reddy and Bear joined him on a huge rock overlooking the rushing waters.

"Hey, Wrangler, here ya are, loafing away when ya could be workin'," Reddy quipped.

"Oh, hi. Yeah, I was just sorta dreamin' about seeing real people in a few weeks, 'stead of having to look at all of your ugly mugs," he replied.

"Wal," Bear growled, "Joe jest left to scout on top 'n see whut the conditions is like. Likely he'll hev to sleep out tonight

79

in order to git as fer as he needs to . Should be back late tom-morrow."

"Wow! This soon. I've been looking forward to this time, but somehow, I guess I just hadn't figured it'd get here."

"Well, Dan, it's here," Red Elk explained, "and Bear, Joe, Jack 'n I were talkin' this mornin'. We'd like to stick together as an outfit, and sure would like it if'n you stuck with us, too. What do you say?"

"Say? I say great. But ... just where do you plan to go from here? I sorta, well, I just need to know where, I guess, before I say yes." Dan stammered his way through that speech as he looked from one to the other's eyes.

"Say, youngster, the three of us, without Jack, talked it over," Bear answered, "and we sorta feel like maybe YOU should tell us where we can go or cain't go..

"After all, it is you that's shakin' the law, not us."

Dan was struck through with a cold shock at that statement. How could they know? He studied awhile before he answered the gravelly voiced man of the mountains. Once he regained his composure, he spoke.

"How did you know? I mean ... I never told any of you! How? Tell me, please." That last was a plaintive cry for help.

"Well, Dan, ole pard, it showed in yore eyes that first mo-ment I found you on the high plains. I suspected then.

"And while we've been down here, you've often had that hunted look in those same eyes; mostly when you've been thinkin' for a spell.

"Then Bear noticed thet whenever anyone called thet mean, poor excuse fer a man Johnston an outlaw, you flinched. Oh, not much, but enough." Then Reddy went on, "We ain't askin' to know, pard. We jest need to know whar we kin and whar we cain't go."

Dan steeled himself, and proceeded to tell his story, sparing no details. He had to stop several times to regain his composure, but when he finally finished, he felt all the better for it.

There was a pregnant silence for several minutes, then Bear broke it with a quiet, yet determined statement.

"Kid, thet is the rottenest treatment I've ever heard of, and ya kin bet I'm gonna stick to ya no matter what. If'n it comes to gun play, count on me, cause I'm yore pard fer life."

"And you kin add me to that, pard, 'n Joe too, I'll bet when he hyars yore story," Reddy added.

After another long, thoughtful pause, Dan said, "Thanks, fellas, you don't know what that means to me, but I sure don't intend on any more gun play in my life."

"Now you look," Reddy quickly spoke, "I've been workin' at least an hour a day with you on that very thing. You've learned how to throw that pistol quickly and can shoot darned real good with it. I didn't spend all that time with ya fer nothin', cause yore shore gonna hev to bore thet Johnston sooner or later. You kin bet on it, Dan, fer he's gonna push it!"

"I don't think so, Reddy, at least I hope not. And as for you guys buckin' the law for me, I won't hear of it, you understand?"

At that, Bear's huge head suddenly snapped up and turned towards the downstream end of the canyon. He had all the appearance of a bird dog on point.

"Listen!" he snapped. In a little while he grinned, and added to the other listeners, "Joe's comin' back a-ready!"

"Then it's either extra bad or extra good on top!" Reddy exclaimed.

With that, they all started rapidly to the little cabin, all aglow with excitement mixed with trepidation, for all were ready to leave their beautiful little canyon for the real world.

It was a full two hours before Joe reined his dripping wet and heaving horse up in front. He dismounted as though he'd just been out for a ride and strode past them into the cabin, where he poured a cup of coffee, then began to strip his wet clothes off to exchange for dry and warm articles.

Jack quickly left to care for Joe's horse, stripping the gear from it and then beginning a rub down with a dry blanket. He walked the animal in a small circle as he did so.

All were waiting impatiently at the table for Joe to speak, which didn't happen.

"Say, you," snapped Johnston, "do ya aim to keep us waitin' here all day afore ya tell us what ya seen?"

Joe barely lifted his eyes from the coffee cup as he replied,

"No, just until Jack's in here, so I do not have to tell it twice."

"Shoot! He don't matter no how," the grouchy outlaw shot back, "he's just a no count kid whut don't pull his weight!"

Reddy started to stand, but Dan's hand on his arm held him down, and Dan spoke instead.

"Listen you, Jack's done all the working and cleaning here, and just because you consider that woman's work doesn't make it any easier to do! He's not griped once, and we've not missed a meal, so he's as much a partner in this as anyone, especially the likes of you!"

"Aw, don't get yore back up, the kid 'n I've become good friends, but I don't think he rates a voice in this."

"Well, he does, and he will have," said Reddy, and the matter was closed.

Before long Jack came stomping in and tossed his coat onto his bunk, flopped down on top of it and crossed his hands behind his head as he leaned back against the wall.

"Well, we're all here," Joe started, "so here's the way it looks. I know I left expecting to be gone for at least two nights, but I got on top with so little trouble that I couldn't see going any further.

"Apparently it was a pretty mild winter up there, and we can push on out within a week!"

"That settles that," Reddy exclaimed, "fer I was gettin' concerned about drivin' some of the mares that are gonna be foaling. This way we should have all the trailing behind us before they do, and we shouldn't lose any colts! We'll leave five days from now at daybreak."

"No, let's wait three extra days, so we can cross the creek out here easier, and we'll be less likely to hit flooding in some of the other areas as we head clear out north, "Joe suggested.

"O.K., eight days it is," Reddy agreed, and a festive mood struck them all.

"I'm gonna fix that big ole tom turkey that Bear brought in yesterday," Jack piped up. "We'll celebrate seeing the outside world again. I don't mind tellin' you all, I've missed people, especially girl people!"

They all laughed, as Jack had become the target of numerous pranks in an effort to cheer him up, as had Dan, for both had become rather morose in the past few weeks.

Reddy and Bear both knew the reason for Dan's mood now. He'd obviously been dreading leaving the quiet seclusion of Wild Horse Canyon. With a knowing glance at each other, they reaffirmed their support for their young friend.

The two Indians were of the background that gave them the abilities to adapt to whatever life handed them. If solitude it was, then they could make the most of it. If it was to be civilization, then so be it.

Bear Rollins, the mountain man, was, by choice, one who preferred few people around him. The outlaw Johnston wouldn't fit in no matter where he went, so he stood the winter well also.

Therefore, the two younger men of the group, Dan and Jack, didn't hold up as well to the several cold months of isolated canyon life. But with a decision made on leaving, Jack became his old self, though Dan still struggled between a desire to see people and a fear of being caught. His nights remained lonely. For him, there was little comfort.

THIRTEEN

It was exactly a week later, at 2 A.M., when Bear and Joe both sprung bolt upright in their bunks.

"I heerd a gunshot!" Bear exclaimed.

"Me too," answered Joe, "quite a ways off, but it definitely was a rifleshot."

"Thar, thar's two more. Handgun, this time," said Bear.

Reddy had risen by now and lit a lamp. "Hey! Johnston and Jack are gone!"

Thet consarned outlaw is up to no good, you bet on it," was Bear's reply as he tugged on his buckskins.

They all were soon dressed and went cautiously out the door. Dan ran for the small corral by the cabin where their day's horses should be, to find the bars down and all stock gone, including Sheba!

"Hey! These horses are gone!" he yelled, and no sooner was the first echo of his voice sounding from the canyon walls than the four of them were in a full run for the fenced in canyons behind them.

When they had covered the distance and stood panting for breath at the gates, the moonlight revealed to them a pair of empty corrals.

"Now how in tarnation did those jaspers git the hosses outta hyar without we heard them?" Bear raged. "We got two sharp redskins and a mountaineer, and they snookered a hunnerd hosses by us in our sleep!"

"I don't know, but I'm worried about those shots that finally did wake up our redskins and mountain man," Joe replied. "We've got to start out as soon as possible. I'm afraid Jack may have suspected something and tried to stop that dead man alone!"

The others glanced knowingly at each other at Joe's reference to the outlaw as a dead man, each one grasping the significance.

Dan interjected his thoughts, "Look, I agree, but there's just no way one man is driving a hundred head of stock at night, even in daylight, for that matter!

"I figure he's selected the best horses and scattered the rest in order to delay us. There simply has to be some riding stock nearby!"

With that he elicited a shrill whistle and called out, "Blue! Blue! Here big and ugly!" Then another whistle.

Off in the darkness, quite a distance away could be heard a nicker, then the thud of large, heavy hooves. They continued awhile, then ceased.

"Blue! Come here Blue!" Then the whistle.

This time the hooves came much faster and steadier, as the big roan became sure of his master's voice. In a couple of long minutes he came crashing up to Dan, obviously skittish and upset.

Dan finally grabbed the ragged mane and made a valiant effort to swing astride. Blue was just too big! Bear quickly grabbed Dan's foot and gave him a heave aboard, where upon Dan kneed the intelligent brute towards the cabin.

Finding his rig in the dark, he slung it to Blue's back and was cinching up when the others trooped in on foot.

"Dan," Reddy spoke, "you've gotta ketch more hosses, a real big job in the dark, mebbe impossible, but ya gotta try!"

"Consider them caught, Pard, dark or not!" And he was gone into the night.

Determination is a great taskmaster, but in spite of Dan's assurance, it was fully an hour after first light before he rode wearily into camp with three of their horses in tow.

"They've not scattered too badly, fellas. In fact they're bunched up pretty good, but down canyon instead of up. It looks like around twenty head of horses started up a wide sloping bench down there about a mile. The rest were right in that same area.

"He left some of the really good stock, so catching these wasn't too tough once I found them!" And with that breathless speech out, Dan slipped to the ground and headed for the cabin, totally starved.

When he came out eating some cold biscuits and jerky, the others were saddled, with provisions behind all four saddles for a week. They had prepared these packs while waiting for Dan's return.

"Make sure you've plenty of ammo, and that them rifles are loaded men!" cried Reddy as he made for his mount. They were soon pounding off behind Dan towards the canyon exit.

Wild Horse canyon begins to narrow down gradually, until it peters out to a mere ten yard wide crevice filled with the rushing waters of the creek. That continued for nearly a quarter of a mile before opening into another, lower canyon.

While the water's exit path was not negotiable, about half a mile back upstream was a sloping bench that was easily wide enough for wagon passage should one desire to remove the boulders and trees from it.

The slope was gradual enough to provide a fairly comfortable climb of two thousand feet in about four miles. It turned into the canyon wall about a third of the way up to become a wide crevice of its own. It was there they found Jack.

Dan saw him first, for his big blue roan was eager to climb and was in front of the others, but he suddenly shied and leaped back at a form directly ahead by a boulder.

Dan leaped off with a loud cry of "Jack!" and ran to him. As he knelt by the lad he could see the red froth of blood on his lips, and heard the barely audible breathing as it gurgled with each exhale.

He tore the bloody shirt open, to find two ugly holes staring at him. One was in the chest, the other lower down, just below the ribs. Jack was barely conscious.

The act of tearing open his shirt had started the bleeding again, and Dan began trying to stop the flow just as the others knelt.

Reddy tipped a canteen to Jack's mouth, allowing a few drops to trickle down, then tried to talk to him.

"Jack! Darn you kid! Why'd ya try to stop that thief by yoreself? When you saw him slippin' out ya shoulda woke someone else, boy!"

The youngster coughed, and with a look of pain not born of bullet wounds gasped out his confession.

"I was helping him. He's been planning this for weeks, and told me if I didn't help him he'd burn my folks out. He'd been hurting me from time to time, too, just to keep me down.

"I'm sorry, I couldn't help it!" Then he lapsed into a fit of coughing and passed out.

`Reddy leaped up and began to cut a nearby sapling, working quietly and rapidly. Joe stalked down the shelf to another and began to do the same. Bear pulled the bed roll from his saddle and began to pierce the edges of the tarp with small holes. Dan realized quickly that the three were instinctively working like a well-oiled machine to build a travois to haul Jack back to the shelter of the small cabin. He applied himself to binding up the two holes by tearing Jack's shirt up for bandages.

It was about two hours before they placed the now feverish body, limp and seemingly lifeless, on a bunk. Reddy stirred the fire to life and broke out his warbag. In it were herbs used by his people for healing, and Red Elk was known among his cowboy peers as well as his native family as one who had studied hard the medicines of his people and learned well.

Through the rest of that day, young Jack Varley lay on the edge of life, clinging only by a desperate thread. Every breath came raspingly and haltingly, each one the result of the amazing tenacity the human body has for life. Around ten that night he regained consciousness for a few minutes.

He wept openly as he gasped out the story of his part in the theft.

Johnston had stolen all the ropes he could, leaving only a couple he'd missed, and as they roped the best of the horses he'd tied them on cut ropes to each other's neck, and when he ran out of rope, he quit. They had two bunches of mustangs of fifteen each when they were done.

He sent Jack on with those, and proceeded to drive the rest of the horses out as quietly as possible. The outlaw then took all of the horses from the small corral, including Sheba, and rode off to join Jack. It was at the turn in the trail that Jack could no longer abide the outlaw's treachery, and he jerked his rifle from its saddle sheathe and hurriedly fired at Johnston.

He missed, and the outlaw answered with his six-gun, not missing. Jack pleaded with the men to leave him and go after Johnston right away, he pleaded for them to forgive him, and repeatedly sobbed as he did so.

"Now listen, Jack, we understand, and we're not holding anything against you. Understand? Now you just calm down and be quiet, you're making matters worse for yourself, and we want to pull you through. You forget everything for now; we're not leaving you, and we want you for part of this crew!"

After this from Joe, the young man did rest somewhat easier, but awakened often from fitful sleep, or coma, or whatever it was, and repeatedly asked for someone they'd not heard of to hold his hand.

Dan sat with him through the night, holding his hand and washing the fevered brow often. He finally fell asleep from exhaustion, but dreamed nightmarishly of the Chelseas, Johnston, and his parents.

When Bear's huge hand on his shoulder awakened him, the gray of dawn was upon them. Dan sat up, startled, and quickly grasped the hand he'd let slip from his, only to gasp and drop it as though burned. The hand that had been alternately hot and sweaty, then cold and clammy now was simply cold and lifeless. Young Jack Varley was dead.

On his face was the terrified look of one alone, blank eyes staring lifelessly and hopelessly into space, with a set to his mouth that suggested a final struggle to remain, a struggle lost. Dan lost all his composure and sobbed openly and bitterly at this wasted young life, all over greed, until Reddy and Joe were wakened by the noise.

"Aww no!" Reddy cried out, Joe only dropped his head in his hands for a moment, then began to utter the soft death chant of his people, a mournful, eerie sound coming soft and low.

Joe was the most educated of the four, but sometimes the more learning one does, the stronger the ties to their background become, and at this moment, Joe was once again Five Ponies, Comanche warrior, and no one else.

Bear's reaction was totally different. He set about getting a large meal, preparing enough for several meals at once. Then, as all was cooking on the fire, he began to pack for a long ride. Reddy, after a short walk outside, pitched in, and their actions soon spurred their comrades to join them.

"Hyars the way I see it," Bear spoke as they worked. "We bury Jack out hyar in the grove where he liked to sit an' watch the crick, then we should split up. Now Joe, I know yore the best tracker, but I'm pretty fair myself, an' that varmit is draggin' twenty or more broomtails with him, so he'll not be hidin' tracks well at all. So, I'll take Dan and that monster hoss o' his'n an go after Johnston. You two git busy roundin' up what hosses ya kin, so's we don't lose our whole winter's work.

"It'll be a heck of a job, cause them hosses is still wild, so don't kill yourselves gittin' all of em, jist do whut ya kin and then head out after us. We'll mark the trail real plain. After we git the varmit, an' we will git him, we'll stay put. Thet sound right to you, men?"

Reddy quickly answered, "Sounds perfect, Bear. That way you'll hev thet Sharps 50 along to knock the snake outta the saddle long range, 'n iffn he tries to haul outta there on any hoss but Sheba, Dan can run him down. But Dan, I don't need to tell ya that a race between the roan an Sheba would likely mean one of 'em would be run to death 'n the other would be wind broke, so wait fer the right time to try such a ride so's to lessen the chances of a long race.

"An' I want you to take extra ridin' stock so's to switch off, 'cause ya know he's goin' to do so. Joe 'n I kin ketch us a couple o' hosses out hyar, so's you take all the stock we got out hyar now."

Joe agreed, adding, "Let's get poor Jack put to rest, and get on with this. I want a rope around Johnston's neck before another week is out!"

Dan shivered at the statement, but steeled himself to the fact that this had to be a ride to the death. Johnston had written his own sentence by adding murder to horse stealing, and a court of law was not necessary, in his opinion, to carry out the sentence. He would not only ride with Bear on the manhunt, he would do so with the resolve to capture or kill, no holds barred. He was satisfied with his decision, but not at all comfortable with the carrying out of it.

FOURTEEN

Water dripped copiously from the huge oak trees that filled the large level park as the day dawned gray and wet. A constant rain had fallen all night and a foggy haze slipped in in place of the morning sun. Steam rose mingling with the smoke of the small campfire as the wet logs dried out next to it.

Two wet and hungry forms crouched near the fire waiting for the coffee to boil and the venison to roast. A drizzle continued to fall, assuring them that the day would be a long one. It ran from their hat brims to the back of their slickers, cropping in rivulets around them to soften the layer of leaves beneath their ragged, worn boots.

The hobbled horses had been brought into camp and stamped impatiently from their picket line, wanting to be allowed activity that would help them warm their soggy bodies from the penetrating dampness and chill.

As Bear Rollins handed Dan a tin cup of coffee he offered his thoughts. "Reckon we're no more than a day behind him now, Dan. You want to keep yore eyes open today. We don't wanta ride up on him without we first see him and have the upper hand. That varmint would as soon back shoot us as nothin'!"

"I don't know where he's headed, Bear, but we've been two weeks on his trail, and it seems to me he's headed north most of that time. Where does that put us now?"

"Wal, Danny, my young friend, if'n you've never been in Utah afore, yore certainly thar now. Thar's a pass outta hyar bout two day's ride from us that opens up into a long valley what has two towns with railroads in them. They runs east outta the valley clear into Colorado, where they joins up with that track that drops down into Arizony.

"We gotta ketch this skunk afore he hits thet first town, as it's a horse dealin' town, an' he'll find a good market there fer them hosses, sure."

With that speech ended, Bear suited action to words and grabbed the not-quite-done meat from the fire and sliced off a huge hunk, slapped it between two cold biscuits from the previous night, and began to wolf it down, chasing it with the scalding hot coffee.

Dan followed suite, and when the gray dawn had completed its task of nudging aside the night, it found them saddled and riding, and at a fairly rapid pace, as the tracks were easily seen in spite of the rain's attempt to wash them away.

After four hours of gradual climbing they emerged from the dense forest onto a crest of a ridge. The landscape dipped sharply away to the floor of a wide canyon several hundred feet below, with a floor nearly devoid of vegetation and strewn with boulders. It appeared to be some ten to fifteen miles long, gradually descending all the way.

Bear let out a satisfied grunt and pointed down its path. Nearly halfway down its length, Dan made out several horses, strung out nearly single file, with one rider behind them. Johnston!

"No, Dan Kade, hyars when thet big hoss of yores makes the difference. You switch yore saddle over to him whilst I talk." As Dan put the order into action, Bear went on, "To the right hyar is purty flat country fer nearly twenty miles, then thar's a rocky descent right at the mouth o' this hyar canyon. It's dangerous and steep, but yore horseman enough and thet's horse enough to handle it.

"You run this devil an' run him hard till ya git to a huge sandstone rock the size of a house. It'll be off ta yore left, and ya cain't miss it, fer it's small at the bottom an is balanced like it could fall anytime. Only it won't. Cut jist to the right of it and you'll see the desert. Give this big hoss a few minutes rest, walkin' him slow. then hit thet trial down hard, an' I think we'll hev the varmint boxed.

"I'll take all the hosses with me, but I'm gonna push 'em hard, so don't loaf. An' remember, this man is gonna die, whether one of us shoots him, or we hang 'im! So don't take no chances, you hyar?"

"I hear you, Bear, don't worry, cause I want him!" Dan answered.

Blue stamped impatiently as Dan finished cinching up, and was off as soon as Dan hit the leather. He pounded down the rocky flats as though the very devil was after him, and Dan could not but marvel at the power and speed of this horse he'd come to love as much as Sheba. He let him go full out for at least two miles before pulling him down some, but he still ran him hard, as Bear had commanded.

For what seemed like days the big brute pounded on, down gradual slopes only to erase the slight climb back up as though he were still going down. He leaped the smaller rocks as a rabbit clears a fallen tree and cut and swerved by the larger ones as if they were mere shadows to be erased.

On and on, forcing the miles to flow beneath them like the eddies of a river he flew. Dan rode bent low over his neck, occasionally patting and stroking as he talked to the now lathered brute as they flew on.

They broke out close to the rim very briefly, and Dan caught a quick glimpse of the canyon floor ahead of them and far below. It was void of life! The gallant Blue had taken him past the outlaw!

Instead of a walking rest to begin the descent, Dan hauled the big fellow down to a fast lope for three miles and could feel the massive stride return to a full, easy stride. He had no idea how far this horse could go at an all out gallop, but he knew he'd never ridden another that could come even close, including Sheba! How he hoped and prayed that it would never come to a race between the two!

As he sensed the muscles beneath him begin to strain to be allowed to go all out again, he sighted the rock Bear had spoken of about a mile ahead. He allowed Blue to stretch out again, but not to full speed.

He paused at the huge rock to take a look for the trail, and there it was, just as Bear had said it would be. Dan couldn't help but wonder if there was any part of these mountains that Bear Rollins hadn't traveled and didn't know!

He faced the big roan down the steep, rock-strewn trail with the realization that after he and Sheba's descent into the Grand Canyon with Red Elk, this was nothing. The horse was able to keep to a very fast trot or slow lope all the way to the bottom. "Old son," Dan told the horse, "you've got a cake walk here. Someday, if you get too cocky, I'll take you down a real trail!" Then he chuckled, for he received the same ears forward response that Sheba would have given.

Upon his arrival at the bottom he turned up the canyon and looked for a likely place to stop the herd and is driver. He'd settled on a spot that appeared to have had a rock slide on one of the walls and was choked down to a gap roughly fifty yards wide. The perfect spot if there was such a thing.

Dan had just drawn his carbine from the saddle sheath when the boulder beside him virtually exploded in his face. He faintly heard the angry whine of a ricochet bullet as it screamed away.

Instinct flung him from the saddle to a spot behind the same rock, and he fought frantically to clear his burning eyes of the painful dust that had filled them. Blue had jumped wildly from under him and could be heard pounding away down the canyon. Dan's eyes were watering profusely and had begun to clear somewhat when he heard Johnston's voice!

"Well, big shot, let's have you stand up here and see what kind of scurvy scum you are! You didn't figger I'd seen ya tearing along that rim ahead of me did ya? Oh yeah, you were a fur piece off, but thar's no mistakin' thet ugly blue hoss o' yorn."

Dan's eyes were now cleared enough to see the outlaw facing him and realized that his back was to the direction Johnston had been coming from. That placed Bear behind him instead of Johnston!

"I'm gonna put a rifle slug in yore guts, Kade, then I'm gonna find thet blue roan and put several in his! So jist watch the barrel o' this here Winchester 'n see if'n you kin see the slug come out!"

Dan's hand flashed to his pistol as the rifle barrel came up, but a thhhwuupppp sound swished by his ear so close he felt as well as heard it, accompanied instantly by a sudden slap as the outlaw was flung backwards as though some giant hand had reached out and smashed him. He bounced off a rock, twisting sideways and falling as he did. His rifle flew from his hands when he hit, but with some sort of amazing strength he came to his knees, clawing for his pistol. As it came out of the holster, Dan's own Colt leaped in his hand, and before the report even sounded, a small hole appeared in Johnston's temple as his head jerked violently back. He was dead before he fell.

Dan walked unsteadily to the outlaw, gun at the ready, and when he found no pulse, he actually heaved a sigh of relief. Then he sat down on the nearest rock to try to get his equilibrium back. The shock hit him quickly, and with the nearness of his own death coupled to killing again, he trembled and fought off a sickness until Bear came riding up several minutes later.

He put his big hand on Dan's shoulder in fatherly fashion and said, "Son, I shore am sorry I couldn't a did fer thet varmint myself, but thar just warn't enuff o' him showin' past yore own self fer me ta get a killin' shot in. I'm awful sorry fer thet."

Dan experienced a new and different shock at that. "You … you mean you shot that close to me on purpose? Why, I felt the air from that bullet go by me!"

"Had to. Warn't no other way, son."

"How … how far away were you? It seems I barely heard the rifle, and then it was as he was falling."

"Aw, not that fur, maybe four hunnert yards or so. I saw whut was agoin' to take place and figgered I'd better really pound leather to git as close as I could. I saw ya pop out onter the rim fer a second, fergot ta warn ya 'bout thet spot, and I could tell he did too, fer her really sent they Sheba flyin' ta beat ya hyar."

"Sheba!? He was on her? Then--how far ahead of him was I there. When he saw me, I mean?"

"Oh, 'bout five mile. No more. I tell ya, I was really glad to be straddlin' that dun o' mine, he shore sent some dust up gittin' me in range o' you two. He ain't as fast as these two great horses o' yorn, but as long as I got this buffler gun, ta extend our range, I mean, he'll shore do!"

Dan was slowly coming out of it, and realized that the sooner Johnston was out of sight, the better.

"What'll we do with him, Bear? We don't have a shovel with us, and even if we did, I doubt if we could dig here in this rock."

"Wal, we'll jest slide him over by thet rock slide thar 'n tumble some stones over 'im so's the coyotes cain't get him. Don't wanna poison no coyotes, now do we? But first, let's ketch thet hoss o' yorn and get these others bunched together. I'm afeared if'n we leave the ropes on them any longer, they're gonna gald somethin' fierce. I noticed a couple of 'em with sores on their necks as it is."

It took no effort to find either Blue or Sheba, as Dan merely whistled twice and the two of them came around a huge boulder together. They trotted up to Dan and nuzzled him affectionately, the two of them nearly knocking him down.

"Hey, you two! Take it easy here," he said.

"Shoot!" burst out Rollins. "Them ain't hosses! Them is big ridin' dogs, the way they act."

Dan chuckled at that as he pulled their ears and petted them, thinking as he did so how much he was going to miss Sheba, for he'd been developing a plan. If he could assure himself that the railroad could connect up with the proper runs to get her to Arizona, he intended to ship her and Ira's fancy saddle home. To take such a chance of being located didn't please him at all, but he figured he could move on north quickly and avoid detection.

The two of them mounted up and in short time they had everything in hand. They salvaged enough long pieces of rope to rig a makeshift picket line to hold the stock long enough to bury the remains of Mr. Johnston, former horse thief.

After removing all of his belongings, they simply dragged him to a spot beside the rock slide and tumbled stones over him. That done, they placed several larger ones on top so that nothing could dig the body out, and returned to the horses.

"Say, Bear, what do we do with his things? I mean, there's a couple hundred dollars here, besides his guns and saddle."

"Wal, he sure ain't needin' 'em, Dan'l, so I'd guess we should appropriate 'em as payment due fer our troubles.

"You run the varmint down and did fer 'im, so you jist keep it fer y'self."

"Oh no, not a chance!" Dan replied. "If you hadn't parted my ear with that buffalo gun of yours, I'd be dead meat right now instead of him!

"I'm going to need a saddle and rifle fairly soon. I'll take those, you take the money."

"Now, I tell ya what. Thet's O.K. by me, but you take that fancy holster rig and Colt, too. It'll look might good on an honest man fer a change."

With the unpleasant task done, they both realized that they didn't want to try holding the horses in this dry canyon. So, they removed the ropes from all the horses, and began the few hours drive to the green grass and running stream beyond.

They were well situated in a nice grove of trees with a temporary rope corral up by supper time. There was plenty of grazing among the trees, and the stream ran right through it, so they determined to remain there until Reddy and Joe caught up with them.

As they sat around their fire in the darkness, Dan laid out his plans to ship the mare back to old Ira Nelson.

"Wal now, Danny lad, thet's real white of you. And, I happen to know thet connections kin be had all the way to Flagstaff in Arizona, and ya kin wire him ta pick the mare up thar. But I'll tell ya this, my young friend, that hoss is gonna miss you, fer she's jist like a hound dog whar yore concerned. Her eyes are always on ya,, 'n she follers ya around all the time."

"I know it, Bear, and it's not going to be easy to let her go, either. I've come to absolutely love her a lot. More than I ever thought a man could love an animal, but shoot, she's closer to being human than some people I've known."

"Thet's fer sure. Now, not to change the subject, but I'm thinkin' on leavin' in the mornin'. Reddy 'n Joe are tryin' ta drive the wilder hosses 'n track us at the same time. I'll take two hosses 'n a little pack 'n beat leather back thar and help 'em out.

I know these hyar mountains, 'n I kin make some all fired good time, 'n thet'll help them make better time in turn."

"That's a good idea, Bear. I'll just laze around here, patch saddles, and sleep. Sounds pretty good to me right now."

With that, they rolled into their blankets, and sleep soon captured them. It was the sleep of the dead for Rollins, for he hardly moved all night, but it remained the fitful sleep of the hunted for Dan. Would he never be free from the dreams?

FIFTEEN

B y the time dawn opened its sleepy eyes and decided to stretch itself into the darkness of the grove, it was too late to catch the wrangler and the mountain man in their bedrolls.

In fact, it was necessary to search in two vastly different directions to find them, as Bear Rollins was already seven or eight miles along his journey by then, and Dan Kade was stalking a small herd of deer in the opposite direction. He'd sent all the food with Bear that the worthy was willing to pack, and needed replacement.

The herd of ten or so that he'd seen from a ridge were still in the same place, but he could see a restlessness beginning to prevail among them, as though they sensed a danger. So it was that by the time he'd spent two hours sneaking up on them, his rifle was at the ready when they suddenly gave a start and bounded off across the meadow. He had decided against wasting a shot at that distance when a large doe slipped on a small embankment and half fell. Dan quickly snapped the Winchester up and dropped her to the ground as she attempted to rise again. This time she stayed down.

He dressed her out and went about cutting the choice parts off of the carcass, then he hung the remainder in a tree to keep it safe until he could return with a horse to pack it back to camp for jerking. Oh, how he was tired of venison, especially jerky. And how he longed for a big beef steak smothered with onions, potatoes, peas, and on and on his tastebuds wandered away with his imagination in tow.

He arrived at camp and set about roasting a large haunch over the fire, with a dutch oven of sourdough bread and some more coffee, and the last of his beans.

As he sat down to his meager fare, he saw the ears on several horses shoot up, and they quickly turned to the north to look for the source of a yet unheard sound by Dan.

He tensed, then retrieved his rifle from its scabbard. Then, thinking better of it, he replaced it and secured his big, double-barrel shotgun and set it by him, then continued his meal.

The tin plate was clean when he at last heard the sounds that had alerted the stock. He could hear the creak of wagon wheels and the clink of trace chains somewhere in the distance. He stood up and tied down the fancy holster that the outlaw had forfeited to him, grimly disappointed in himself for thinking of trouble every time strangers approached. Was he becoming hardened? Or just over-reacting?

Some twenty minutes later a wagon laden with supplies came into sight over the small rise to the east, a team of draft horses tugging it on its way, with two men seated high above the payload.

Dan slipped the thong from the Colt's hammer in reluctant readiness, and stood as the vehicle approached the grove and his fire. When they were still fifty yards out, one of the men hailed him with a "Halloo the camp!"

"Hello yourself, come on in!" Dan called back, and stood waiting.

When the wagon drew to a halt beside him he looked the two occupants over. One was old and grizzlied, with white shaggy beard hiding his dirty shirt, as the map on his face showed time's unkind treatment to the leathery skin turned brown and wrinkled by sun and years. His companion, however, appeared to be somewhere around forty, and exhibited the cared for look of one who valued life and those he shared it with. It was he who spoke up.

"Hi cowboy. We smelled your fire and saw the smoke and figured we'd best check it out. I'm Gordon Montgomery, my house is about five miles over that next rise there to the north-west, and this is part of my spread. So, I'm sorta naturally curi-ous when I find a camp. You passin' through, lookin' for work, or it's none of my business? Which of the three?" he asked.

The question was delivered good naturedly, but Dan sensed that there was a no nonsense backing behind it.

"Well, Mister Montgomery, I'm holding these horses here 'til my partners catch up with me with the rest of our herd. We've wintered in the canyon country and gathered a sizeable bunch of mustangs, all of which we intend to market as soon as we find a railhead."

"First, it's Gordon, not mister, and second, how'd you get out in front with that large a string? Seems like it'd be better to muster them together?"

"Yes sir, it sure would, but we had us some trouble with one member of our crew, and this is the result. I didn't have any idea whose spread we were on, or even where we were when we anchored down here. It just seemed like a place where one man could hold thirty plus head the easiest. If you like, I'll move them on."

"Oh no, not at all. I'm a horse rancher and I know how the rustling business can put things out of sorts. That IS what you are saying, isn't it? That one of your crew took off with these?"

"Yessir," Dan replied.

"And I gather you must have caught up with him some-where?"

"Yessir."

"Well, that's good." and without asking, he seemed to know the fate of the horse thief. He continued, "Where do you plan on going to find the railroad?"

"Sir, I just don't know. One of our crew, Bear Rollins, he knows this territory, so I plan to stay put 'til they get here."

"I see," the rancher replied. "Well, I tell you what. I need some good stock, and if these are broke good, I could be inter-ested."

"Well mister," Dan said, "these horses here aren't broke, they're gentled. There's a big difference."

"Say, I like your attitude, young man. How many 'gentled'

head do you have?"

"'Round thirty that are for sale. Along with between forty to sixty head of 'broke' horses. It depends on how well the roundup went. You see, the rustler scattered what he couldn't drive out."

"I see. Well, I tell you what. I'll come out here tomorrow and look this stock over. If it's good horseflesh, I'll give you forty-five a head for them, and thirty a head for the rest. That's two bucks a head less than you'll get at Boomstick, but you won't have to drive them any further. You tell your pardners that, and you can make up your minds between you."

"I'll sure do that Mister Montgomery, but I'm thinking that we've nothing better to do than drive horses, so we'll probably not take advantage of your offer. I'll put it up to the rest of the crew, though."

"Good enough. Is there anything I can bring out in the way of supplies tomorrow? As you can see, we've just restocked and can spare plenty."

"Well sir, that's very kind of you. I could use some beans and bacon. I'm out of most everything."

"I'll make you up a pack, no charge. We'll see you tomorrow morning. So long, wrangler!" And with that the grizzled old drover beside him, who had not spoken a word, whipped the team into a trot and they rattled and squeaked off.

Dan stood and watched them, vastly relieved that the rancher hadn't asked his name, but warmed by the very act of meeting someone after the long, lonely winter.

What should he do about his name? He spent a lot of time pondering that question as he sat by his fire working on the saddle he'd recently acquired from the departed outlaw.

He took some spare leather from his pack, and spent several hours mending the rig, and also carefully arranged a thong set up to sling the double barrel ten gauge from the pommel on the right side. His rifle was already slung to the rear on that side, so rather than alter that to the frontward position that he preferred, he simply opted to leave it as it was.

The double rigged outfit was a good one, probably stolen at some time past, and he concluded that between the saddle, bridle,

Winchester and fancy Colt and holster, Johnston had shown an expensive taste.

By supper time everything was in top shape, and he had nothing to do but cook more venison and reflect on a name. After much deliberation, he decided to retain his first name, for simplicity, and last initial. He ended up with changing the last to Kase, a simple enough change that he hoped would be effective.

As he stirred the fire to heat a last cup of coffee, he began to feel a certain contentment he hadn't felt for months. He only hoped the night would not bring the dreams and their faces back to him again. With the coffee gone, the horses checked on, and the spring chill assailing his resting place, he rolled into his bed-roll and called it a day.

As was the custom and habit of the wests' working men, Dan was up before first light, fire going and coffee grounds from the previous day boiling. It would be his last unless the rancher Montgomery thought of it. He surely hoped that would be the case.

The eastern sky was beginning to glow with the morning's joy of arriving on time when he heard the horses begin to stomp restlessly. Taking up the big Greener, he made a round of the rope corral, stopping to pet and make over Blue and Sheba as they pestered him the entire time.

Blue was like a big dog and followed Dan everywhere he could, often giving a playful nudge with his huge nose, the results of which was sometimes a sprawling forward that left Dan on his hands and knees. Such was the case this time.

"Cut it out, you big lug!" He picked himself up, retrieved the double barrel, and turned to his camp just in time to see Gordon Montgomery sitting his horse beside the fire with laughter consuming him.

"Good morning sir! You're sure early today!" Dan called out.

"And worth it it is too, son, to see a playful kitten of that size in action. What a huge steed he is!" the rancher replied.

"Well, sir, he's just as smart as he is big," Dan replied, "I've never worked with a horse as willing and eager to learn as he is..

But, as you can see, he can be a pest!"

"Yes," the rancher chuckled, "that is rather obvious. It's also a sign of intelligence, according to my own experience with these amazing animals we call the horse.

"Tell you what I'll do, Dan. I'll give you a thousand dollars for him right here and now."

Dan looked him straight in the eye and answered, "Mr. Montgomery, I wouldn't take your whole ranch, horses, hands, kids, and all for Blue. He's not only all I really have in this world, for right now, he's about all I need."

The rancher smiled at that, and with the smile still on his face he made his next offer. "I don't suppose you would part with the mare then, would you?"

"No sir, not at all" Dan replied.

"I thought not. So how about a colt from the two of them, I'd make you a very attractive offer!"

"Well sir, I guess I'd better explain something to you right now. You see, the mare isn't mine, but belongs to a good friend down south of here, and I'm not free to do something like that, even if I wanted to."

"I understand, so what would it take to get that fellow's name from you so I can pester him? That's the finest mare I've ever seen, bar none!" the rancher exclaimed.

"Yes sir, she surely is that, but … Well- I uh, well I … " and Dan's voice trailed off, as he stood there unsure of himself.

Montgomery was a wise man of experience with range riders, and sensed his young rider's hesitancy. "Look, I didn't intend to pry. But if there's a problem you'd like to talk about, I can be very closed-mouthed. It would seem that you've rid the range of one more thief, and we owe you for that. So, if there's any way at all I can be of help to you, I'll be more than glad to do so, and forget anything that happens during the process.

"We're alone out here now, so there's no one else to hear or know anything about this conversation, so what do you say, Dan?"

"To tell you the truth, sir, I'd like to stir up some chuck while I think about it. I think there may be some help you can give me, but I need a little time to think this over, OK?"

"Sure!" the rancher replied with gusto. "I skipped breakfast myself just so we could eat together. In fact, I sorta pride myself on my cooking, so I'll whip up grub while you make the coffee."

"Coffee! Real, honest to goodness, fresh, never boiled before coffee!" Dan exclaimed. "You've got a deal!"

With that exchange, the two started preparations with the typical efficiency of experienced campers, and were soon enjoying a scrumptious meal together. They engaged in small talk of their life's pleasures and other things of that sort during the meal, and by the time they had washed the utensils at the stream, Dan had determined to trust the kindly rancher.

"Well," he said, not sure of just where to start, "I think I'll take you up on your offer, sir. I have a really tough decision to make, and it involves the mare and her safety, as well as the need to return her to her rightful owner as soon as possible."

With that introduction, he proceeded to tell Montgomery of his flight on Sheba, without explaining the actual crime involved. Instead, he just explained that his actions were justified in his own mind, and now that several months had passed, he wanted to send Sheba back to his friend, but without revealing his whereabouts. He also needed to be reassured of her safe arrival.

His companion pondered a bit, then arose to walk around the fire slowly, obviously deep in thought. Then he spoke. "Tell you what we can do, Dan. You said you came from south of here. I have a shipment of horses going to Colorado in two weeks. I never send horses anywhere without an escort to see that the right person gets them. Never!

"So, the railroad links up with a southbound track that goes all the way to Flagstaff, in Arizona. I'm willing to send my man on that far to see that she gets there. We can wire your friend to meet the train and secure his horse, provided he can show the proper identification, if he's a true friend, he'll not ask any questions. Sound OK?"

"That sounds just great, but how can I pay you? We haven't sold our stock yet."

"Tell you what. I need more riders for the summer, especially good riders, and more so, good wranglers. If you'll sign on, I'll pay you forty a month and found, and your crew the same if they want to come with you. If, at the end of the summer you've done the job I think you're capable of, we'll call it square and add a bonus for all of them besides. How about it?"

"Naturally I can't speak for the others, but that sounds great to me. But, if they don't go for it, we've agreed to stick together, and I'd have to honor that. What then?"

"We'll work that out after they decide. If need be, I'll still help you out, and we can work payment out after you've sold your stock. But Dan, I really need good riders, and I need them now. So try your best to persuade them, OK?"

"Yes sir, I will, I surely will."

The two new friends spent the rest of the morning looking over the stock in the rope corral, with Gordon Montgomery ending up being very impressed with the quality of horses available.

"It's obvious that you've spent a lot of quality time with these mounts, Dan. I tell you what, I'll raise my offer to match anything you can get at the railyards, and if that's agreeable to your pards, driving them to the ranch will be your first official job.

"You talk it over with them, and let me know. Meanwhile, I need to be getting back to the ranch, there's a lot to get done before I'm ready to ship, and not a lot of time left."

They shook hands, with Dan hoping that the rancher didn't notice the lump that suddenly came to his throat at the thought of Sheba leaving so soon. He had known for sometime that this moment was coming closer and closer, but had chosen not to dwell on it. Now that the time had come, he wasn't as ready to meet it as he'd thought.

He strolled out to the rope corral and spent the rest of the day with her and Blue, playing little tag games with the two of them just as a child would play with a dog. Then he curried and groomed both, spending all the precious minutes he could at the task. Hunger escaped him until the darkness of night began to drape its mantle of gloom over them. Even then it was hard to leave the two for his campfire and food. He was only beginning to discover how much love a man could develop for an animal companion.

He had known the love of parents and family as well as the

love of horses all his life, but the depths to which a man could reach with that love had not become real to him until he was deprived of it in several ways. This was but another step in his learning process as a man.

It was a late moon that shone down on his little camp before he found the solace of sleep.

Three weeks went by with Dan working with the horses as much as he could to keep them all in line. He knew that a wild mustang could revert back to its former ways quite easily. On Thursday of the third week he was just beginning to think about breaking for supper when several of the horses suddenly lifted their heads and looked towards the southerly route that had brought them here. A short time later he heard a distant hello drift softly to him. The boys were here!

His excitement at the prospect of seeing his only friends again totally overwhelmed him, and a lump appeared in his throat that rivaled the pounding in his chest for attention. He ran to Sheba and vaulted to her back, with no saddle or bridle, and charged out to meet them. She was eager to run, and simply jumped the rope corral like it wasn't there, and he was soon reminded of her tremendous speed as she carried him the short mile out to the oncoming herd.

As he approached the herd his heart dropped a notch, for it looked as though there were no more that thirty head left! That was barely more than half of the number they had of the rough stock. Then he saw Red Elk on the near side and kneed Sheba in his direction, waving his hat as he did so.

The two friends came to a halt side by side and shook hands with grips that told more of their pleasure at seeing one another than volumns of words could have.

Dan spoke first. "I'm sure glad to see you guys, I was starting to talk to the coffee pot 'cause the horses wouldn't listen any more!"

"Coffee pot? Why talk to that? Ours hasn't been any use to us for a week, 'cause we're out! And while we're at it, it's sure good to see you, too!"

"Say pard," Dan replied, "I've been visited by a guardian

angel, and I've got lots of coffee in camp. I'll go on ahead and get some boiling if you think you can get these broomtails there without me!"

"Without you? Listen you Arizony wrangler, we got them here without you whilst you were here loafin' an' doin' nothin. You get on back there and cook up a week's worth o' grub, 'cause we're powerful starved. And more than a little tired of rabbit and squirrel meat!"

Dan laughed, kneed Sheba around and raced her towards camp. He didn't start cooking however, instead he prepared to let the horses through the makeshift gate into the corral. After they were securely inside, they closed it up and then went to the fire site before starting their reunion.

As they all pitched in to prepare a meal Reddy caught Dan up on their excursion. "We tried our best to get all the stock we could, but they reclaimed their freedom so quickly that we woulda had to make a drive. Plus, the nags had split up into several small groups, and they jist weren't worth the time. So, hyar we are, quite a bit poorer than we planned on bein'.

"But we've talked it over, and we wanta go back next winter to make another sweep, only this time, we'll be more careful pickin' our help."

"Count me in, fellas" Dan replied, "I'd sure hate to leave a chance to spend another glorious winter with you go by. Why, I can't remember when I've had more fun or better company!"

"Hyar now, you ranny, don't you go ta makin' fun of us, or next time, you do the cookin'!" Reddy shot back.

"Why pard, what ever in the world makes you think I'm not serious?" Dan returned with an innocent look.

His only reply was a "Hmmp!" and a dirty look from the dark eyes that were fixed upon him. The Comanche cowboy turned to his eating like a man lost at sea for weeks without another sound.

Once the four had completed their meal and the cleanup chores they settled in to coffee and lively conversation. Dan could hardly wait to spring the pending sale on his friends. He finally felt the time was right to do so, and related his visits with Gordon Montgomery, including his offer of jobs as well as the purchase of the stock. "And we'll not only be driving the horses fifteen miles less this way, but we'll be paid to do it!" Dan finished.

"Say pard, I take back what I said about you not doing much, I guess your time of leisure wasn't wasted after all. I vote we take this feller up on his offers! What say, you two?" Reddy exclaimed.

"Sounds good to me" Bear replied, "I've been on this range several times, and this hyar feller Montgomery has a good rep. I think I remember huntin' cougar fer him a few years back, and he paid right smart."

"Sounds good to me, too" Joe answered, I'm anxious to settle down to some good food and recreation once in a while. I think the world of you three, but I could use a little change of scenery, believe me!"

"Ha! Hyar we go agin" Reddy shouted, "He's gonna go and get tangled up with some paleface squaw and get us all run outta the country, iffn' they don't hang us instead, that is!"

They all laughed at the expression on Joe's face at that sally, then Bear arose to unroll his blankets and prepare to bed down. The rest seemed to take this as a signal to do likewise, and snores were soon drifting through the campsite, giving Dan a sense of peace he'd not had for many a night. He was coming more and more to feel that these men were now his family. They couldn't replace his dear parents, not even his wayward brothers, but they were certainly close to doing so!

The following weekend found them spending a well earned day off in the town of Boomstick, so named by the Indians because of the dynamiting required to clear the roadbed for the railroad as it came through the mountain pass. The stock had been delivered to Gordon Montgomery's Rocking M ranch, and their cash was now safely tucked away in the local bank, with the exception of the small sum that each retained for some recreation and expenses, of course.

Dan was pleased to discover that none of his friends were inclined to waste their time or cash in the saloons, but would rather use their time in a more quiet manner. They trooped into the general store as one and quickly descended on the clothing section, with even Bear purchasing some new outfits to replace his ever-present buckskins.

Neither Dan nor Reddy could resist the temptation to ride him a little, and in answer to their good-natured prodding, he said "Hey now, you fellers, you ain't the onliest ones to have a little sophistication. Them there 'skins are the berries fer the wilds, but us men of leisure got to have some respectable duds, 'case the girls see our hidden values what shines above your shallow flirtations. Got it?"

"Ifn' your hidden values shines so, how's come they're hidden, Bear?" was Reddy's quick reply, and the jesting went on from there in a never-ceasing manner.

After they left the store laden with their purchases, they deposited their goodies in the borrowed buckboard, and as the others wandered off in one direction, Dan set off to the rail station to meet Montgomery's straw boss, Lane Glover. The two were to discuss the following Monday's arrangements with the rail clerk, making sure that Sheba would be on a lightly loaded car, and further assuring that the saddle and trappings would also be properly cared for. Glover was a seasoned old hand with the look of wisdom that comes from the years, accompanied with the look of authority that spoke of the ability to take care of himself in any situation. Being Montgomery's most trusted hand, the supervision of the stock being shipped always fell to him. And, though he thoroughly disdained these trips on that "Consarned bumpity train" he willingly went along with the rancher's wishes, for he himself liked the security of personally delivering all stock to its rightful purchaser. It was he that would accompany Sheba to Flagstaff. At Montgomery's advice, Dan had filled the foreman in on the background of the matter, and had found a very understanding ear. He was now at peace with the trip, for he felt the mare was in good and capable hands.

Once the arrangements were made, they wired Ira Nelson in Metzal to inform him of the probable arrival. Lane would wire him again from Colorado as soon as he had a firm date. With that taken care of, Dan then moved on to find his friends and join them for lunch.

Their talk was that of spring plans and dreams, focusing on their good fortune to be employed by one the likes of Gordon Montgomery, the great accommodations for the hired help, and the generally good cheer that seemed to permeate their introduction to the hands already there. When Joe made a comment concerning that fact, they were informed by Glover that the congenial rancher would tolerate no troublemakers in his crew.

Coupled with the excellent wages he offered to loyal hands, it produced an atmosphere that was good to work in. It promised to be a good summer.

Monday dawned bright and sunny, and Dan rode Blue beside Sheba as they made their way to Boomstick and their separation. He was strangely at peace with the moment, and thoroughly enjoyed the ride. He had intended to ride her and lead Blue, but decided against it, for he was not willing to take the chance of stirring up his doubt at relinquishing the mare to Lane Glover's capable hands for the ride south. The moment would be poignant enough as it was.

He could hear the turmoil ahead as the other stock was being loaded on to the rail cars. As he rode up, Lane met him at the entrance to the corrals.

"Over here Dan, I've made sure we can load beautiful there on her own car last. I'll be riding in that car myself, most of the way. I like to stay near the stock cars on a trip like this, and the crew always lets me make a car pretty comfortable if I get here in time. I will say this, I've never had a lovely passenger riding with me before!"

Dan laughed at that sally, and was feeling better all the time about the trip. When the time came, he led Sheba up the loading ramp and unsaddled her, placing Ira's saddle and bridle on the floor at the other end of the car. "Here's the trappings, including Ira's rifle and saddle bags. I've tried to replace everything I'd used in them, and put some little gifts in there to try in a small way to show my gratitude. I also put a letter in there explaining why I chose to do what I did, and why I didn't get her back to him earlier than this. It's not much, but it'll have to do."

"Well, son, I'll see to it that she's all dressed up and her hair done proper when her owner claims her" Lane informed him with a chuckle.

Dan joined him in the chuckle, then went back to the curious mare and spent several minutes stroking her. The wise ramrod found an excuse to leave the car and let Dan have his time alone with this precious cargo. As the sounds of loading dwindled, and Dan sensed the time was near, a lump began to grow that rivaled the size of the rail car. He put his arms around her neck and hugged her silently for an eternity or two. Then he stepped back, wiped the tears from his eyes, rubbed her silky nose goodbye, and ran from the car. He had just about reclaimed his composure when Sheba whinnied, a sound much like a child calling for its parents, and he was all broken up again. He leaped on big old Blue without touching a stirrup and charged out of town like the devil himself was after him with his heart broken once more, but this time over a faithful companion sent away by his own hand. This time, it was right that his heart be broken, he told himself, and he found a little comfort in that thought.

SIXTEEN

Two sweating, heaving horses pounded into the stable area of the Slash N in full stride, pulling to a sliding halt almost as one. One rider nearly fell as he dismounted, grabbing a stirrup to maintain his balance.

"There, see, I told you so Tom Seever! You are not ready to race like that yet!" Allison scolded as she dismounted hurriedly. She ran over to the recipient of her sharp tone to assist him if necessary. She had long been aware of the fact that you didn't help Tom unless he really needed it. He had seen to that fact in a very definite way.

He smiled at her in a tolerant way and allowed her to help him as he went to the front porch of the house and set down on the step. "Allie, I swear you think you're my mother or some-thing ," he teased her. "How do you think I'm going to get along if you go back home some day?"

She patted his hand and replied "I'm sure Julie will take care of you when I go back. I've certainly tried to make that clear to you."

She was immediately sorry for the reply, as they had quar-reled about this very thing only three days before. Tom had finally gotten up the nerve to profess his love for her, and to pro-pose in nearly the same breath. Allison had feared this moment for months, so was prepared for it with a rehearsed answer.

She spent several minutes explaining to Tom that though she

loved him, her's was not a love of romance, but a love of brother and sister relationship. A love conceived by association and need, hinging on the mutual respect developed between nurse and patient. She had been doing good until that point, when Tom bucked and accused her of feeling sorry for him. It then took her several minutes to reverse his misconception, but felt in the long run that she had done so.

There had existed between them a heavy silence for a couple of days, and today's ride had been suggested by Tom to patch up their relationship. They had ridden several miles, had a picnic, and ended up racing the last two miles back to the ranch.

During their picnic, Allie had tried to subtly let him know of young Julie's love for him, with some mild repercussions. These had been smoothed over successfully, and she feared her last remark would fire them back up again. Such was not to be, however, and the tired rider let the comment go on by without answering it.

After a brief rest, Tom was ready to move into the ranch house and claim the oversized couch before the empty fireplace. Allie thought of the sign of new strength this demonstrated, for just a few weeks ago, he would have been in bed after a bout like this. She went to the kitchen and got him a plate of cookies with milk, returning to sit with him to help demolish the snack. It was only half gone when Ira entered and called to her.

"Allie, could I talk to you for just a minute?"

"Yes uncle, I'll be right there. I just need to see to it that this cowpoke is getting some of his energy back," she replied. With that, she settled Tom in, and then trooped out to the kitchen. There she found the kindly old Ira waiting for her with a grave face.

"Why uncle, what on earth is wrong that you would look so serious?" she asked.

"Well lass," he replied, "I need to know your plans for the afternoon. Were you planning on another ride today?"

"I did plan to take Tom out for a short and very, very slow one, yes. Why do you ask?"

"I"d like for you to change your plans, if you would. Just give Tom a long walk instead, for I need for you to be close by today. I have some folks coming that will want to have a discussion with you about his recovery and the time involved. It's very important that they see you as soon as they arrive."

"Who would it be, uncle? I really can't help as far as any medical knowledge is concerned. They need to talk to Doc Pritchard about that," she said.

"I'd really rather not say, lass, for they won't want you to be drawing any foregone conclusions before they talk to you," was the only answer she received, and she knew her uncle well enough to know that the matter was closed. She spent the better part of the next hour trying to determine what and who could possibly be involved in this rather secretive matter.

When late afternoon was upon them, she talked Tom into a walk around the buildings and corrals, and they were on their second trip around when she spotted the two seated spring wagon on its laborious climb up the road to the ranch from Metzal valley. It was about thirty minutes away, so the two had time to finish their walk and still get Tom settled in before its arrival. Allison's curiosity was about to burst, but she knew she would have to wait.

When they were back in the house, Tom shuffled her off to the porch to await the wagon then went to the kitchen to get his own snack. He was becoming more and more self sufficient with each day's passing, thought Allie, and she had just stepped onto the porch as the wagon rattled up. Ira had slipped up to stand beside her as she emerged from the house, and smiled with delight as she gasped loudly and began to weep softly with her joy. The two people seated in the wagon's back seat were her parents, Paul and Ida!

"Oh! Oh! Mother, Dad! Oh my! Oh my!" And with that profound statement she fell upon the road-weary couple with hugs and kisses that threatened to drown and crush them, crying and laughing at the same time.

The stocky built, graying man who was one of the recipients of this attack simply beamed in silence, the smile amplifying the slowly forming wrinkles in his weathered face. His sturdy torso showed the passing of time, yet defied its aging effect by remaining as hard as nails from the years of being work-hardened while building and maintaining a successful horse ranch in Idaho. Time would have to wait a long while before claiming this man's being for its rocking-chair society. He was just too busy to allow it to slow him, and the enthusiasm for life radiated from him despite the years.

The athletic lady beside him who was presently engulfed in Allie's arms showed even less of time's cruelty. Ira's younger sister Ida stood nearly as tall as her husband's five foot, ten inches, and her honey-brown hair exibited none of the graying tendencies assailing him. She was neither heavy nor thin, but a lady who still showed the beauty of her youth seasoned with the wisdom of a long and prosperous life. Lines were trying to force their way into the finely chiseled face, but with little success. Her gay laughter could be heard as she teased her only child about their complete surprise.

"You certainly didn't think we intended to leave you here much longer, did you child?" she asked gaily. "You've gotten out of several month's chores as it is. We can't abide much more of this loafing around and allowing your uncle to totally spoil you, now can we dear?"

"Oh Mother, I just didn't expect you and Daddy to come all the way down here to retrieve me!" Allie moaned. "Why ever did you do this? It must have cost you so much in time and money!"

The resonant bass voice of her father finally sounded out. "Listen, daughter, would you deprive your poor old mother and dad of a vacation and visit to this ornery old rascal's poor excuse for a horse ranch?"

"No, Dad, but I'm, well, I'm shocked, that's all! And you, you sneaky, underhanded, low-down, mean old wonderful uncle. I'll get you for this!" she scolded Ira. "The idea, letting my folks come to see me and not even telling me! That's not fair!"

"Well now, Allie, I just don't know how to take that little speech. Am I all those bad things you said, or the one good one? Besides, who ever told you that life would be fair? Certainly not me!" he answered.

She dashed over to him and tackled him with a huge bear hug, smothering his face with kisses until he surrendered with a laugh and drew away from her. "Whoa, there, lady, no one gave you permission to try to drown me!"

"Oh uncle Ira, I just love you so! But you must realize that a girl doesn't like surprises that have her folks showing up without a chance to spruce up so she'll look her best!"

"Now girl, I bet that these folks of your's think you look just fine," the delighted old rancher returned.

"I dunno Ira" Paul answered with a laugh,"she looks a little heavier to me, like she hasn't been working very much and needs the fat run off of her. I'd say we came for her just in time to keep you from totally spoiling her."

"Dad! Shame on you!" Allison scolded. Then, after a pause, she exploded into a startled question. "Wait! Did you say you came for me? Does that mean I'm going back with you? How soon do you mean? Or were you teasing again? Or …"

"Whoa there girl, I can only answer one at a time! Slow down!" Paul interrupted with a laugh. "We plan to stay and visit for a couple of weeks and then go on back home. We came down by rail and stage, and we plan to have three going back instead of two. That answer your questions?"

For an answer she simply hugged him silently for a very long time, relishing the thought of home and parents once again. Then Tom entered her mind and she suffered a pang of regret at the thought of their parting on less than happy terms. She did love him, but as a dear friend whom she didn't wish to see hurt. Julie simply must win him over in a hurry!

She glanced his way only to find him looking intently at her, and she quickly looked away. Ira stomped into the house, pausing to hold the door open for his guests, and everyone quickly followed suit. They were soon chattering away and catching up on everyone's lives as Mary served them refreshments. Allison's concerns were soon forgotten amid the excitement of the hour, and she didn't think of the subject again until she was long in her bed that night. She drifted off to sleep with Tom on her mind, worrying about his feelings for her.

The next week and a half were filled with excitement as Allie visited with her folks, rode with Tom, and tried to remember all the little messages she wanted to leave with everyone. It seemed an impossible task to do all that and pack too. Tom seemed to be a little aloof, and that weighed heavily upon her as well. Finally, in the middle of the second week, she was cornered by that worthy as she was leaving the barn.

"Allie, can we talk?" he asked. The serious look on his face drew her to a halt, and she nodded the affirmative.

He drew a quick breath and started in a quiet, subdued voice. "Allie, I've probably put you through a bad time these last few weeks. I can't apologize for loving you, but I can tell you what I've discovered about myself during the last few days.

"I know that my love for you was and is genuine, but I've been thinking about what you said about it being a result of your caring for me as I healed. You were right, Allie. I see that now and I can live with it. I just wanted to tell you while we were alone, so I could relieve your mind of any guilt feelings about causing my feelings for you. I'm sorry if I've caused you any grief, dear Allie. I just hope you can forgive me."

Her eyes filled with tears of love and relief, and she leaped forward to grab him in a death grip type of hug as she wept quietly and allowed her tears to flush away the frustration and fears that had clutched at her heart for days. Now she could go home with her folks to their beloved ranch with a clear conscience and quiet heart. She was freed from her burden.

Tom was smart enough to remain quiet until she had spent her emotions and stepped away from him. He smiled shyly and said, "Gosh, Allie, if I'd known you were that upset about it, I'd have made you feel guilty enough to marry me. Then you'd have to love me!"

She cuffed him playfully on the head and proceeded to scold him about teasing at a time like that. As they bantered back and forth Julie came out onto the back porch of the house to empty a pail of mop water, then turned to disappear into the kitchen once more. "Look there, ,Tom Seever. There's a girl who loves you so much that she can't think, talk, see, or dream of anything or anyone else! You know that, don't you?" Allison asked him.

"Aww Allie, what ever made you think that? Why, she's just a kid!" Tom replied.

"Ha! And how old are you, Mister Seever?" she shot back. "Are you twenty yet?"

"Well, yes, last month," he answered.

"So here we have a man of the world who's trying to marry an old maid that's twenty four saying that a young lady of eighteen is just a kid" she half teased.

"Now listen, you old maid, there's a lot of difference between eighteen and twenty four. Julie's never been off of this ranch, and I've been on my own since I was twelve. I think there's a little difference there as well. So what do you have to say to that, miss lady of the world?"

"What I have to say is this, mister man of the world; maybe I am six years older than her, and maybe you have been on your own a long time, but that young lady in the house is just as adult in her thinking as either one of us! She's had the responsibility of caring for everything in this house but the cooking since she was twelve. Now, how much have you been responsible for besides your own backside, huh, big britches?"

Tom took a step back at that impassioned sally and took a close look at Allison to see if she was serious. It was clear that she was. The serious look she wore was too much for him and he burst out laughing. The harder he tried to stop, the funnier the look became to him until he was roaring uncontrollably. And the harder he laughed the angrier she became until she began to push him around.

"I don't see anything funny, buster, so just stop it. I'm serious!" she snapped.

"Aww, I'm--I'm sorry Allie," he stammered, "It's just that you've never looked so angry before, and you've never used those kind of words. Look after my backside? Big britches?" And he began to howl with mirth once again. This time she began to see the humor in what she'd said and began to laugh with him. But she also started to push him around again, subtly easing him towards the watering trough as she did so. As soon as she had him backed close to it she plowed into him with her shoulder and knocked him back another step. The end caught him at the knees and he started to tumble backwards into it. The action of falling startled him and he quite naturally reached out to catch himself on the only thing close enough to stop his fall: Allie!

There was a short squeal of fear, a splash, and two very wet people, all in quick succession! Two of the hands came running from the barn to help, then stopped to look closer at the two drowned rats, and became useless as aids, for they lost all sense of anything but laughter at the sight.

"A fine lot of help you two are!" Tom laughed, "Help us out of here, will you?"

Allie was spitting, sputtering, and trying hard to be mad, but it just wouldn't come to her.Her long hair was plastered to her face, and rivulets of water ran down over her whole being like a cascading falls. She knew she was a sight! Uncontrollable laughter finally claimed her and she ended up lying on the ground in tears, adding several pounds of mud to her outfit as she shook with glee.

The first two hands that were attracted to the ruckus were Bud and Vern, and the two of them stood in wonder at the scene before them. Bud then made the mistake of betting Vern that "Allie's wetter than Tom, lot's wetter. Betcha two bucks."

Allie wrestled her way to a standing position and winked at Tom, who nodded and eased his way away from the trough. Allie then accosted the unsuspecting pair with a feigned vengeance.

"How dare you two stand there and make bets without making sure I'm not hurt! Who do you think you are?" and she railed on at them as she slyly and subtlety herded them just like a cowboy would head a few horses towards the hungry looking trough. The two astonished hands looked haplessly at one another as the little whirlwind attacked them. It took little more than a few words to back the confused Bud close enough to the trough that a quick shove from Allie started his arms windmilling and his mouth putting forth cries of "Oh no, you wouldn't! You little--"

Whatever Allie was became lost in the sound of the splash as he sprawled his full length in the water that had claimed another victim. Vern lost his composure and began to laugh at his pardner's misfortune, not realizing his own impending doom.

"Some--some pard you are, help me outta here you hyena!" yelled Bud. Vern, still howling but not thinking, stepped forward and bent over to offer his hand to the soggy Bud. Bud grabbed the offered member and jerked hard on it, and when Vern caught his balance momentarily his other hand darted up to clasp the front of his shirt. It was then that Tom entered into the fray and gave Vern a hearty shove. The sinister watering trough had claimed another soul!

Then complications set in, for Vern saw an immediate path for revenge on his friend. He simply laid down on Bud so that that worthy was held under much longer than was comfortable. As the bubbles started to rise from the struggling cowpoke Tom and Allie grabbed the prostate Vern and hauled him off his unfortunate companion. Bud came up sputtering and swearing at Vern, then realized his surroundings and quickly shut up. By now everyone within earshot, including those in the house, had been drawn to the scene.

It was also at this time that Ira happened to ride up from his daily rounds with Dick and Allie's dad, Paul. The three set their horses and looked on, Ira with feigned sternness.

"And what, may I ask, is going on here? Bud? Vern? What are you two doing away from your chores? Come on, speak up!"

The two hands looked at one another with astonishment to think that they were being singled out when they had nothing to do with starting the whole thing.

"Aw boss," Bud blurted out, "We was innocent, honest. This here invalid was in dire trouble and me and Vern here was trying to bail him out when this fireball attacked us both! Right, Vern?"

"I see. And am I supposed to believe that this fireball whipped you both, along with young Seever? I'm not sure I need hands that can't whip a lady when they out number her! Now GET BACK TO WORK!" And with that he had to turn his head to keep the two wranglers from seeing his laughter.

"But Uncle" Allie broke in, "They really were just trying to help. It was all my idea to get them wet as well as Tom. You can't be mad at them, they're innocent!"

"Ha! Those two? They don't know the meaning of the word. But I'll relent on the punishment I had planned for them. But they better watch their step."

"B-b-b-but Boss! We didn't deserve any punishment, so we really shouldn't be watched close because of this," blurted out Vern, clearly shaken by his fair employer's obvious displeasure.

"Whut wus our punishment, Boss? I'd rather take my medicine than have you think you gotta watch me!" cried the crestfallen Bud.

"No Bud, I'll not impose so severe a thing on you, thanks to my niece's confession. I think it would be unfair to send you to town in Dick's place for supplies. 'Specially since you're innocent."

"To town!" they both cried in unison. "To town?" Then Bud, once again forgetting his whereabouts, began to cuss to himself about "These women can get a guy in trouble without him even being around!"

"All right, Bud, that does it, get that worthless pardner of your's and get the wagon ready to go to Metzal. And see Mrs. Garrison for her list before you go. My list is on my desk. And be quick about it!"

"Yessir!" They yelled, already on the run to the stables for the team.

"Now, Ira," Dick said. "I just can't believe you didn't know that a cowboy will do anything to get to go into town. I guess I'll have to teach you a little bit about these men, after all."

Allie came over and laid a wet hand on Ira's knee and said "That was sweet of you to let them go, Uncle. I was afraid you were really mad at them."

"No lass, but there's nothing in the rules that says that the rancher can't have some fun too, is there?" And with that he dismounted and scooped up two hands full of dust and poured them over Allison's head! She screamed and tore off towards the house on a dead run, making threats all the way to "get even, favorite uncle or not!"

"Uncle Ira Stevens!" Julie shouted. "I can't believe you did that. That was terrible! How dare you!"

He simply smiled and approached her in a menacing manner, getting more into the mood of the moment with each second. She squealed and hid behind Tom, grabbing onto his shirt with both hands to use him as a shield.

Never one to push a good thing too far, Ira stopped and relented, reminding Julie that she couldn't hide behind just any good-looking man she chose. That caused a good deal of laugh-

ter at her expense, and Tom put his arm around her to guide her
off to the house and safety, never giving thought to the fact that
he was getting her wet in the process. She was so taken up in the
excitement of actually having his arm around her that she never
noticed until he released her inside the door. When those by the
watering trough heard her startled cry at the discovery they completely broke up with howls of mirth.

"Well," Ira said, "that should keep the two of them busy for a
while. After all, they have a party to get ready for, and that takes
all day even when they're not a shambles!" He was referring to
the dance he had arranged for the McCord's departure celebra-
tion. Paul quietly reminded him that the dance wasn't until the
next evening, bringing a threat to manage the same type of mischief on the following morning!

"Boss, I think you've caused enough ruckus for one week,"
Dick reminded him. "Let's just let them recover from this one
and allow nature to take its course. Say, did you see the look
on my Julie's face when that rascal put his arm around her? I'm
afraid she's got a real case on him."

"I know it for a fact," Ira replied. "All you have to do is see
her watching him!" At that sally they all chuckled and led the
horses off to the stables to be retired for the day.

Bud and Vern returned very late that night, and upon seeing
Ira's office light on, both postponed the unloading long enough to
deliver the information they had picked up in town. Ira opened
the door at Bud's soft knock to let them in.

"Say, Boss, you shouldn't just open the door anytime some
ranny beats on it," Bud scolded. "You never know when some
broke saddle tramp is gonna stop in fer to rob an honest man."

"Is that why you came up here, Bud Raymond Holly, to see
if I was on guard?"

"Now you know it ain't, dag blast it, I jest want you to be
more careful. What we came up fer was to let you know that we
saw those two Kade brothers in town. They'd jest come in from
the north country and it peers as though they weren't too happy
'bout the trip. Thet Martin, he don't say a lot, but the bigon', Art,
he done told us thet they lost the trail fer sure."

"Boy, that's too bad, I hate to hear that. Well thanks, boys, you were right in disturbing me. I hope the trip to town taught you both a lesson" he finished with a grin.

"Yep, sure did boss," Vern offered. "From now on we're gonna cause trouble every day so's we can be true martyrs."

Ira shook his head and waved them away, chuckling to himself at the wrangler's turning the tables on him. How he loved these free-spirited hands of his. They were certainly a unique and wonderful breed!

Eleven o'clock the following morning found Tom Seever watching intently down the road at an approaching buckboard and two mounted horsemen. Guests were starting to arrive already for the night's activities! The people in this remote part of the earth didn't see much social life, and when an occasion to meet with others came along, they always made the most of it, sometimes staying until the rooster dismissed them with his morning cacophony. Youngsters would be bedded down in any nook and cranny that would afford comfort and quiet while the adults danced and talked the night away. There would be time to sleep another day when others weren't around.

"We got visitors comin', Ira!" Tom called into the house. The light, spry footstep of the older man signaled his approach, and he soon stepped through the door to squint down the road in an attempt to identify the first arrivals.

"Looks like John Kade's team, don't you think, Tom?"

"Well, I sorta thought so, but I couldn't figure the two riders out, unless a couple of hands happened to meet up with them on the way."

"You weren't awake yet when the boys got back last night, but they came up to tell me that Art and Martin were in town yesterday, that's gotta be them with John and Sue."

"I take it there's no good news, or you'd have told us in a hurry," Tom stated.

"No son, none at all. Let's get down to the stables and get the boys located so they can take care of those horses right away. I hate for guests to do their own stock." With that, he suited actions to words and struck off towards the stable.

Early afternoon found everyone gathered in the large living room catching up on the latest news. Big Art Kade was relating their efforts to the rest.

"We found Dan's tracks the second day, over by the rim. It took another day to find where he went up, for it was a hidden trail that looked like horses used it pretty regular. There's a huge rock in front of the opening, and you just can't see it 'til you're on top of it. But you can't hide that sort of thing from Martin, here." he finished with pride .

Martin quickly added "We found where he'd camped on top, then he set off to the northwest. There are places in those mountains where no one is going to trail with any success, but I lucked out and found his camp about three days' ride from there. 'Course, it took us five days to cover the same ground while trailing."

Art interrupted Martin by jumping up and heading for the door. "Say little brother, you almost let me forget the telegram for Mr. Nelson." And with that he was gone from sight.

"Oh yeah, Mr. Nelson, the telegraph operator came looking for your two hands yesterday right after they left. Said he had a real important telegram for you. Art told him we were coming out here today so he sent it along. He sealed it in an envelope and all," Martin explained.

Art re-entered with a rather fat envelope in his hand that he handed to Ira. Then he went on with their story of the efforts to find Dan.

"The closest we came to Danny was up north of Flagstaf. We run onto a little village of trappers there that had sold him some supplies and they remembered his horses. The one fellow tried every way he could to trade him out of both of them, but nothing doing! Said they told him that snow was coming soon, and not to go on north or he'd get caught. Well, we went on from there and got caught ourselves. Lucky for me that little brother here never forgets landmarks! He got us back to that village and we wintered right there.

"I never got so tired of the same people in my life! Ten trappers in six cabins, with cards and whiskey for the long months. We didn't want anything to do with either one, so we were sorta outcasts. I'll tell you, though, we'd never of survived without that place."

Susan Kade began to softly cry at that, as she perceived the hidden meaning behind Art's comment. Dan had more than likely perished in the winter's fury.

The dark silence was suddenly broken by Ira's "I'll be hitched! Look at this, all of you!" And he held up the three page telegram.

"This is from some rancher from somewhere north of here who says that Sheba is being sent to Flagstaf by rail, and someone will wire me to let me know when to meet them! You know what that means?!"

As they all looked at him with astonished, questioning faces, most shook their heads.

"It means that Dan is alive, you slowpokes!" cried the old fellow. "He has to be alive to send her back, and he has to be alive, or she wouldn't be alive to be sent back!"

"Quick," John Kade shouted, "Where did the message come from?"

"No luck there, John. It says that the sender paid off the operator to leave that off, and that there's no use to try to find them. He also explains that I'd better have some good proof of who I am when I get her, or his man won't turn her over, and it won't do any good to try to learn anything from the deliverer, for he'll be hired in Denver."

They had no way of suspecting that this last statement was a lie, and were disappointed at not having a chance to send word to Dan that he was free and clear of any charges of wrong doing.

The mood at the dance that night was especially festive, for at least all knew that their young friend was alive and well. It was only two days later that a tearful farewell took place in Metzal as most of the county inhabitants gathered to see the Mc-Cords off. The last sight Allie had of her patient was that of a young man with his arm around a youthful girl of eighteen! Her heart jumped with joy at the thought of their possible romance. She knew that cowboys were notoriously fickle, and placed her trust in that knowledge. She would miss all of them terribly, but looked forward to reuniting herself with family and childhood friends. Her last thought that night as she dozed off was that it was a pretty good world to live in.

SEVENTEEN

Southern Idaho had seen three winters come and go since Allison McCord's return to the home ranch, and it had been a happy three years until recently. She had experienced plenty of time riding and dreaming of the love she couldn't shake that still haunted her. Why did she have to dream of one whom she'd never meet? Then, a sinister cloud invaded the area in the form of a new neighbor thirty miles to the west. That cloud now held her family in its clutches in a real and fearful way.

The McCord ranch lay nearly in the middle of a flat, lush valley at least fifty miles wide between two mountain ranges. To the west lay the Sawtooths, not to be confused with the Colorado range by the same name, with the continental divide to the east. The terrain was a gently rolling mixture of green grass, oak groves, and clear, mountain streams. Its beauty had captured Paul and Ida McCord at the first look they'd experienced together, and within a week they had settled into the present location to raise the best horses they could. The ranch complex showed the steady growth that ensued, for the main house was a rambling structure surrounded by the various stables and other out buildings.

The house faced south, with a series of corrals leading at least a quarter of a mile further in that direction. They were strategically placed on either side of the lane so that stock being driven into the ranch could be diverted into the proper corral by simply opening a wide gate which would then stretch across the lane and affectively block it off.

As one looked down the lane from the house, they would see the main barns off to their left. These were comprised of two very big two-story structures with three smaller single story stables wandering off behind them to the east. The nearly empty bunkhouse and foreman's quarters was to the right. The foreman was the sole inhabitant at this time.

Their new neighbor was clear to the west side of the valley nestled among the foothills of the Sawtooths. This ranch had been a small cattle operation until the new owner took over, but he had announced that he intended to become the area's biggest and best horse rancher. He had then proceeded to try to buy off Paul McCord's government contract.

Paul was a man who knew horses, and had carefully bred a strain of tall, rangey riding stock of consistent coloring that the Army preferred. The newcomer also wanted to buy that stock to make it his own. When he was informed that there was absolutely no way this could occur, he had gotten ugly and made threats. It appeared that these threats were now being carried out. A hired gun had shot one of their young riders, supposedly in a fair fight, and let it be known that others would follow. When that rider healed sufficiently he had ridden off, and by then he was the last, including their foreman.

A short time later a new foreman was found, an older fellow with the toughened exterior of a warrior who had seen many troubles and had taken them all on, spurs in and full speed ahead. He said he needed a change of scenery, that he'd been too long in one place. His name was Lane Glover.

Allison struggled to be released from the harsh grip on each of her arms as two ruffians held her fast between them. Lane Glover, the new foreman, lay on the ground close by as her mother tried to stop the flow of blood that cascaded from his temple. It had been an especially brutal blow that fell, an unnecessary one at that. Lane had merely protested the action of the two thugs when they accosted Allie.

Her anger at the confrontation had gotten the best of her temper, and she had attacked the tormentors, forcing them to retaliate. Her father, Paul, also was bleeding, but from a pair of bruised and cut lips suffered when he reached for his gun. One of the ruffians had jumped forward and smashed him with a fist, then wrestled his weapon from him.

There were five of the invaders in all, led by Harvey Croft, the straw boss of their adversary. He was a bad man, especially if one should ask him, and taunted the rest of the range continually. It was said that his boss was a one-armed man whom no one had ever seen since the day the deed was signed. Croft was telling the McCords of the wrath they were about to face when one of the men uttered a low "Rider comin' Boss."

Allie looked quickly down the lane to see a horse the likes of which she'd never seen before. It was several hands higher than any riding stock she was familiar with, and appeared to weigh at least sixteen hundred pounds. A veritable behemoth!

The rider astride him looked to be around six feet tall, but the size of the animal made it hard to tell. She could see that he was a well built man with his gun tied down after the manner of these gunmen who were presently molesting them. She assumed that he was one of them until Harvey Croft told the man nearest the lane to "handle him."

As the pair got nearer all could see that not only was this horse big, but it was very unusual. The head was mammoth, and the ears were mule-like, with huge brown eyes that protruded from his head as though they expected to see in every direction at once. It was this fascination caused by the animal that allowed the rider to get completely up to them before anyone spoke.

"Just ride on out, buster, you're not welcome here," Croft said in a menacing voice.

"I can't help but notice the two brave men holding that young lady sorta rough over there. Maybe she doesn't want me to leave," came the soft reply. As he spoke he took in all the details of the scene he'd just ridden in to.

Harvey Croft was used to others jumping when he spoke, and was instantly furious. He crouched and hovered his hand near his gun and repeated the order. "I said move out!"

The next move was so quickly and smoothly executed that it just seemed to Allison as though there was no movement involved. The stranger dismounted on the wrong side of the roan monster and the command "Back, Blue" was heard spoken sharply but softly. The mount showed extraordinary grace as he fairly jumped two great strides back to reveal the rider standing facing Croft. Harvey discovered that he was staring down the cavernous twin barrels of a ten guage Greener with both hammers eared back to a full cock!

The quiet man held the shotgun level at the waist in an almost nonchalant manner, but it was obvious to all that he meant business. The next order came in that same soft voice, but with a sharper edge to it.

"Mister gunman, if you don't unbuckle that belt and drop that hogleg, I'm gonna cut you in two. Plain and simple. And if any of these big, brave heroes of yours even blink, I'll make two of you for that, too. Now move."

It wasn't easy for Harvey Croft to do, but he swallowed hard with rage and reached for the leather thong that tied the holster to his leg. He froze at the order, "NO! Leave that tied."

Then a cold fury gripped him until he was nearly blind from it. He came close to drawing his last gun on a human, but was able to get hold of his emotions in time to stop. The gunmen of the day prided themselves in their well-oiled, smooth-working, and clean weapons, and a true gunman spent several hours a day in practicing and caring for them. If he did as told, the thong would hold to his leg and cause the big blue Colt to drop into the dust at his feet when the holster swung upside down. He knew it was a deliberate move to disgrace him.

Choking with anger, he stood without moving until the barrels tilted up just enough to stare into his eyes. In a blind rage he did as told, and actually winced as though struck at the sodden thud the pistol made in the deep dust. The holster and belt quietly brushed against his leg as they swung gently from the drop, adding to the frustration. He would kill this brash wrangler, and very soon, he promised himself!

The rider looked at the two who held Allison. "Do you two want this to be your last day to ever hold a girl, or would you rather let go of her and live to see another, more willing subject?" he asked. "If you prefer the last, I suggest you move over there by your hero friend."

They looked at Harvey for their instructions, and when they didn't move right away, he glared at them and growled out, "Do as he says."

As they complied, the rider closest to the lane spoke up. "Mister, I ain't liked any of this from the start, and if you don't mind, I'd sure like to climb into that pinto's saddle and get goin' to somewheres else! How about it?"

"What's your name, cowboy?" asked the stranger.

"Skinny. Skinny McGuire. And that's a name you won't ever hear around these parts again, if I get my way. That's a promise!"

"You're a yellow coward, scum!" yelled Croft. "If you do this I'll hunt you down and shoot you myself!"

"You've got to live, first, mister big mouth," McGuire answered, "And somehow I jist don't think that's gonna happen."

The shotgun holder spoke softly "Fork that pinto and get out of here, kid, but shuck the shells out of that sixgun first. And be careful how you do it. Then, when you get to the end of that lane, turn left. You'll meet a mountain man and two Comanche wranglers real soon. They're driving twenty head of horses, so you can't miss them. Tell them to turn in here and to hurry it up, we may have some hangin' to do by the time they get here. You do that, and you can go."

"I'll sure do it, mister, and thanks!" And with that reply, the holster was empty, and the chambers of his gun soon followed suit. Then he was on the mount and spurring his way south down the lane.

"Uh … Look, sir, I … Well, I don't care much for this neither" spoke up the fifth party. He'd been next to Skinny, and looked to be nearly as young.

"You've had no part in what's happened here?"

"Uh … Well, yes, I, I sorta smacked Mr. McCord there in the mouth when he went for his gun, but I had to do it mister! I saved his life! If I wouldna' done that, Harv there woulda' shot him, sure!"

The rider looked to Paul for confirmation, and when he nodded assent, the stranger simply waved at the other horse with his shotgun. "Get!" was all he said to the kid.

Then he turned to Paul. "Sir, would you mind holdin' this thing for a while? I think I'd better finish this little chore right now."

Paul wiped his bloody mouth with the back of his hand and nodded. He strode over and took the big Greener and held it on the three remaining toughs. He smiled as he said "I sure hope this has hair triggers so I can accidently blow someone's head off!"

"Yes sir, it surely does that, so you be careful. Two things I need to ask of you while you watch these three. First, is there a chance we can borrow a corral for a day or two to keep our stock in? And second, do we need to hang these three for this? I don't know what all they've done, but it seems to me that to take hold of so pretty a young lady in that manner should justify it."

"I'm gonna kill you, you pilgrim!" shouted Harvey. "If you didn't have that shotgun, you wouldn't be nothin'! You wouldn't dare stand up to a real man!"

The other two men had turned a pasty white at the mention of hanging and were obviously scared at that point.

"Look here, mister. We was just followin' orders. You can't be serious about no hangin'," said the nearest one.

"You mean to tell me you aren't men enough to refuse to do something a snake like this tells you to do? All the more reason to hang you, just for being cowards where a lady is involved!" was the reply.

"Mister, you jist don't know who you're up against there," joined in the second rider, "That's Harvey Croft, and he's the worst gunman in these parts. Only a crazy man would cross him!"

"Bah! He's nothing but a two bit, would-be, tough guy who likely preys on old men and punchers who aren't even sure how to load a gun, let alone be good with one! I'll show you what I mean. Tough guy, do you want to back up that threat?"

"Sure, be real brave! You know good and well that that piece is dirty and likely to hang-fire on me," Croft shouted.

The rider looked over at Paul, still with the shotgun at the ready and spoke. "Sir, would you cover these three for a bit? I have a chore to do."

"With pleasure, son."

The stranger strode over to Harvey, bent down and secured his gun, then turned his back to walk away. He went to the saddle bags on his big mount and fumbled around a bit until he drew out a cloth bag. From the bag he drew the cleaning apparatus for his own guns and proceeded to efficiently disassemble the gunman's Colt. Within five minutes time he had cleaned, oiled, and reassembled the weapon. He then replaced his own gun with it and proceeded to draw and dry-fire the gun several times. Each time he drew, all who watched failed to see the beginning motion of the draw. The gun just seemed to appear in his hand and click loudly on the empty chamber.

This task done, he calmly reloaded the pistol, then looked Harvey in the eye from two foot away. "Harvey, my friend, you look sorta stupid, standing there with that gunbelt hanging like that. Buckle it back up."

As soon as Harvey had done so, he slipped the freshly cleaned Colt back into its normal place, then stepped back three strides and spoke softly, never taking his eyes from Harvey's.

"Mister, likely you'll try to do just what you've threatened some day. I don't like clouds over my head, so let's get on with it right now. Make your play."

It was just a little too much for Harvey. The man had ridden in and upset his little party, then had faced him down with a shotgun. Next, he had called Harvey for exactly what he was; a careful bully, and then had shown more speed than any of the people there had ever seen with Harvey's own Colt. Now he stood just five feet away waiting willingly for Harv to make his draw. The would-be gunslinger swallowed hard, shifted nervously on his feet, and began to tremble. Though he crouched with his hand hovering over his gun, it wouldn't move. He couldn't force it to! As sweat ran down his handsome features, he saw the others begin to smile with contempt, and had the sudden sound of hoofbeats in the lane not disturbed them, he might have been forced to try and draw just to save face, for the smiles branded him a coward.

All eyes but the stranger's looked at the drovers coming

down the lane, and Paul McCord quickly ran to open a gate and divert the driven horses into the nearest corral. As soon as they were in, he closed the gate and looked over the three men who rode up to the group. One was a huge mountain man who fitted the big blue roan that stood beside him, the first rider's horse. The other two were dark, copper-skinned Indians in white rider's clothes. The big man spoke.

"Wal now, Dan'l, what ya gone and got y'self inter this time?"

"Just a little misunderstanding, Bear. These rannies were trying to hurt a few honest- appearing folks, and I butted in. Those two over there were holding that pretty young lady rather tightly, and not in the normally accepted way. I think they were afraid she was going to whip their leader, there, the tinhorn.

"If you'll look over there at the wrangler on the ground that the nice lady is trying to bring around, you just might see something familiar about him. I figured if anyone would hurt Lane Glover, they needed to be taken down a bit."

"Wal I'll be durned, it is old friend Lane!" barked out the big one. "Looks to me like we'll hev to postpone the reunion til a bit later, though. He don't look so good, Dan. What'er we gonna do with these fellers?"

At that question the two Indians exchanged a quick conversation in the Comanche tongue, to which the big man got very upset and replied vehemently "Consarn it , NO! We told you two savages the we wouldn't tolerate such doins again towards a white man! We'll jist hang 'em and be done with it. I ain't spendin' no three days watchin' another man try to die. I've seen my last o' that! You red devils hyar me?"

The two looked abashed at the attack, and subsided into silence. As Allison blanched white with fear she could have sworn she saw the nearer of the two wink at her, and began to worry at the next move.

"I'm going to give it to you straight, you punchers. You can ride out of here on the condition that these people say so, but if I or any of these men ever see any of you again, you'd better pull iron, 'cause we're going to shoot first and ask later. If that's not acceptable, make your play now." With that, the man called Dan stepped back to face all three, and the Indians both hit the ground so quickly that Allie wondered how it happened. They both assumed the same crouch as Dan, and waited.

The two toughs who had held her moved quickly towards their horses, and noting that Harvey seemed rooted to his spot, the one spoke to him. "Harv', you comin' with us?"

When he received no recognition from that worthy, he almost gently took the gunman's arm and guided him to his horse. Still seeming to be in a daze, he mounted and rode off with them, the three of them heading west at the end of the lane.

By the time the toughs were out of the lane, the three riders had Lane Glover on his way to the house. He was semi-conscious and mildly responsive. As soon as they laid him on the bed they were directed to, introductions were made.

"Young fellow, I'm Paul McCord, owner here, and this is my wife Ida and daughter Allison. It seems you already know Lane over there. I'm sure glad you happened along when you did, that bunch came in here real ugly like, and were getting worse."

"No thanks neccessary, sir. I'm just glad we could get them out of here without bloodshed. My name is Dan Kase, this is Bear Rollins, and these two savages are Red Elk, our leader, and Five Ponies. He prefers to be called Joe."

Allison's heart had fairly leaped within her as Dan started to say his name, she had thought he was going to say Kade. Then she was startled again when the Indian called Joe bowed low, took her hand and kissed it, then said in perfect and very proper English "I'm so very glad to make your acqauntance, Miss Allison."

Red Elk stepped forward and held out his hand. "You gotta watch this ranny, maam. He fancies himself a lady killer, and, wal, he jist ain't got the charm what the rest of us does. And by the way, ya kin call me Reddy."

At that rendering, Ida let out a squeal of mirth. "I think a bunch of bad men were just played for suckers. You two aren't Comanches at all, are you?"

"Yes maam, we are, and we was talkin' real Comanche langauge. 'Course, thet don't mean we'd really do anything like whut Bear thar hinted at. You'd be amazed at how many would-be tough guys fold up their tents and run when they hears injuns about to go on the warpath and torture them a little!"

Laughter erupted instantly, and as the tension drained from all of them as a result, they turned their attentions to Glover. He was semi-conscious yet, but the color seemed to be returning to his face. A concussion was likely, but it appeared to them that he would recover. After making him as comfortable as possible, the men returned to the corrals.

EIGHTEEN

Paul McCord leaned on the corral and gazed at the twenty head of horses it held. They ran small for the most part, but were exceptional riding stock. They showed stamina, with a hint of speed, but it was obvious they were best suited for all day stints. He said so to the newcomers.

"Yes sir, thet's egzactly whut they're fer. We been working to get hosses thet kin go from first light til way past last light. These are the ones we've settled on fer our breedin' stock. We've spent the last four winters in the canyon country trappin' wild mustangs, and have kept the best of each year's catch," replied Reddy.

"No kidding!" exclaimed Paul. "That's a lot of work for four fellows. So what brings you this way?"

Bear answered him. "We saved all the profits we could from the nags we sold, and hope to get our own spread. ya see, Mister McCord, we found out we get along better'n any other folks we know, and we wants to stay together as a crew. Reddy there, he's our ramrod, since the whole thing wus his idee, an' he thought we should look fer permanent stompin' grounds. It didn't take much persuadin', fer we was gettin' tired of jist seein' each other's ugly mugs all winter!"

"Yes," Joe continued, "and we heard there was a good ranch for sale up this way, so we took a chance on the accuracy of that report, and here we are. Can you tell us where the Twin Forks spread is?"

"Oh my," Paul groaned. "I sure can. You just ran their fore-man and two of their crew off my ranch. You're too late, fellows! This fellow, Jude Chesterson, bought it up about a month ago. He's been trying to cut a wide swath ever since. I'm not sure just where he's from, but he's been pretty sick, I guess. Really a pale fellow, with only one arm. In fact, I imagine healing up from the loss of that arm is why he's so pale. I don't know how he lost it, but the whole shoulder and all is gone, so it must have been pretty bad. I don't know if that has anything to do with his lousy disposition or not, but he's a miserable man to deal with.

"In fact, I'm positive that he's responsible for my crew run-ning out on me. After the last boy got shot and killed by Harvey Croft, it wasn't long 'til all of them cleared out. Even my fore-man. Then Lane, there, came along, and offered to hire on. I told him the score, and he wanted to stay in spite of it. I just hope he pulls through this. They hit him awfully hard."

"He's a tough old bird, mister McCord," replied Dan. "I just want to find out why he isn't with Gordon Montgomery any more. You see, we worked for them for two summers, and they were like brothers. I can't imagine him leaving."

"Meanwhile, we got us a problem, fellers," Reddy spoke up. "What we gonna do with these broomtails here 'til we decide where to go from this place?"

"I don't see that as a problem, fellows. You're welcome to keep them here for as long as you need. That's the least I can do. In fact, I'd sure like to hire the four of you 'til this is settled. I'm really concerned about the safety of Ida and Allison. Since I don't know how Lane is going to do, I'd sure rest better at night knowing you were on the job. What do you say?"

"I really don't know about thet, we'd have to palaver a while on it. ya see, we realy want to git started ranchin'," Reddy an-swered.

"It has been a lot of long winters on the way to this point for us, fellows," Dan interjected, "But since it's taken this long, what would another summer hurt? We'll have even more money saved by then. I'd sure like to finish what I started."

Bear nodded his assent, and Joe just looked at the house with that dreamy look they all knew so well by now. Reddy laughed at that and held out his hand to McCord.

"Wal, ya got yer crew, boss. Whut do we do first?"

"First, we talk. This thing today will cause a war, no doubt about it. Then, we eat. Every one eats at the main house, for our cook quit, too, so let's just wander on up there and make plans 'til supper's ready."

"Food? Real food? Not Bear's cookin'? I'm sure ready fer thet!"

"Hey, I never heard no griping 'til now on thet cookin'," Bear exclaimed.

The five of them set on the porch of the rambling house until mealtime, discussing plans and strategies. It was decided to keep two of them at the ranch at all times until Lane was up and around. The other two would patrol the range and tend to all they could that needed done on that front. It was agreed that Paul would attempt to find at least six more hands as soon as possible. His was probably the toughest assignment. With these plans made and supper out of the way, they moved into the bunkhouse and drew straws to see who would take the first watch. With Reddy grumbling about the outcome being fixed, the other three went to bed as the non-plussed Comanche went out to assume the watch. All hoped it would be a quiet night except for Reddy.

"I'd sure like to scalp some idjut, jist to make this night watch stuff worth while," he muttered.

As the first light began to reflect on the light frost in the morning, the triangle sounded for breakfast. Upon completion of a silent meal, Ida approached the men.

"I'm really worried about Lane," she said. "He isn't any different this morning at all. I think we should get the doctor in Crosstown to come out and look at him."

"I'll go git him," Bear spoke up. "I'll head out soon as I git saddled. Where is this Crosstown, and whut's the Doc's name?"

"He's Doctor Simms. You'll find Crosstown by riding out the back way there to the north, go 'til you hit the road going northwest, and go left on that. It's a good two hour ride at a normal trot," Paul answered.

Dan had stood the second watch in the night, and was now bringing the big blue roan out of the stable for his morning grooming. It was more of a ritual of love than a necessity, and the two of them performed it every morning when it was possible. Dan began to curry and brush while Blue did his darndest to playfully nip his beloved master every chance he got. This would result in a smack from Dan on whatever part of the brute was closest, whereupon Blue would assume a hurt, innocent look as though he'd just been beaten for nothing. His antics soon had Allison chuckling from her vantage point on the porch. Reddy stepped up to her side.

"Them two go at it like thet all the time. I never saw the like. Thet hoss shoulda' been a dog, fer all I kin see."

"It's hard to believe that he's a hardened killer when you see him with that horse, isn't it?" Allison asked.

"What!" Reddy exclaimed. "Now you jist wait a minute there, young lady. Thet ain't no hardened killer. Why, Dan there's about the softest hearted feller I ever done met! Why would you say somethin' like thet?"

Taken aback by his passionate reply, she hesitated before answering. "Well, I-I guess because he wanted to kill Harvey yesterday. He--he seemed to relish the thought of hanging those two men, also."

"Miss Allie, 'scuse me, but you've read him all wrong. First off, hangin' those two was jist a bluff to make them think twice about ever crossin' ya agin. An' to maybe make them skedadle outta hyar on their own. And second, yes, he would hev killed thet skunk iffn he'd hed the guts to draw. But ya see, Miss Allie, Dan there's a purty good jedge of men, and he jist knew thet feller'd never draw on him."

"Then he's--he's never killed anyone?"

"I didn't say thet. Yes he has, but they either needed killin' or they left him no choice. He's only good with a gun 'cause I make him practice with it at least an hour a day. ya see, back there in his past is some turrible hurt, an whar we was goin' ya run inter some purty seedy fellers whut would jist as soon cut yer throat as look at yu. I saw right away thet this feller wus gonna git killed iffn I didn't teach him otherwise. So I took him under my wing an' did jist that.

"No maam, Dan there, he's one of the finest fellers on God's green earth, an' one of the gentlest. I could tell ya stories thet would curl yer purty hair 'bout Dan Kase, but they all were 'cause of some turrible tragedy, nuthin' o' his own doin's."

"Then I'm afraid I've judged him wrong, for I've been somewhat frightened by him since yesterday's incident," Allie replied. "But I still don't understand how he could be gentle and kill at the same time. Surely there's a conflict there!"

"Wal, let me tell ya about whut happened two years ago down in Utah, an' maybe yu'll see whut I mean. But ya gotta promise never to tell anyone thet I told yu! Deal?"

At her assenting nod, he began his story of terror and sorrow. "We was workin' fer a rancher name of Gordon Montgomery, who wus Lane's old boss. It wus the second summer we'd sold him our hosses from the winter's ketch, an' we really liked it thar, fer he wus a prince of a feller. Lane wus the straw boss, an' a finer straw boss never forked a hoss!

"Mister Mongomery hed him a son named Jeremy whut wus jist twelve years old. He wus the world thet man lived in! He jist existed on Jeremy's love, an' the two o' them were like the legs on a hoss; whar ya found one the other wus right next to him.

"Wal, thet wus common knowledge 'round those parts, an' six no-good rawhiders got the idear thet they could make their fortune offn thet love. They kidnapped the boy, an' left a ransome note on his saddle. They put some blood on the note from the boy's hand jist to let us know thet they meant business! We were told how they cut him to git it later on by one of the guys while he wus dyin'.

"Mister Montgomery, he wus some upset, an' paid the ransome jist like they told him to. He wouldn't let us go after them fer fear they'd kill the boy. Then, wal, they didn't let him go like they promised. They took off fer the mountains to wait 'til he sold his ranch fer more ransom. We finally got wind of it, an' told him thet these kind would jist bleed him dry an' likely not do anything they promised.

"Wal, he finally let us go after them bums. Now Joe, there,

142

an' Bear, they's the finest trackers in the country. Ain't nowhere ya kin go but whut they cain't foller yu. We was three days out when we found a bad lookin' camp. Thar was a lot o' dark stains on the ground by the fire, an' we could see whar somethin' hed been drug away. Bear found the boy in the bushes. They'd cut his throat an' never even bothered to bury him.

"They didn't do it 'cause they knew we were on their trail, either, 'cause they couldna' known at thet time."

He paused to let that sink in, as well as to gather his emotions. Then he continued. "We was all cold with the need to kill, right then. It was the worst thing any of us hed seen, takin' a boy's life like thet fer nothin'. We figgered we was two days behind them fellers by then, and Dan, there, he jist up and took off on thet big ox he calls a hoss. They wasn't hidin' their tracks none, an' Dan is a pretty fair tracker, hisself, so he jist spurred thet beast an' left us eatin' his dust.

"It was four days later thet we heard the shootin'. We could tell thet Dan had gotten further and further ahead of us, an' figgered they'd found him out and ambushed him. Wal, we shoulda known better.

"Here he'd caught them TWO days earlier an' pinned them varmits down fer thet long. We found later thet he'd ridden daylight 'til dark at nearly a full run fer two days, stoppin'only when he couldn't see to track any more. Then he dry- camped, an' was off at first light. Thet big horse kin run fer a week without stoppin', Miss Allie! I swear he kin!

"Anyhow, we skirted 'round 'til we could see the layout, and Dan had them vultures pinned in a little setback in the rocks where they couldn't climb out or nothin'. I could see whut I thought wus the bodies of two of them by the fire, but realized later thet it wus one feller whut had been blown in two! I knew then thet Dan hed tried to take them alive, an' they'd said no.

"I found out later thet he'd slipped up on them in the dark and held them up with thet big Greener o' his'n, and thet dumb cluck hed tried to draw on him! Dan let both barrels go and backed out of there, but the rest wus a little smarter than the first one.

"Wal, to make a long story even longer, we got around thar

in several different places an' started to shoot inter the place whar they wus, an' ended up killin' one and woundin' two others pretty bad. There was this really dirty lookin' feller layin' thar after we had 'em whipped, bleedin from about a dozen places, and the other wounded feller pointed him out as the one whut killed the boy. Said he told the lad to quit cryin' an' when he wouldn't, he jist killed him.

"Since he wus busted up pretty bad, we knew he wouldn't make it back. We talked it over, decided thet all of them varmits would be hung back in Boomstick, so why take them back."

The wrangler paused, and seemed to be done talking, so Allie asked breathlessly, "You--you mean you hung them there, without a trial?"

"No, Miss Allie, we had a trial. The one wounded feller told us everthin', and the other fellers sided with him. So, since none o' them tried to stop the one whut did it, we figgered they wus as guilty as him. Jist to make it a little better fer them, we hung them first, to sorta let him watch whut was gonna happen to him."

"You--you m m mean you could just kill them like that! Didn't it seem terribly cruel and evil?"

"Yes'm, it did, and it was, but it was also necessary. Whut they did condemned them, not us. We jist carried out the sentence. And if the truth were to be known, Dan there voted against it, but the rest of us are a little more realistic when it comes to justice. We outvoted him, and we stretched the ropes without him, fer he wouldn't help us, or watch. So you see, Miss Allie, he ain't a hardened killer at all, jist a very good man whut sees the real picture, and ain't afraid to carry out the needed things in life, even iffn it means takin' a life."

"I see. Thank you, Reddy, for setting me straight, I've misjudged him unfairly, and you've saved me from a grave mistake. I think I'll go talk to him and thank him for yesterday."

She patted his arm as she left and strode towards Dan and Blue. Reddy stood looking after her and smiled to himself.

"I think we might have a complication coming up hyar. Thet girl has the look of a young lady about to fall fer someone, an' thet someone jist may be Mister Dan what's-is-name," he muttered under his breath.

Allison tripped up to the mildly feuding pair and let her presence be known.

"It surely seems as though he's not all that happy with being groomed. Are you sure it's worth the trouble?"

Dan laughed and replied "Oh yes, if I don't do this, he may pout! He's just a big, overgrown baby!"

"He certainly is --- weelll, uh, a unique animal," she said.

He laughed again and said, "You can say ugly, it won't hurt either of our feelings. We both know that looks are deceiving, and he doesn't even care, just as long as I feed him and love him all over all day. He's really spoiled."

"Where did you get him? Is he a certain breed that we haven't seen around here yet?"

Another laugh. "I think he's all breeds mixed together, with all of the good features but the bad looks from the others mixed in. We caught him wild four years ago in the northern Arizona canyon country on our first winter in Wild Horse Canyon."

"How'd you ever tame a horse as big as him?" she asked.

"Well, to tell you the truth, I think he was just waiting around for a human to catch him and take care of him," came the answer. "The first time I saw him, he was looking me straight in the eye. And the first time I put a rope on him, he just backed up a bit, even though he could have drug the saddle off my horse, and was pretty nervous about it. Just the same, I was able to touch him without fear of losing my hand, and it was easy from there on out.

"He's only been rough with two men since I've had him, and he tried to kill both of them. I guess it's a sixth sense he has, for both of them were very bad men."

"Do you think he'd let me ride him?" she asked.

"He would, as long as I told him to. And any of my pards can, but he doesn't like it if they do."

"Well, he's safe, I could never get all the way up there!"

He smiled and spoke softly, "Kneel, Blue."

The big fellow instantly stretched his off-side leg forward and pulled his left foreleg under him, thereby kneeling until his broad back was at Allie's waist.

She squealed with delight, "He's adorable! You've taught him tricks!"

Dan smiled tolerantly, and replied, "Adorable isn't one of the names I've heard for him. As to tricks, he just loves to please me, so it was easy. I'd seen that done in eastern Arizona at a rodeo, and always liked it. Reddy showed me another one that's even more useful out in the wilds. Up, Blue."

As soon as the horse was on his feet, Dan barked out, "Blue, down flat!"

Allie jumped back and cried out, for the horse dropped flat as though shot, then lay perfectly still.

"Oh! Oh my! That's marvelous! But----what good is it?"

"If you need a rest for a rifle, and need it quick, he's as good as you'll find," Dan answered with pride.

Allison immediately became sober. "So. You still think in terms of shooting, even when training your horses? I had hoped that Reddy was right when he said you hated to fight. It seemed too good to be true, I guess."

"Now wait a minute, Miss Allison. I only taught him that at Reddy's suggestion. And where we've been, it very well could have had its usefulness. I hate shooting and killing, but I hate bullying and pushing people around even more. I refuse to apologize for something like yesterday, even if you don't appreciate it!"

His vehement comeback set her back on her heels, and she quickly realized her error. "I'm so sorry, Dan," she spoke quickly, "I was wrong to judge you like that! I do owe you a huge debt for yesterday. We all do! Please forgive me." And with the saying of it, she lay her hand on his arm and looked into his eyes with a pleading that no man could have refused.

He smiled and just nodded, for her touch and look had rendered him speechless. They held each other's eyes for a few breathless moments, then she whirled and fairly ran towards the house. Partway there, she stopped and looked back, smiled and waved with a weak little gesture, and continued on. She stopped again at the door; just long enough to see that he still watched her, then disappeared from sight into the house.

Dan stood there for what seemed an eternity, just watching

the door that had swallowed her up. After a while, he mused to himself, "Look out, Kade, that one could steal a heart too easily. And an outlaw can't afford such things."

At the thinking of it, his heart dropped, and he slipped into a depression for the rest of the day. It seemed so unfair that he dare not make permanent plans, like love and family, because of murderers like the Chelseas. Gloom claimed his day.

NINETEEN

The noon meal was nearly over when the sound of hoofbeats on a moderate run was heard. Ida jumped excited-
ly to her feet and ran to see if it was Bear and the doctor, which
proved to be the case. As they entered the house, Doc Simms
was talking to them at a frantic pace.

"We'd been here a lot sooner if this behemoth hadn't made
more business for me in town! If you've got a gripe, see him.
Now where's the patient?"

Ida quickly showed him to the room where Lane lay in a
semi-stuper, while the rest of them just looked at Bear expectant-
ly. Reddy finally broke the silence as Bear commenced to shovel
forkfuls of food into his cavernous mouth.

"Wal, let's hear it, ya overgrown, walkin' chuckwagon.
What's he talkin' 'bout?"

Bear stopped long enough to look up before resuming his
meal, then supplied the details, sketchy though they were, between bites.

"Wal', the Doc, there, he wus in the resteraunt, an' it's jist got
a big doorway 'tween it an' the saloon, thar, so when I went in
an' asked fer him, some fellers in the bar wanted to know whut it
wus I wanted him fer. I 'lowed as to how it warn't none of their
business an' told 'em so.

"I guess since there wus three of them, they figgered different. The one dandy said thet iffn the Doc wus fer Lane in

thar, he wusn't leavin'. I 'lowed as how it weren't none of their business agin, an' we hed us a little scuffle. Thet's all." With that account, the mountain man returned to his attack on the unfortunate plate of food before him.

"Little scuffle!" the high pitched voice of Simms came from the other room. The burly doctor emerged with an exasperated look and gave his own account.

"Look, if the bartender hadn't seen who started it, this moose would own half of the Pink Lady by now, just in damages, not to mention my bill for the two broken arms I had to set before we could come out here! Little scuffle, my Aunt Sally! He nearly destroyed the place!"

Paul McCord stood looking at the big man as he finished off his plate, and just shook his head. "You mean to tell me you cleaned up on three of Chesterson's toughs and don't show so much as a scratch? That's incredible!"

"Aww, Paul, they wusn't so tough, they wus countin' on them guns I took away from them when it all started. Some people jist don't realize thet a gun don't always make a feller bigger."

Joe interrupted their discussion. "It seems to me that this is an indication that the man over there on the west side intends to start a war over this thing."

"I'd say thet you're right about thet," Reddy broke in. "Those fellers hed to have orders to do somethin' like thet."

"It looks to me as if we should be on the alert for that type of thing to be starting on our home range. Whoever is assigned to the range duties had best be careful. I don't have a good feeling about the whole situation," Joe continued. "Bear, let's you and I take the range duties this week, if you can force yourself away from that table, that is!"

"Looky hyar, ya redskinned renegade. Iffn I gotta be in the saddle from light to dark, I gotta hev some energy! But I guess this'll hev to do, so let's get on with it."

The light-hearted banter continued until Paul began to explain the boundaries of his ranch and what they could expect to find within those boundaries. As soon as he was done, the two went off in different directions to start their patrolling.

It was nearly an hour later that the doctor emerged from the room where Lane Glover was laying. He went to the kitchen and helped himself to a cup of coffee, then sat down at the table.

"I've got some stuff here that'll help the pain Mister Glover's having, other than that, he should start to show improvement in another twelve hours or so. If you don't see any change by tomorrow morning, send for me again, but don't send that big mountain man, the town can't afford his visits!" And with that announcement, Doc Simms downed the final bit of the coffee and moved to the door. He was a brusk man, not given to long explanations or unnecessary visiting. He always figured he "had too much to do to waste daylight."

Ida walked to the door with him and offered payment, which was promptly refused. "It was worth it just to see Chesterton's hardcases properly stomped. That man is going to be trouble for this area yet, you mark my words."

Paul asked him, "What do you mean by that, Doc?"

"Well, he has the big shots in the territory convinced that he should be something big himself, no matter what it takes to achieve it. Of course, he doesn't tell them that. But it's just a matter of time before he gets rough in trying to buy out several well established ranchers around here. This one included!"

"Why are the big shots, as you call them, falling for his talk?" Ida asked.

"I'm not exactly sure, but he claims to have the backing of a lot of railroad big-wigs, and a couple of Army buyers as well. In fact, there's supposed to be a big shindig at the Twin Forks ranch in a month or so for a bunch of them. He's probably going to make his play for power then. I hope the place burns down by that time!"

"Iffn he messes with this bunch of rannies, it jist might happen, Doc," Reddy put in. "Fer now, I think we've got a couple of pitchforks waitin' fer us, Danny me lad!" And with that, the two of them made their way to the barn and stable area.

When Bear and Joe clumped into the house that evening it was nearly dark, and they found Lane Glover seated in the over-stuffed chair in the living room, eating from a tray on his lap. He looked up at Bear's whoop of joy and smiled. The two riders ran over to shake their old boss' hand, with Bear's grip causing him to flinch and growl at the big man.

"Darn it, you big ox, don't go breakin' that paw of mine, I'm gonna need it to ride herd on you characters. I just want to know what I've done to deserve this kind of punishment to have to put up with you four rannies again!"

"Say, you mossy-horned old renegade, you're glad to see us and you know it!"

"Yeah, I am. I couldn't believe my eyes when I saw that big blue roan trot up the other day. Even through the haze, I had to know him. And that meant you guys were right close, so I felt a lot better right away. 'Til I tried to stand up, that is!

"What in the world brings you fellows up this way, any-how?"

"Now, we'll get into that a little later," Joe answered, "What we want to know first is what brings you up here? What in heaven's name happened between you and Gordon?"

"I was afraid you'd want me to go through that, and it's pain-ful to do. After you fellows came back from the manhunt with the sad news about little Gordon, he just never recovered.

"You can remember how that little guy went every where his Daddy went, so it didn't really come as a shock when he told me he was going to sell out and go back east. Mira had family there, and he figured on resting a while and then going to work for them.

"I was at wit's end trying to make him see that running wasn't the answer, but it didn't work. The new owner talked me into staying on, but then I ran across some information about the kidnapping that was mighty interesting, and I ended up following that lead up here.

"It seems as though there was one more person involved in that deal, a guy who was the brains behind it. He got the ransom money and didn't show up to meet the others as planned, and that's when they decided to hold out for more money. My infor-mant pointed me in this direction with a fair description, and I figure this person is actually responsible for the little boy's death. If he'd split the money with the others as planned, they would have let the little tyke go.

"So, here I am, and I think I"m close, but I can't be sure yet."

"Who is it, Lane?"

"I'd rather not say just yet, 'til I have something solid to go on, OK? I know you fellows have a big stake in this, but I don't want to influence your thinking. That way, if I"m wrong, I'll have four clear heads to help me see it."

Reddy offered his hand and said, "I sure appreciate yore stand, old pard, so I'll honor it, but soon's ya know, I want to pull on the rope with ya that hangs the snake!"

After the evening meal was over, they moved to the living room for a war parley. Joe and Bear were the first to speak.

"I have a concern for the horses on your range, Paul," Joe started out. "I saw a lot of shod tracks that were not that old on the western part where I patrolled. I realize this is a small ranch as far as square miles, but the stock that's out on the fringes is subject to being easy pickings.

"Correct me if I'm wrong, Paul, but you said your range was twelve miles north and south, and sixteen miles east and west, or around a hundred thousand acres. Or a little more than that, right?"

"A hundred and twenty-two, to be specific," Paul answered.

"Well," Joe continued, "the way we see it, we should bring the herd in as close as we can to home territory, and bunch them in two different places. This will split the herd enough to keep from over-grazing an area, but still keep them within a smaller perimeter to make patrolling and guard duty easier.

"The only problem with that is that we need more riders to get the job done in as little time as possible. Riders we don't have!"

Dan spoke up, "I'm not so sure we can't get it done with what we have, Joe. I think your idea is a good one, and it seems to me that four riders herding, one patrolling the rest of the ranch, and one on guard here would be able to carry it out. Reddy and I could take Paul and Miss Allison to do the round-up, while you and Bear split the other duties.

"Since you two have already seen the range, you're familiar with it, and Paul and Miss Allison know it well enough to guide us."

"Nothing personal, Miss Allison, but I assume you're a good rider?" Joe asked.

Before she could answer, Dan spoke up. "She sure is. You should have seen her on Blue today! She worked him in the corral for a while, and I saw that she was good, so I suggested she take him out a mile and then let him out on the way back. Yes sir, she can ride!"

Allie blushed at this testimony of her prowess, and added, "I thought Flame could run, and I would have put him up against any horse within a hundred miles. But, oh my, how that big brute can fly! I thought I'd be blown off him by the wind!

"But you men forgot to include one little step in this. You forgot to ask Miss Allison if she would help! Well, I won't. At least not until you stop this Miss stuff! It's just Allison, or better yet, Allie. OK?"

Dan looked at her with admiration, while Reddy chuckled and nodded. "Ok, Allie, it's a deal. We start tomorrow at first light. Bear, I'll feel best if you take the guard duties here. Then in a couple of days, Lane should be up to the task of riding with Joe to scout out the next roundup on the other sections.

"Any questions? If not, let's hit the hay, it'll be a short night at best."

As Allie passed by Dan she looked at him with a smile and said in a low voice, "Thanks for the vote of confidence, Sir Galahad. That was nice of you. And thanks for letting me ride that wonderful animal you have that's disguised as a horse!"

And with that, she patted his arm and moved on towards the stairs, leaving him open-mouthed and speechless. Reddy quietly took his arm and guided him to the door, saying goodnight as he did so. They made their way to the bunkhouse to turn in.

"Pard," Reddy offered, "I think you'd better watch that one, she's got you buffaloed!"

Dan said nothing in reply. He was still marvelling at the softness of her touch. It lingered on into the night as sleep did its best to elude him. When he finally faded away, it was to the call of the midnight hour; the night would be short, indeed, for Dan Kade, outlaw.

Red Elk, Paul, Allie, and Dan were working the northwest section of the ranch by mid-morning the next day, and had split up into pairs to search out the shallow draws and creek beds for stock. Their plan was to start working the horses towards the center of the range, then make one big drive from there. Dan and Allie were riding together in an especially rugged area when they became split up as a result of coming onto two groups of horses at once. It had been nearly a quarter of an hour since Dan had last seen Allie, which really wouldn't have been that unusual had it not been for the circumstances.

Dan got his bunch started in the general direction he wanted them to go, then ran them a little to insure their excitement would keep them going that way for a while, then circled back to find his partner. He spotted her going down a draw just as he topped a sharp rise, and his heart fairly jumped to see two riders suddenly ride into her path and stop her. They were a couple of hundred yards away and below him to his left.

Allison was following the tracks of two horses that had eluded her and was totally engrossed in them when the two confronted her. She gasped and wheeled her mount around to run, but saw a rider emerge from some brush to her right to cut her off. He swung a rope with the loop already formed and his intentions were clear to her.

Allison frantically looked around for another way out, saw none, so she dropped as low to her horses neck as possible to avoid the rope. Just as his arm reached its height to release the loop towards her, dust flew from his ribcage just under that arm, his face contorted into a shocked expression, and then went totally slack. All in the same split second he flopped from the saddle like a sack of rocks, dead before he left the stirrups. The report of the rifle came on the heels of the puff of dust from the rider, and was enough to cause Allie to put the spurs to her horse and leap the falling man on her flight to safety.

On the ridge, Dan had whipped his Henry rifle from its scabbard and dropped from the saddle to rest the barrel on the big roan's back. Blue had been trained for this type of moment, and knew instinctively to hold perfectly still. He barely flinched at the crack of the rifle that swept the rider from his horse. Dan

154

was on his back again before the first echo of the report sounded from the opposite banks.

The other two riders did not show a great amount of intelligence, as they shot off in pursuit of Allie. They weren't gaining on her, but she was headed for a steep area that Dan saw would slow her considerably. He touched Blue with the spurs that the big horse only felt in dire times, and the race was over in no time. As Allie turned in the saddle to check the pursuit, she saw Dan directly behind her would-be abductors, and smartly turned to her right to clear herself from the line of fire should he decide to shoot. The riders turned at the same point she did, and as they did so, Dan unleashed his Colt at the nearest one, and knocked him from the saddle. He fell in front of the other's horse, who jumped so violently to avoid the fallen one that it fell, spilling its rider into the brush.

The outlaw cursed and came up clawing for his sidearm, but stopped when he found the barrel of Dan's Colt a mere six feet from his face.

"You'll want to pull that Colt real slow-like, Mister," Dan said, "and drop it where you stand. That's good. Now back away from it.

"I want to know what you had in mind, and who sent you to do whatever it was you were going to do, Mister, and I don't intend to fool around with you very long to find out. Now talk!"

"Go ahead and shoot, sucker, I ain't tellin' you nothin, and you ain't gonna face me down like you did certain other cowards. So you just do your darndest," the rider answered defiantly.

Dan knew this one wasn't likely to be bluffed, so he issued his orders without further attempts at learning anything from him.

"I don't intend to waste my time on a bum like you, Mister. So hear me, and hear me good. We're riding out of here, just long enough to get her back to the ranch, and then I'm coming back. While I'm gone, you'd better get this scum on his horse and out of here , 'cause if you're here when I get back, I will bore you. And if he's here, I'll look you up pronto, and finish this job right. Now back up some more while I get that gun."

"No man takes my gun and gets away with it, you. You'd

better leave it right where it is! And how am I supposed to catch those horses, they're spooked bad about now?"

"You should have thought of that before you tried this little stunt, Mister. You catch them, and you do it quick, 'cause I'll be back in less than two hours, and I won't be so squeamish about boring you if the lady isn't here."

With that, Dan collected the weapons he could find, unloaded them, and threw them as far as he could in different directions. Then he mounted up and herded Allie out of there as fast as possible.

They were nearly half way to the ranch when they ran across Reddy and Paul driving a small bunch of horses in the same direction. They reined in and Dan filled them with a hurried account.

"I'll head back thet way and check on those jaspers, Dan. You take these hosses on back and stay there. We've got to have another war parley before we make another move!" Reddy offered.

The others merely nodded their assent and went after the herd with a rush to get them moving as fast as possible towards home.

At the ranch, they herded the thirty-odd head into one of the larger corrals, and rode on to the stables. Paul tied his mount to a stall, asked Dan if he minded taking care of him, and moved rapidly off to the house, obviously shaken. Dan led Blue and the other horse into the runway between stalls and helped Allie down as she pulled her horse in beside them.

"Well, Sir Galahad, I guess that's another time I owe you for. I hope you don't have to make this a habit for very long," she quipped. It was plain to Dan that she was shaken up, and needed to tease to ease her tension.

"I'll tell you something, young lady, I hope not. But if I do, I hope you're on that strawberry roan of yours the next time. This other nag just doesn't have the speed to help much! I was afraid they were going to get to you before we could!"

She was obviously pleased with his praise for her favorite, Flame, and was about to thank him when the mischievousness of Blue took over. He reached over and gave Dan one of his big shoves in the back with his huge nose, fairly tossing him against Allison.

The two of them were pushed against her horse, and catching hold of the saddle to keep from falling, Dan ended up with his face scant inches from her's. He was suddenly captivated by her eyes and their closeness, for she stared unwaveringly into his own. He couldn't have stopped his reaction had there been a gun to his head. He leaned to her and kissed her tenderly on the lips, lingering for a brief moment before withdrawing.

He was about to stammer out an apology when she reached up just as quickly and returned his kiss, holding to him as a drowning man holds to a log.

For what seemed 'til the end of time they stood there in each other's arms, then, as though they were suddenly awakened, they both stepped back with a start. Allison gasped a little surprised sigh, while Dan simply stood motionless for a moment. After that brief pause, she stepped to the side and started for the house on the run. That lasted for a total of two or three steps, then she whirled to face him.

He stayed rooted to the spot like a schoolboy awaiting the wrath of an angry teacher, but she only smiled a radiant smile that set him on his heels, and left him rocking there as she spun around and resumed her rapid trek to the house. It would be many minutes before he moved from his place, and then it was the impatient prodding of the big roan that awakened him.

"Golly, Blue. I think I've gone and done the worst now. I don't know if I can ever face her again, after that! And she kissed me back! And then smiled! Golly, Blue."

He then went about his tasks with a schoolboy demeanor, wondering around in a kind of foggy manner until the only thing left to do was return to the house. It was at that point that he came back to earth with a thud, for he now had to face Allison, ready or not. Could they act normal? Would everyone sense something? What could he expect?

With pounding heart and dragging feet he made his reluctant way to the kitchen to wash up, and it was with a thankful heart that he found it deserted. But he still had to face mealtime sooner or later! He suddenly chuckled at his frantic state of mind over a simple kiss, for he realized that the shooting of two men was a much more traumatic event than that, and he'd completely forgotten the seriousness of the afternoon's events. With that realization pressed upon him, he strode into the living room to find Reddy just entering by the front door. The rest of the crew was already there, gathered up by Paul as soon as he had hit the house. Joe was not yet in from the range, but it was very early, and he would be brought up to date as soon as he arrived after dark.

Dan could tell by Reddy's visage that there was more wrong than even he knew about. The Comanche brave came out in him as he took his place in front of them to relate the latest events.

"I shore don't know how much Dan and Allie hev told yu'all, but whatever it is, it ain't near as bad a news as whut I've got to share since checkin' up on those scum what Dan left back thar."

"I haven't told anyone anything yet, pard, but it sounds as if maybe I'd better do so as quickly as possible," Dan answered. So, for the next few minutes, he and Allison took turns giving the details of their morning. When they had finished, all looked to the Indian for his extension of the news.

"Wal, it's a durned shame, but we've got ourselves some of the lowest life men on God's green earth to fight against," he began.

"Dan, did you shoot thet last critter once or twice?" he asked.

"Just once," was the reply.

"I thought so. Wal, when I got back to whar ya said I'd find them, you was right. The wounded one wus still thar, dyin'. I recollected as to how ya said he wasn't all thet bad hit, so I give him some water an' got him up a little, an' he wus able to talk some.

"His partner could only ketch one hoss, so he jist plugged this one so's he didn't hev to mess with him. Told the feller he wusn't worth haulin' back, an' thet he knew too much to let live!

"The bum fergot to make shore of hisself, an' this wounded feller hed enough strength to tell me most of whut they hed planned before he cashed in. It ain't good news, folks!"

Ida had been listening intently, but with a sudden expulsion of breath, she got up and left the room, saying she couldn't take hearing any more. Allison stayed put, but was getting whiter by the minute.

Reddy continued, "It seems as though the Twin forks is out of control now. This hyar Chesterson feller wants all he kin git, an' has let thet would-be gunman, Cross, hev free reign to do as he pleases. And it pleases him to think thet iffn they kin git Miss Allie, you folks would cave in an' sell out. But he told these varmits thet he intended to hev her fer his own!"

Allison gave an involuntary gasp and looked quickly at Dan. He clouded up like he was going to rain, and instinctively laid his hand on his gun. The thoughts that welled up inside came out in a rush.

"I should have killed him when I had the chance! Why in the world did I think I could change someone like him instead?"

Allison slipped over to where he was standing and placed both hands on his arm tenderly. "You did right, Dan Kase. Trying to spare a life is always the right way first. I wouldn't want it any other way."

She spoke the last with such feeling that her dad and the others looked at each other with knowing glances. What Dan and Allison were yet to learn had just become obvious to those who knew them best. Love had arrived!

Lane Glover stepped in and took over the planning from that point on. Their first point of agreement came quickly, that Allie was never to be left alone from that time on. Then the logistics of getting the rest of the horses close to the ranch proper was cared for. As they were finalizing the next few day's schedule, Joe arrived to do away with all the plans they had just made. He stormed through the door, bloody visage dark with fury, his coal black hair disheveled and hatless. A groove along the left side of his head had bled profusely before closing, and several cuts marked his face.

He forsook his normally perfect English as he blurted out in anger. "The dams broke and there's the devil to pay! They've run off a couple hundred head of two year olds to the northeast.

"Six of them jumped me from different directions and we had a running battle 'til I got to some rocky ground. Then the tide went out on them!"

159

The others just stared at him in shock. The battle for the valley had been launched.

TWENTY

Paul McCord spoke up with a finality in his voice. "I see what he's doing, people. Their plan is to run off the stock I have contracted to the army, and in fact, that's just what they've done! That way, we can't meet the contract terms, and we lose it! Those were the two year-olds that were ready for delivery when our hands were run off. Well, it isn't going to work! We've worked hard for this ranch, and this bunch isn't going to ruin all that!

"Joe, you get in the kitchen and get yourself cleaned up and fed. Allie, you get enough supplies sacked up for three men for a week. Dan, you and Reddy get three horses saddled, and three others on lead ropes ready to go. Get a pack horse saddled, too.

"Bear, you and Lane go to the bunkhouse and get your's and Joe's ammunition and gear for the trail ready. Joe, Bear, and I are going after those horses in an hour. Lane, you'll be the guard at the home sight, here. Dan, I want you to take your field glasses out to the knoll about a mile to the north there, the one with the scrub oak thicket on top? I want a light 'til no-light surveillance of the area where the other horses have been bunched, and if anyone tries to take any more stock, don't interfere, but follow them. That way, we can get good evidence on them.

"Reddy, I want you to try your best to turn Indian! I know it'll be rough, but I want the Twin Forks ranch watched closely for the next few days. We want to know every move they make, and if possible, who made it. If any crew rides out in this direction, you're to get here first, no matter what! Take the fastest horse out there, your's is maybe the most important job of all. When you ride that way, hold a little north, and after you've gone five miles or so, you'll be able to make out a wide gap in the mountain range to the west. Head straight for that, and you'll come out close to the spread. The Otter river runs north and south there, with the Beaver joining it from the west. Just a mile north of that, the White joins it from the northwest. Twin Forks ranch lays halfway in between the two on the west side of the river.

"About a mile this side of the river there's a bluff that slopes away sharply towards the river. That's a good place to spy from, as the brush is thicker'n hair on a goat, and plenty high. Now, does anybody have any thing to add?"

Dan spoke up, "Take Blue, Reddy. Nothing on this range is going to catch him, and he doesn't need a lot of graze for a couple of days, so you won't need to risk leaving the cover during daylight."

"Thanks, pard, I'll do thet. I'll go get my gear and be back soon. Paul, you tell Ida thet I don't need nothin' but some cold biscuits. I'll go Injun, as ya said."

Fifteen minutes later the group had gathered outside the house again, as preparations had taken less time than expected. Allison had just stepped up beside Dan to speak when a figure came around the corner. She gasped with fright at the sight before her. There facing them stood a lean, slender form in buckskins, warpainted face, and bow and arrows at hand. His feet were encased in the tall moccasins known to the Comanche warriors, some of the worlds' best horsemen. The brave spoke to her in the gutteral dialect of a southern tribe, then broke into a grin as he added, "An' iffn ya cain't understand thet, pretty lady, yu'll jist hev to let Mister Kase thar interpret fer yu."

Allison gasped, "Reddy, is that you? It can't be! What in the world are you doing?"

"Wal, now, make up yore mind, lady. Is it me, or ain't it?"

"But, why the outfit, and the war paint? I don't understand at all."

"Look, the buckskins blend in to the woods better'n other clothes. Moccasins are quieter, and a bow is not only silent, but scares the britches off anyone thet gits shot with it. As fer the war paint, iffn anyone surprises me, this usually shocks them fer a couple of breaths, and gives me a chance to move first. Sometimes thet's the difference 'tween livin' and dyin'."

With that said, he turned abruptly and stalked to the big blue roan, swung into the saddle and was off at a moderate, ground covering lope. Dan explained to Allie that this was the lovable wrangler's way when faced with an unpleasant task. He disliked discussing things of that ilk with others, for they could cloud his judgement with their own thoughts. Right or wrong, the Twin Forks outfit had a sinister force to deal with in Red Elk, son of Dark Cloud, Comanche chiefton.

Allison watched him go and said to Dan, "It seems to me that he should have at least taken a rifle."

"Don't worry, you just didn't see the Colt in his waistband or the Henry in my scabbard. He's loaded for bear."

She gave him a look of thanks, then replied, "I'm so glad. I hope you'll be extra careful out there on that hill, Dan Kase. I don't want you hurt, either."

The last was said with such feeling that Dan actually shuddered inwardly. Her meaning was as warm as the touch of her hand as she took his and squeezed with feeling

He could not have replied otherwise if someone had a gun to his head. "I'll be careful, but you do the same, only more so. I couldn't stand for you to be hurt!"

They were interrupted by the sudden hubbub of the rest loading their supplies and leaving. The magic of the moment was gone, and Dan took that opportunity to mount and flee before he went too far and could never get free!

TWENTY-ONE

One week later, in the little railroad town of Dry Springs a hundred miles to the east of the McCord ranch, three bedraggled and trail weary men sat their horses by a corral at the railroad loading pens. They overlooked a herd of fine horses that occupied the corrals.

Paul McCord spoke first. "I can't believe their gall! They haven't even changed the brands!"

The gravelly voice of Rollins expressed the thoughts that each was entertaining. "Thet tells you whut kind of critters we're dealing with, Paul. We gotta expect them varmits to back shoot us or worse iffn they gits the chance. So don't let your guard down fer even a second! They's gotta be summers in this hyar burg, an' I aim to see them first, no matter whut!"

The others merely nodded their assent, and as one, they turned their horses toward the main street in search of a meal and their prey, in that order. Locating a small restaurant, they tied the mounts and entered, to find it bustling with activity. Paul grabbed the nearest available table and was joined instantly by Joe and Bear. Joe's eyes were constantly searching for a familiar face as they awaited the arrival of a waitress. When she finally appeared, Joe was so engrossed with his scrutiny of the patrons that he totally forgot his customary flirtations.

They talked strategy throughout the meal, once it arrived, and within a short period of time, were on the street headed for the nearest saloon, the most likely place for men such as they sought.

Dry Creek sported three such establishments, all within a block of one another, and the first one netted nothing. The second was the largest of the three, and it was there that they scored a direct hit. As soon as he entered, Paul immediately recognized a uniformed officer, his cavalry dress blues spotless and pressed to perfection. Paul turned to his companions and whispered, "That's Lieutenant Leeds. He's the purchasing agent for the Army that I deal with."

Joe's reply was quick. "And the three men with him are three of the five that I was shooting at back on your ranch!"

Bear said nothing, but slipped away to his right and proceeded to make his way quietly around behind the three and their table of fellow gamers. The saloon faced east on the street, with the bar to the right as one entered the door, with the card tables to the left, filling an area some thirty feet wide and easily that deep from front to back. It was indeed, a large establishment for the small town of Dry Creek.

Knowing that no one in the place had ever seen him, Bear calmly walked right up behind the three that Joe had pointed out, and positioned himself against the wall in what appeared to be a relaxed position against the wall. Paul walked directly towards the table as Joe sidled off to the left. As they approached, one of the three players from the Twin Forks trio turned to Bear with a growl.

"I'd rather not have anyone behind me when I play, fellow, so move it if you don't mind."

Bear just smiled and shook his head, remaining in place. As the scruffy-looking rider started to stand, Paul McCord spoke up from directly in front of them.

"Hold on just a minute there, fella. We want to have a little talk with you and your two friends here."

The ruffian stopped halfway out of his seat and looked at McCord. "Mister, I don't know who you are or what you want, but I got nothin' to say to you but to get this scum out from behind me!"

Paul looked from one to the other for a tense moment, then spoke loudly enough for the whole bar to hear.

"You and the two other civilians here stole those horses yonder in the loading pens from me, and we're here to get them back and hang the lot of you. Now make your move or drop your guns, whichever you want. It's your choice, but you're dead men either way!"

Lieutenant Leeds jumped to his feet with a cry. "Wait! I purchased those horses from these men, and aim to send the bank draft to you! What in the world are you trying to do, McCord?"

The man by Bear had paled visibly at the accusation, and made his move at that point. He leaped from his chair with a shout and swung towards Bear, drawing his Cotl as he did so. The big man was as quick as a cat, and promptly knocked him senseless, sending him sprawling acrossed the table in the process. The short puncher to Paul's left raised a gun from under the table, then froze in an almost comical position as he felt the barrel of Joe's pistol on the back of his neck. In the two seconds required for this to take place, the third outlaw succeeded in drawing and firing wildly, the bullet missing Paul and smacking into a patron standing behind him to his left. Paul's own weapon was at full cock when the fury of the mountain man struck the hapless thief. Rollins was just getting started now, and grabbed the man by the neck with his left hand. He picked him bodily from the floor while slapping him repeatedly back and forth with the big right paw at the end of his other arm. The gun went flying, then the body of the thief quickly followed as Bear soon tired of this and solidly busted him in the side of the head with that huge fist. He crumpled to the floor senseless, joining his first companion in a heap of rags and unconscious flesh.

Paul's assessment of the big man went even higher than ever before as he witnessed the unbelievable strength of the man. He was grateful that he didn't have to take a life in this crowded place, or anywhere, for that matter.

"Somebody call the sheriff," Paul said, "We've got some horse thieves to lock up."

Someone yelled out from the door that the sheriff was already there, and the crowd parted to let a huffing figure through. Sherrif Haynes was a portly man of fifty, with a long, reddish gray, handlebar mustache and a couple of day's stubble that had escaped the razor. He made up in experience what he lacked in physical ability, for he had been the first elected lawman in the state, and had been in office ever since. He was a man not prone to worry about appearances, and often used his less than professional demeanor to his advantage. Many a man had felt he could easily coerce this tobacco chewing lout, only to find himself wondering when the fellow was going to slide his next meal through the bars to him.

Several men started talking at once, but stopped at a glare from Haynes. "What's going on here, McCord? And why isn't someone getting poor Lenny there to the doc? Come on you numbskulls, get a move on! Get him outta here!"

Just as Paul was about to speak, Leeds barged in loudly.

"I'm glad to see you, sheriff! I have no idea what's gotten into McCord there, but he came in here with these two strangers and accused his own riders of stealing horses! I've already issued Army vouchers for those horses once, and I don't intend to pay again! I've heard that he's about to go under, but I didn't think he'd stoop to trying a stunt like this! I'm pressing charges, lock him up!"

Paul's mouth dropped open in disbelief, and he found himself speechless. The old lawman wasn't that impressed with Leeds, but didn't let on. Instead, he surveyed all the men involved with a slow, careful, studying gaze, then motioned to the unconscious rustlers.

"Young feller," he said as he looked Bear in the eye, "you made 'em thataway, supposin' you cart one of 'em over to my office while your two pards here bring the other one. And be easy with 'em, too, okay? We'll all work this out over there."

Leeds started to protest loudly, but was cut off immediately with a stare from the old lawman. "I said we'd care for this over there, sir, and that's just what we're a gonna do. Savvy?"

The sputtering officer impatiently stalked off in the direction of the jail, followed by a rather unusual procession of the sheriff and his charges. Upon arrival, he herded them into the little bare room that served him as office. The only furniture in the place was a rolltop desk and two chairs. On the back wall was the usual gun rack holding a couple of shotguns and three rifles captive. The potbellyed stove held a coffee pot, and that concluded the contents of the place.

"Well," Haynes began, "I want to hear Mr. McCord's story on this first, then I'll listen to the rest of you. And I won't put up with no interruptin' each other, either, so just wait your turn. You'll all get to talk."

Bear spoke up quickly. "Beggin' yore pardon, sir, but kin I put this varmit down sommers? He's likely to git heavy iffn I gotta hold him too long."

The lawman smiled at that, and motioned to the back where the cells were. "Put'em both back there, on the bunks in the cells. I won't lock the doors, yet, but they'll be best off there."

"Really, sheriff, I must protest this treatment of these men and myself! I've aready told … " Leeds began, only to be interrupted by a cold stare from Haynes.

"And I already told you how it was gonna be! So shut up and wait your turn! Now, Mister McCord, let's hear it."

Paul spent a good deal of time telling the details of the last few days, starting with the running off of the crew by Harvey Cross, and leaving nothing out. He finished with the statement that he, Bear, and Joe had tracked the rustlers to the loading pens, and found his herd there.

Sheriff Haynes looked at Paul's two companions, and asked, "And what might your names be, gentlemen?"

"My name is James Anderson Rollins, sir," the big man growled out respectfully. "My friends calls me Bear."

Joe started to choke and chuckle as he looked at Bear. "James Anderson Rollins? James Anderson Rollins? You never told us that! You've been holding back on us Bear, and us pards for more than five, no, six years! Shame on you!"

"Now young man, just what name might you have that's nearly as respectful as this little feller's?" Haynes spoke up.

Joe composed himself, drew himself to his full six feet height, and replied, "I am Five Ponies, son of Nah-Toe-Hay, great Comanche chiefton." Then he added with a chuckle, "But my friends call me Joe."

The kindly sheriff smiled at that, and asked the two companions, "Would you say that your bosses' story here is just like you'd tell it?"

"Absolutely!" they cried in unison. Joe added, "And any liar or horse thief that says otherwise is likely to find a couple of renegades on his trail."

The last was not lost on the ears of Haynes or Leeds, and the latter paled at the insinuation. He remained silent until the sheriff looked at him with lifted eyebrows and nodded.

He spoke with an angry quiver in his voice when he finally did so. "I don't know what you people are trying to pull, but the Army has a contract for those horses, and I've made the purchase according to that contract. Any disagreement between McCord and his men is of no interest to me. I intend to wire for the necessary rail cars to ship them immediately."

"Those horses go nowhere until the money is in my bank in town. You try it and I'll stop you if Sheriff Haynes doesn't!" exclaimed Paul. "It's not my fault you paid for horses without seeing proper identification. Those men don't work for me now, and never did. They stole those horses, and it looks to me as if you're out some money for your carelessness, Leeds!"

The trooper was now nearly out of control, with only the stare of Haynes enabling him to maintain a semblance of calm. He protested to the lawman as to his intervention in the matter.

"Really, sheriff, I don't see how you can legally stop me. These men I dealt with are known to me from before, and the Army has jurisdiction over this matter of the shipment of their horses."

"Leeds, I've known Paul McCord for over twenty years now, and he's a man of his word. If he says these aren't his men, then I don't know or care where you knew them from before, but it looks mighty fishy to me. I'm holding these three back there on suspicion, and you can feel lucky I don't hold you.

"Now, Paul, I'm asking you to leave those horses here until there's a full investigation with the Army and I working together. Without a signature from you, these horses can't be sold anyway, so you'll either get your money or the horses in the long run. And I'd appreciate if you, Mister Rollins, and Mister Five Horses there stayed in town 'til we clear this up. Shouldn't take more than a couple of days. Okay?"

"Five Ponies, sheriff, Ponies," Joe spoke up. "And it's sorta important that we get back to help out as quickly as we can, for they're very outnumbered back there."

"Just the same, I want you here. They'll get by for a couple of days without you." With that, he looked at Paul, who nodded his assent.

Leeds started to stomp out when Haynes stopped him. "Lieutenant, you stick around, too. I do have the authority to hold you if I feel it's warranted. I'm wiring your commander to get here to help clear this up, and you'd better be around when he gets here. Savvy?"

"I'll be here, all right, and you'll wish I weren't when my superiors get done with you!" And with that, he rushed angrily to the board walk and soon disappeared towards the hotel.

Sheriff Haynes looked to Paul and told him, "I'm really sorry to have to ask you to stay, for I've no doubt you're needed there, but with the Army's stuffed shirts in on this, it's for your own good. I'll see you for supper tonight at home, and bring those two renegades with you, okay?"

Paul simply grinned his yes and led the others out to find the telegraph office. He intended to wire Ira Nelson for the hands that were so desperately needed.

On the way, Bear queried, "How does thet sheriff know you so well, Paul? It's near a hundred mile from the ranch to hyar."

"I know, Bear, but it's also the nearest railroad to the ranch. I've shipped stock from here since the railroad moved in, and before that, Marcus Haynes was the federal marshall in this territory. He's only been sheriff here since they established county law and he could stay closer to home. He used to be the only law we had back home, now there's hardly any law enforcement at all.

"We've tried to get another federal marshall appointed for our area, but so far, no help at all. That's why we're in this fix now. That's also why I'm determined to stop this crazy man over on the Twin Forks place! Here's the telegraph office, why don't you two go get us a room at the Emporium a couple of blocks down that way while I send this? I'll join you in the restaurant where we had lunch after that."

The two wranglers nodded assent and moved on down the

street in the direction of the hotel, and Paul sent his wire. It read, "Ira, shooting trouble here-stop. No hands left to speak of- stop. Need four or five good men who don't mind a scrap-stop. Send them to Dry Springs-stop. Horses and map will be waiting at Emporium hotel-stop. Thanks, we're desperate-stop."

That task taken care of, he proceeded to the eatery, wishing all the way that he could at least send his two riders home to help there.

TWENTY-TWO

It had been two full weeks since Paul and the others had left in pursuit of the thieves, with every waking moment of Dan Kade's life spent in misery. He had carefully avoided Allison as much as possible, for he didn't know how to tell her that he was a hunted man with no right whatsoever to ask a woman to commit to him knowing that sooner or later she would more than likely have to see him found and taken away to prison, or worse, shot by some trigger-happy lawman.

The tremendous pressure of that, coupled with the all-consuming love for her that refused to stop growing, let alone go away, filled his days with remorse and his nights with restless dreams. He seemed to be walking in a daze most of the time, and in order to avoid her, he arose well before daybreak, and rode in to a cold meal at the bunkhouse long after night had fallen. This routine had begun to take its toll, and he looked drawn and haggard to the point of frustrating Lane with his refusal to cut back on his hours. Though the crafty foreman was sure he knew the source of Dan's troubles, he was hesitant to approach him directly about it. The day came when he could no longer keep silent. That night, when Dan rode into the darkened interior of the stables, the faithful old hand was waiting for him.

He lighted a lantern as Dan dismounted, smiling at the drawn Colt staring at him. "Just a mite jumpy, aren't you, son? I wanted to have a confab with you, so I stayed up later than usual. I didn't figure to startle you like that."

"What'd you expect, with me spending my time on the watch for vermin all day, total peace and calm?"

Lane smiled his big engaging smile and shook his head. "No son, I guess I didn't. You've a right to be spooked, what with the hours you're spending out there. And that's what I want to talk to you about.

"You can't keep on like you have been, it's takin' its toll on you. I just don't think it's necessary to put the time in that you are. The way I see it, the early hours 'til mid-mornin', then right after noon time, and again from just before evening meal time 'til dark are the most likely times for those snakes to make a move.

"So, the way I see it, you could get back in here for some rest between times and change your eatin' schedule accordingly. You've lost weight, boy, and you look like death warmed over. What do you think?"

"I think you should take care of this end and mind your own business," Dan growled, immediately sorry for his gruffness with this trusted and loyal friend.

"Uh-huh! Really testy, aren't we, boy?" Lane replied, not at all offended. "Seems to me that you'd also be a might easier to get along with if you'd spend more time at the house talkin' to someone besides that Bay horse of yours. If I didn't know better, I'd say you were pinin' for that big, ugly Blue horse of yours!" He ended this last with a chuckle.

"Aww, I'm sorry, old timer. I didn't mean to bite your head off. I'm just tired and on edge these days. And Bay isn't the best of company. He doesn't even mutter at me for the long hours!" He smiled at the foreman with this last, and turned towards the bunkhouse.

"Now just you wait a minute, Dan Kase!" Lane spoke, "I'm not done yet! I'm dead serious about you cuttin' back on your hours out there. You can't avoid Miss Allie forever, so why try?"

Dan turned a pastey white color as the blood drained from his face with that last sally, and turned on his heel to look into the kindly, steel-blue eyes of the old Texan.

His voice was barely above a whisper when he spoke. "What do you mean by that, Lane? Don't tell me it shows that much, old friend! Please tell me it doesn't show that much!"

"Dan. How can I tell you that without lyin' to you? It shows every time you look at the house with that moon-eyed look on your face. And every time you leave this bunkhouse, you look at the house, so that means that look shows up all the time, even in the dark! Why don't you just go up to that girl and tell her how you feel? My word, man, you ain't the first feller to fall in love! The fact that you and I are here shouts out that fact, loud and clear!"

"You don't understand, old timer. I can't be telling an honest, noble girl like Allison that, for I sense that she feels the same way about me! It's a plain and simple fact that I've got to ride out of here as soon as this trouble is cleared up, and I can't be misleading her to think otherwise!"

With that impassioned outcry done, he sat down on a nearby bench and hung his head in morose, desperate fashion, cradling it in his hands. He remained there as the foreman sat down at his side and placed a gnarled, rope-worn , but kindly and gentle hand on his shoulder.

Lane's voice was soft and filled with compassion as he spoke, "Son, don't forget that I know your story. Remember, it was me that delivered that mare to your friend in Arizona. And just remember, too, that I know just how far it is from here to there! There's some of the most rugged mountains in the west 'tween here and there, and literally hundreds of miles of them, at that. Why, son, I don't see how in the world anyone from down there would ever wander in here that knew about you!

"'Sides that, it's been at least five years since that happened, and I'm sure they've given up on findin' you by now. There's no doubt in my mind that you and Allie could settle down here abouts and never have a worry.

"I think you should just come clean to her and let her decide for herself! Now, what do you say?"

Dan groaned from beneath his hands, "No, Lane, no, no. Those were lawmen that I shot down. They never stop looking for killers of lawmen! I just can't do it to her, I've got to leave as soon as this is over!"

"Well, son, you've got to do what you think is best for all concerned, but I think you're wrong. But whatever comes, you know I'm with you all the way. I like you young fellers. A finer lot never forked a saddle, and if this turns out right, I'd be proud to be numbered as one of you when you ride away, for I know you can't leave without those other three going too.

"But for now, I'm still your boss, and I'm tellin' you that I aim to spell you during the times that I mentioned. Startin' tomorrow, you ride in here mid-mornin', and I'll ride out when I see you comin'. Then I'll ride in after a couple of hours. I mean for you to rest during those times while you're in here, savvy?"

Dan looked up, smiled a weak smile in the lantern light, and merely nodded. He knew his friend was right. He was near exhaustion and needed the rest. How he would avoid Allison, he didn't know, but he must try.

The two arose and headed for the bunkhouse, where Dan ate his cold meal and turned in, only to sleep the fitful sleep of one who lacks inner peace and assurance of things to come. Lonely, indeed, are the hunted.

TWENTY-THREE

Some thirty miles to the west at Twin Forks Ranch there was a summit meeting of sorts in session that evening. The sun had barely slipped behind the mountains that stood as sentinels over the ranch before five riders arrived to tie their horses to the hitch rail in front of the house.

Twin Forks was a bachelor's spread, that was obvious. The house itself stood among several oak trees and had been constructed of the same when the original owner established the place. It was a long, low structure perched on the side of a knoll with the trees in close around it on all sides but the front. That area of the house sported a high porch that stretched the full length of the building, with the floor of the porch being about even with an average horses back. The steps leading up to it were well worn and many. The original house had been added to, with a roofed breezeway connecting the two halves. This had been the route chosen to provide sleeping quarters for hired hands when they became a necessity for the previous owner.

The section to the right of the steps provided housing for the owner, with the hands living in the left-hand section. Cooking facilities were housed in a building immediately behind the main structure. The barns and associated storage buildings were to the north side of the main house, to one's right as they approached the ranch from the front.

The visitors clomped the stairs to the porch, to be greeted

by a bulky looking man with permanently angry features on his pouchy, unshaven face. He was a large man with the left sleeve of his shirt pinned up, for there was no arm or shoulder to fill it. No one in the territory knew for sure how Jude Chesterson had lost his arm and shoulder, but rumors among the men of questionable reputations claimed it was the result of a shotgun blast from close range. No one possessed the courage to ask, for the man was mean to the bone, and loved to prove it. He greeted his guests, however, with the cordiality of a southern gentleman.

"Lieutenant Leeds, Senator Fordman, I'm so glad to see you! And I would assume these three gentlemen are the interested parties you wrote me of?" he said in his deep, bullish voice.

Leeds spoke first, "Yes, Jude, this is my procurement officer and immediate superior, Captain Thanes, and these two men are Mister John Sadler and Mister Joseph Williams, both of the Idaho and Montana railroad. Gentlemen, Mister Jude Chesterson."

The group exchanged pleasantries, then Chesterson motioned them to chairs on the spacious porch. He had prepared for them ahead of time, for a table holding a bottle of whiskey and several glasses enjoyed the center spot in the circle of chairs.

Leeds, apparently the leader of the group, then took charge. "Gentlemen, I felt it essential that we all meet together like this, so that there is no question in any of our minds as to just how far we intend to go or how deeply we must be committed to each other in order to achieve our goals. This venture will either make us all very, very rich, or it will get us all hung! I don't need to tell you how uncomfortable that can be!"

They all laughed at his mundane joke, and Sadler spoke up, "I want to know first-hand just how you intend to make this rather ambitious project work. How five men can come into possession of an entire valley the size of this one is beyond me, even if it is done outside the law."

"Mister Sadler," Chesterson spoke up, "If you'll excuse my bluntness, that is none of your concern. Just know that it is outside the law, and that how far outside depends on the resistance I run into. What we need to know, is just how you and your friend there can swing the railroad through Crosstown, and if it's a sure thing."

"Sir, I assure you, even if we don't get the owners to 'swing through Crosstown, from what we've seen of this valley, mere ownership of such a rich area would set us all up for life without the railroad. However, I've had some meetings with the board of directors, and we both feel that it's a matter of a vote to make it official, and the deal is secured. Wouldn't you say so, Joseph?"

Williams merely nodded, and continued a close scrutiny of his companions, as one might expect a suspicious individual would do.

Fordman spoke out next, "I would like to know for myself how you intend to get the ranch over east of here, Jude. It seems as though they aren't about to be frightened off, no matter what."

"Well, Leeds here, and the good Captain, made a big contribution to the effort by forcing that Sheriff Haynes to hold those horses until a court settlement can be made. That'll keep money out of McCord's pocket for some time, and in the meantime, we'll get a little rougher.

"If you can push a little of your influence down onto the judge in that case, it'll help, sir. Meanwhile, my man Croft is going to get into that ranch with a couple of men within the next couple of days to grab that daughter of theirs that they dote on so much. I told him to get a move on while the three men are still in Dry Springs, cause they're really short handed now. Then, as soon as they have the girl, we'll make an all-out raid on the horses left, and push them through the same pass that the railroad intends to use on its way to the west side of the mountains. I have a buyer waiting over there that doesn't care where he gets his stock from. I figure that'll break their backs and force them to sell out just to get the girl back."

"So then you'd return the girl, buy them out, and we're in, huh?" Williams asked. "What about the rest of the ranchers in the valley?"

"First, I don't care what Croft does with the girl after they sell, and second, once the rest of the valley sees McCord buckle under, they'll gladly clear out, for he's their leader, and they won't have the gumption to fight with him out of the picture."

"You sound pretty sure of yourself when you speak of raiding him," Thanes inserted.

"Ha! They only have three hands and the women left over there. Old Harvey's scared the rest of them off. With those other three tied up in Dry Springs, they're already whipped."

The talk drifted on to other strategies and subjects, and lasted long into the night. As the men drank and talked, the ranch seemed void of other activity, for the gunhands had retired, not having any dreams of riches of their own to keep them up. There was, however, a silent stirring beneath the porch directly below the meeting. A silent form in warpaint and leather britches, naked to the waist, slipped to the south end of the structure and made its exit in the same manner it had arrived the night before this. Red Elk had seen the preparations being made for visitors, what with the general sprucing up and all, and had decided to get as near as possible. He had taken jerky and canteen, and spent the last twenty-four hours beneath the porch. His duty now was to make his way to the grove that hid that big blue tornado and fly to McCords' with warning and incriminating evidence.

It had been a long day, but a very profitable one!

Three days later, as Dan Kade kept his vigil from the high knoll, he picked out a fast- moving, riderless horse approaching the ranch from the west. It moved rapidly, and would arrive before he could get there, so he fired three shots from his rifle, as instructed by Lane, to warn of the approach. He then tightened his cinch and made a flying mount onto Bay to get there as quickly as possible.

When he thundered into the yard, he experienced a shock. The horse was Blue, all lathered with foamy sweat, and no rider! Lane and Allison were looking the big horse over in dismay, for tha saddle was covered with dark stains that marked the cantle and fenders on the right side, running down to the stirrup in two lines. Someone had been severely wounded in that saddle, and that someone had to be Reddy! It looked very bleak, indeed.

Wordlessly, Dan peeled the gear from the big horse and began to rub him down. Then he looked at the weeping Allie and issued gentle instructions, "Please get me two days' worth of grub ready for the trail, bandages, and whatever else you think of to treat a badly wounded man. Lane, hurry and bring me some oats and shelled corn for this big ox, he's going to need refreshing before we leave!"

"But Dan, you can't ride Blue out there, he's run out!" Allie cried.

"I don't intend to ride him, I'll ride Bay, and lead another horse to haul Reddy with. Blue will take me to him."

"You really think he will?" Lane asked.

"Let's put it this way, if he doesn't, what chance does Reddy have?"

"I get you, pard, come on, Allie, let's get a move on!"

An hour later, a distraught group of four gathered around the big horse and weighed their chances of ever seeing the lovable wrangler alive. Then Dan hugged Allison and her mother, shook Lane's hand in misery, and mounted. He rode out at a slow gallop that his horses were noted for, a speed that ate up the miles, and that both Blue and Bay could keep up for days on end.

It had been midmorning when Blue came into the ranch, it was two hours before dusk when he came to a nervous stop at the edge of a thorn thicket. Dan surveyed the area carefully for signs of hostile riders, then began to carefully search for signs of his pardner. Blue tossed his head and fidgeted around by some shale rocks at the thicket's heaviest part, and upon closer investigation, Dan found slight traces of bloodstains. Reddy!

Still cautious, he refrained from calling out to his friend, and searched silently through the heavy brush for further sign. He had nearly given up and was about to call out when he caught his shoulder on a thorn and tore his shirt. The wicked point pierced his skin and he involuntarily jerked free. As he did, his eye caught sight of a couple of buckskin fringes showing out from under a particularly thick section! He quickly tore away the brush, unmindful of the tearing of his skin by the brutal thorns, and uncovered a bloody and pale body. It was what was left of the Comanche warrior, Red Elk.

Dan immediately checked for heartbeat, and found it to be present, but so weak that Reddy surely would have died in a short time. He began to check for the source of blood, and found a wicked looking hole in the Indian's back, through the right shoulder blade and low enough to have possibly hit the lung. It was swollen and an ugly red splotch surrounded it, for infection had set in.

He set about cleaning the wound as best he could, then applied first, whiskey, to sanitize it, then a poultice of Reddy's own making that he carried at all times, finally binding it tightly.

It was all he could do to get the unconscious body out of the thicket, and he was exhausted after he did so. After taking time to catch his breath, he began to weigh the different ways he had to get Reddy to help. He finally decided on a travois, and while searching for suitable limbs to use for it, he reflected on his best plan of action for the possible survival of his patient. As he tied the travois up to the extra horse he'd brought along, it was obvious that Crosstown was the best course of action. Not only was it probably closer, but a doctor was an absolute necessity if Reddy were to be pulled through.

It was after midnight when the weary little entourage struggled into town and pulled to a grateful stop in front of Doc Simm's house that night. Dan fairly beat the door down before the kindly face of Grace Simm peeked out through the open door to see what the latest emergency was. When you were the only medical aid within hundreds of miles, you learned to take the midnight interruptions in stride, and the good doctor was already in his office preparing a bed for his latest patient, whoever that might be.

TWENTY-FOUR

Four hours later and a hundred miles to the east, while Doctor, wife, patient, and friend slept the sleep of exhaustion, the early morning train puffed and clattered into Dry Springs, Idaho. It was met by the local sheriff, three riders, and a circuit judge. As the cars ground to a stop, five sleepy looking and travel-worn men in range garb descended the steps and limped wearily to the greeting party. The leader of the new arrivals, a tall, slender man nearing sixty beamed with pleasure and hugged the leader of the other party of men.

"Paul, it's great to see you again, even under these circumstances!"

"Ira, I didn't expect you to come! But I'm sure glad you did!" Paul McCord replied. "Let me introduce you to these fellows. Men, this is one of the finest gentlemen you'll ever meet, and a man to stand beside you in a fight or anywhere else. Meet my brother-in-law, Ira Nelson from Arizona!"

As they shook hands, the other introductions were cared for, and Joe, Bear, Sheriff Haynes and Judge Morgan met with Bud Holley, Vern Hanks, and the Kade brothers, Art and Martin.

At the introduction to the Kades, Bear Rollins paled, and asked, "You say your names are Kade? And you're from Arizona? Wal, it ain't much of a chance, but … "

His voice trailed off as he looked over the others' shoulders at the beautiful mare that had just descended from the rail car, and he paled further.

An involuntary exclamation of "Sheba!" bounded from his lips, causing the mare to stop and raise her head. She whinnied loudly at the recognition of old friends, and pulled free of her handler to gallop to the group of men, going first to Bear, then to Joe as she nickered low with pleasure while prancing around them.

The handler came running to apologize to Nelson, but he laughed and sent the hapless worker on his way with a slap on the back and a "That's just fine, son, she's fine!"

Joe and Bear looked at each other with dismay. They had inadvertently given themselves away as far as Sheba was concerned, and now careful explanations would be necessary! But Ira saved them with a quick assessment of the situation.

"You men know this mare? And you recognized the name Kade? And not only that, but this mare knows you well enough to be glad to see you! Quickly, men, where is the man that had this mare when you saw her?!"

Before the two could gather their wits about them, Paul McCord stepped in. "Great scott! I see it now! The Dan Kade that you folks were looking for from down in Arizona has been on my ranch helping us out of this jam for weeks, and we didn't even know it! Dan Kase is Dan Kade!"

He then saw the dismay on the faces of Dan's two friends, and saved them from it immediately. "Joe! Bear! Dan isn't guilty of anything illegal! He was found innocent back there, for the two that he shot were outlawed when he shot them. In fact, the one that lived was sent to prison for life for murder and extortion! Our friend is not an outlaw, if you're concerned about that, he's a free man!"

The two stood in stunned silence for what seemed like eternity, until Ira Nelson broke it with a gentle voice choked with emotion, "Boys, where is that fine young man? I, and his brothers here, want to see him as soon as possible."

"He's holdin' down the fort back yonder, an' a fine job of it, too, sir," was Rollins' quiet reply. "But we don't know how much longer they can hold out, fer thar's only three men thar, 'n the two ladies."

Haynes butted in at this juncture. "These fellows have had to remain here for legal action on a matter involving the Army, but I've talked Judge Morgan, here, into stopping all action until the matter back in Crosstown is solved to everyone's satisfaction. He's also arranged a temporary appointment for me as Federal Marshall again to take care of things there in a legal and final manner.

"I would suggest that we get some food inside of ourselves and the horses and get going as quickly as possible. Our horses and packs are ready and waiting down at the livery. I also have the Army's Adjutant General and ten troopers ready to ride with us, for we suspect crooked dealings from his procurement officer and his aid. So, if you're ready, follow me."

TWENTY-FIVE

Dan had sent a youngster out to the ranch with word of his and Reddy's whereabouts, as well as the situation. He then fell into a deep sleep that threatened to last for days. It wasn't to be, however, for a short time later the good doctor's wife awakened him.

"Dan, wake up, your friend was conscious for a couple of minutes, and kept muttering the same thing over and over. He kept saying, 'Croft, Allie, raid', over and over, then he passed out again. I fear that it spells bad news for the folks at home!"

Dan was up instantly. "You're absolutely right, Mrs. Simm! I've got to head out there! Thanks for what you're doing for Reddy, I'll be back as soon as I can!"

Within a short time he was on Blue and on his way, leading Bay and the other horse. When he was but five miles from the ranch he met the young man he'd dispatched with the message. He was obviously quite frightened as he flagged Dan down.

"Mister Kase! They've got real trouble back there! Some men came and stole Miss Allie and shot Mister Glover!"

Dan tossed the lead rope over Bay's head and put the spurs to Blue all in one motion, not bothering to answer the lad. He knew the faithful Bay would follow as fast as he could, but was no match for the roan. The big horse leaped out with a mighty stride and in two jumps was at his incredible full speed. Those huge muscles never slacked off until he plunged to a halt in front of the house. Dan was off and running before Blue was completely stopped.

He slammed through the front door to pull up to an immediate stop, for he was facing the barrel of a Winchester. Behind it were the tearstained eyes of Ida McCord. When she saw who it was she dropped the piece to the floor and ran sobbing into his arms. He held her for a few moments, then she collected herself and drew back.

"Oh Dan, they have Allie! They came at us from both sides, and shot Lane as soon as they saw him! He's okay, it was just a nick, but he had sense enough to play possum until they left, then he went out to trail them.

"He said to tell you he'd mark the trail plainly so you could make good time."

Dan wheeled without a word and ran to the agitated Blue. He was still ready to run. As he whirled Blue around, Ida shouted to him, "They turned east out of the lane, Dan, towards the trail to Dry Springs, from the looks of it!"

In the turmoil of his mind, he gave thanks for a distraught mother who was still smart enough to observe which way the thugs had gone. It may not have saved that much time, but it was something, anyway.

Dan knew that Lane would follow at a distance, biding his time unless he sensed that Allie was in immediate danger, so after a few miles he pulled Blue down to a ground-eating pace that no other horse would stay ahead of for long. He knew the big horse could do this for days without stopping, so his mind began to relax and plan a strategy for the next step.

It was midmorning the next day, after riding half the night, that he saw the tracks of a large group of riders heading west. He also saw that Lane's tracks interspersed with them for a bit, then his and five other sets left the main body and proceeded east again. If Lane had met Paul and the others, he could understand, but these were many more tracks than that. Well, help was help, so take it when you can, he thought to himself.

He trailed those tracks for the rest of the afternoon, gaining ground all the time, for Lane was doing a good job of marking trail for him. It was growing dusk when he found the graves.

The area was in a cluster of large rocks just at the edge of the foothills of the mountain range, and showed signs of a lengthy skirmish. He found the three fresh graves at the edge of the battleground, all unmarked. After close examination he stepped around a large boulder to stop dead still with a startled gasp. Here was a fourth body, but it swayed at the end of a rope!

He approached gingerly to investigate, and found the corpse to be that of the mean- looking redheaded fellow who had been in on the previous attempt to take Allie; the one who had shot his own kind while they lay helpless. A just ending, Dan mused to himself.

With the question of what had happened and who the other dead were on his mind, he rode out, still following Lane's markings. He was forced to stop before he wanted to, for it had clouded over, and those markings were now impossible to see. He reluctantly made camp and mechanically ate from the supplies in his saddle bags. Sleep came easily, for his body was trail weary and bone tired.

As the first sign of dawn blinked and stretched its rested arms to the sky, the big blue horse snorted and pulled at the reins in his master's hands with the desire to greet the trail at top speed. Dan allowed him a short run to appease him, then hauled him in, for it looked to be a long day.They were an hour into the foothills when they topped a rise that capped a twisting, narrow valley. Their position was well above most of the surrounding territory, and Dan could see over the next ridge into the wooded area beyond. As he scanned the section, a movement caught his eye to the left, and he quickly threw the field glasses up to check closer. The distance was too great for identification, but he could make out two riders moving northwest at a very fast run. As he scanned to the right he spotted a group of riders emerging from a stand of trees at the foot of a steep mountainside. They appeared to be in pursuit of the original pair of riders.

Moving back to the left, he tried to judge just where the two would cross over the far ridge into the valley beneath him. He was about to drop the glasses when he thought he sensed movement to the north of the two, but never verified it. If someone was there, it meant the first two were hemmed in, and would have no choice but to continue in their present direction.

Dan's decision was easy. He was sure that the two riders were Croft and Allie, just because of the circumstances involved, and he had a chance of intercepting them if he acted quickly enough. Blue got his wish to stretch it out, and was soon plunging down the hillside into the valley at a break-neck pace. By Dan's estimation, he should reach them in fifteen minutes or less. He set his teeth in a grimly determined manner and pulled his Henry from its scabbard, levering a round into the chamber as he did so.

Blue was still at a full gallop up the valley when he saw the two break into it from a little gulley just a quarter mile ahead, both of their horses also at top speed. Dan could not help but notice the wonderful run of the horse beneath Allison, and sustained a numbing shock when he recognized her - it was SHE-BA! How this could be tore through his mind like a saw, yet it was unmistakably true! And he saw that Croft rode one of the Twin Forks' best; a long, rangy black that was noted for his speed and endurance. His heart dropped as he realized that the race his friend Bear had spoken of between Sheba and Blue was now on, and Allison's life depended on the outcome. Could he deliberately ride Sheba into the ground? Or Blue? He had little doubt that the big roan could take any horse alive in both endurance and speed, but he didn't know how long Sheba and the black had been at it, and Blue had started at a fast pace several hours ago.

For some uncanny reason Harvey chose that moment to look over his shoulder, and he spurred the black viciously as he cut Sheba with his quirt, urging the two to even more speed. They rounded a bend out of sight for a moment, and then, just as he followed suit, the crack of a rifle spat its proclamation of death into the air. The black pitched headlong into the creek beside it, flinging the rider far ahead. Sheba leaped sideways to avoid the falling mount and veered off to the right, slowing to a stop beneath some cottonwoods.

Croft rolled over several times and came to his feet in an amazing display of agility. He came up shooting at Dan, the first foe in sight, but after Dan's first shot missed, Harvey jerked spasmodically with the impact of the hidden rifleman's second bullet.

He had the tenacity of life to slip behind a tree that shielded him from the rifle's deadly aim, but by then Dan had dropped to the ground and leveled his Colt at the gunman.

"I won't miss again, Harv'! You better give it up while you can, for I won't stop myself this time!"

For the second time in his life, Harvey Croft found himself looking at the barrel of Dan Kade's gun, and for the second time, he hadn't the nerve to continue. He slid down the trunk of the tree that supported him and rolled over with a painful groan.

Dan carefully slipped up and searched him for a hidden weapon, then stepped back to look for his unknown benefactor with the rifle. He sustained another shock, for there under the trees, helping Allison from Sheba's back, was Ira Nelson! It was all he could do to stand, his heart beat so wildly. What on earth could this mean?

He walked on rubbery legs to where the old rancher was holding the sobbing Allie closely, and stood waiting until she gathered herself together and stepped back to look up at Ira.

"Uncle! I--I don't understand what you're doing here, but I'm so glad to see anyone who would stop that crazy man!"

Dan looked dumbfoundedly from one to the other, trying to make some sort of sense out of it all. Allison suddenly seemed to realize that Dan was there and turned to throw her arms around him and held on as though her very life depended on it. He finally found his voice and admonished her gently as he extracted himself from her arms.

"Allie. I, uh, I need desperately to tell you something. You have to listen carefully to me!" he choked out in a hoarse voice. He knew that Ira would tell her if he didn't, and felt the need to do so on his own.

"Allie, dear Allie," he choked, "you need to know who I am, and you need to realize that we can never be together because of it! My real name is Dan Kade, and I'm wanted for the murder of two lawmen back in Arizona! I wanted with everything in me to tell you before, but I just couldn't!"

Allison looked up at him, and did something totally out of character for her. She fainted dead away and fell to the ground!

Dan was able to partially catch her and lower her gently.

Ira went to the stream and wet his neckerchief, returning to wash her face and revive her slowly. He looked up at Dan and smiled his knowing smile, saying, "She'll have something to tell you that just may do the same for you in a minute, and I think I'll let her do the telling, rather than do it myself."

Dan's confused thoughts filed that away as something to learn later, but Allie sat up at that moment.

She cried out, "I"m sorry, but when you said Kade, I - I just lost myself. Dan, oh Dan, listen to me! You aren't wanted at all! You're innocent! Dan, do you hear me!"

He looked to Ira, quite sure the girl had lost her senses, and the old rancher just smiled and nodded. Then he explained softly to the reeling "outlaw."

"She's right, son. The day you shot the Chelseas, they had just been fired, and arrested for murder. At least, that was our intention. I had a wire appointing me temporary marshall for the region, just like our friend Haynes has now, but made the mistake of telling them before someone put a gun on them. When you came up, they'd just held a gun to Doc Pritchard's head and emptied all our pockets and holsters. When they stepped out of the saloon door, all we heard was that Greener go off twice and Jules came flying back in through the window, his left arm shot clean off, and his shoulder with it! There wasn't anything left of Max between his neck and belt, so they just sorta poured him in a box and buried what was left.

"Jules lived, was found guilty of two murders, and was sentenced to life. Folks 'round there were mighty upset that he wasn't hung, and were even more upset when he escaped a year later. He'd spent several months in a prison hospital, and while they were transporting him from there to Yuma, a band of renegade Indians lead by a couple of white men attacked the Deputies, killing all but three. One of the three lived long enough to tell that Jules himself shot the remaining three in cold blood, laughing at them as he did. He's never been found, but if he is, it's the rope for him for sure this time.

"Do you understand what I've just told you, Son? You're a free man!"

Dan just nodded, being totally in a fog at this point. He now clung to Allie as though she might run away, the sobs of relief slowly building in him until he could no longer contain them. After several minutes, as he collected his emotions, riders were heard approaching at a dead run.

The group thundered around the bend and nearly ran them over before stopping. Joe saw Allie and let out a whoop of joy. Dan saw Bear, Lane, and three others dismount and hurry to them. His emotions took another leap as he recognized Art and Martin.

They walked almost bashfully to him, then attacked him in brotherly fashion.

Art fairly shook his teeth out as he shouted at him, "Doggone your hide, little brother, we done nearly froze to death, went hungry for weeks, got skeeter-bit, saddle-sore, and whatever other tragedy you can think of hunting you, and here we find you by accident! I'd break your head if I didn't think Mother would do worse to mine!"

Dan looked incredulously at Art, then staggered to a fallen tree and sat down. He looked up at Allison imploringly, and spread his hands as though begging for the truth.

"Tell me - tell me what he means by that," he spoke, barely above a whisper, "What did he mean about Mother? I saw the Chelseas' burn her and Dad with the house!"

This last came out in an anguished cry for help. It was Ira that intervened, laying a gentle hand on the stricken man's shoulder.

"Son, this is sure more than most hearts could take at one time, but your folks are alive and well. Your Dad came to in time to drag your Mom down into the root cellar. Other than some lung infection, scrapes and bruises, and some minor burns from part of the floor dropping around them, they were fine.

"They were sure you were the one dead until that telegram came telling me to expect Sheba on the train! They've never stopped praying for your safe return, Son, and now they'll see those prayers answered."

Allison drew Dan to his feet and led him away by the arm. She knew the most important thing for him just now was to have

time to gather his thoughts and emotions, and that required solitude. The two of them walked silently for the remaining daylight
hours, finally drawing back to the camp the others had set up.
Dan was to spend yet another sleepless night, but this one out of
sheer wonder at what had just transpired in his life. He was no
longer hunted, and need never be lonely again.

TWENTY-SIX

Two days later a bedraggled looking entourage straggled into Crosstown. Harvey Croft was borne in a litter slung between two horses, his feverish body bound tight with bandages around the chest wound. Ira led the horses, riding behind Dan, Allie, and Lane. The two other Kade brothers rode with Bear and Joe, while the grieving Bud Holley brought up the rear.

Bud Raymond Holley and Vern Hanks had been the closest of friends, and he had seen his friend cut down without warning by the redheaded horse thief. The band had ridden into the kidnapper's camp unknowingly, and before anyone even realized they were there, the outlaw had stood up and calmly shot Vern from the saddle. In the ensuing battle two of the outlaws were killed, one by ricocheting bullets, and the redhead wounded. When Ira told Dan the story he said that "Bullets were flying off those rocks in so many different directions that you didn't even bother to think about ducking!"

Croft had dragged Allison off just before they had ridden in, for no good intent, for sure, and when the shooting started, he held a gun to her head and slipped around to the horses. Sheba had been near, so he grabbed her and forced Allie on her back and the chase was on.

When the smoke cleared, there was no way Ira could have kept Bud from starting the hanging. The little wrangler simply grabbed a rope and tossed it around the unfortunate desperado's neck. He wasn't alone long, for the rest grabbed hold and hauled Red up, tied the rope off, and watched the agonizing and desperate kicking of the outlaw as he strangled to death. Sometimes justice is harsh, sometimes it's cruel, but this western type of justice was always barbaric and hard for Ira to take, so he'd gone off to the horses, and there made the discovery that both Allie and Sheba were gone. That's when the chase had started.

When the riders pulled up in front of Doc Simm's house, they drew a crowd of curious people wanting to know the goings on. Dan had explained Red Elk's condition to them, so he, Joe, Bear, and Allie were through the good Doctor's door before the horses were even near a full stop. Grace Simm met them with a startled look at the intrusion, then with a nod of assurance as Doc appeared from Reddy's room in the back.

"His fever broke this morning around three, but he isn't out of danger yet," he told them, before any one of them could even ask, "But it sure looks better than I would have thought when I first saw him!"

"Can we see him?" Allison asked.

"Absolutely not," Doc answered, "He's talked too much as it is. I can tell you everything he told me, but I'd suggest a lawman be present. It isn't pretty."

"Have you seen Sheriff Haynes or the Army in town?" Ira asked.

"Yesterday there were some Cavalry here, a couple of them asking about Twin Forks ranch, as I hear it. But I've seen no one today."

"Then I want you to tell me, in front of these people, just what this man told you, and I'll take the responsibilty for the information getting to the right folks," Ira told him.

"Well, have it your way, sir. He told me he'd been assigned to watch the Twin Forks place for suspicious activity. He saw what appeared to be a big meeting shaping up, so he made his way in that night and spent the next entire day under the porch, waiting to try and hear what was going on!

"These Indians, I swear! They've got the patience of Job and then some! Anyhow, two Army officers, a politician, and two railroad men showed up. I wrote their names down as he told me this. They showed up and talked of kidnapping Miss Allison and a raid on the McCord ranch in order to get them to sell. It seems their game is to get the entire valley for ranching and to resell in case these railroad men can persuade the road to build this far. It all sounds pretty far fetched to me, but someone shot a man in the back over it!"

He stopped, and looked from one to the other, as though expecting questions. Dan looked at Ira, and said, "I think we need to find Haynes and the General, and soon!"

Ira nodded, and told Allison to stay with the Simms' to help with Reddy. They all knew, Allison included, that he really meant it for her own protection. Then they whirled to leave, comimg up short as Doc Simm spoke up.

"Say! I almost forgot! Your friend in there also heard them plan a meeting with a couple of big-wigs from the railroad and a congressman on the twenty first, that's today. They were going to try to give them the hard-sell on the road extending this far based on their owning the valley and guaranteeing the railroad a profit."

They looked at one another with a grim resolve that meant a meeting held that day would have a far different outcome than that which was planned. In a moment, horses were flashing out of town in the direction of the McCord ranch.

As they left town, wagon tracks were an obvious witness to the fact that the guests were more than likely already on their way to Twin Forks. Dan called a halt to his men.

"Joe! I want you to fog it to the ranch and bring Haynes and the Army to Twin Forks as fast as you can! We're gonna break up that little party if we have to, so don't take no for an answer from the General!"

Without another moment's hesitation Joe wheeled his mount and was off, with the rest turning to follow the wagon's dusty route of passage. It was a grimly determined bunch of riders that descended on Twin Forks a couple of hours later.

For whatever reason, the men automatically looked to Dan as leader at that moment, including Ira. Dan looked across the river at the ranch house and barns for a few minutes to get the layout in his mind, then made his assignments.

"I don't see a bunkhouse anywhere, so everyone must stay in the main house. Art, you and Martin go on down river a ways and cross there, then make your way to the south end of that house. One of you watch the back, the other take the front.

"Bear and Bud, go back upstream and do the same for the other part of the house. Lane, you spread out a ways to my right there, and Ira to my left.

"Once you other four are in place, we'll ride in and confront them with the facts. And be sharp, fellows."

Ira added quickly, "Careful too, men. I lost a wonderful boy the other day in Vern, a good friend who deserved much better. Remember that we're dealing with backshooters and women stealers here, so don't be queasy about dropping a man if you're in doubt!

"And Dan, how about giving me that shotgun of your's for now, this old man isn't as quick as he used to be!"

Dan smiled at that, and as the others rode off, he slid the Greener from the sheath and handed it over. Then he pulled more shells for the wheeless cannon from his saddlebags and offered them to him. The old rancher shook his head and patted his Colt.

"If it comes to more than two of these, I'll not have time for that. I'll just have to try and remember how to be fast again."

Dan had to smile at the seasoned warrior's sage humor in a situation like their's. He looked at Lane's smiling face and realized he was with experienced and reliable men for such times as these.

They looked for the others, and saw they were in place. Dan nodded grimly, and they put their horses to the river's shallow crossing, coming straight in to the front of the house. There was a two-seated wagon parked off to one side, and the meeting appeared to be taking place, once again, on the rambling front porch.

The men occupying the porch had long been watching the group as they dispersed to their respective assignments, and a thick cloud of anxiety surrounded the guests, for they had just been warned that this was an outlaw rancher from across the valley.

Jude Chesterson arose and moved to the top of the steps, staring down the mounted horsemen. With the height of the porch, they were nearly even with each other. Leeds and Captain Thanes drifted off to the side and loosed the flaps on the Army issue holsters at their sides.

"I don't know what your intentions are in coming here, but I'm warning you, these men are very important men, and any outlawry on your part will result in very serious consequences," Chesterson said.

"Not half as serious as the consequences you're going to face, Mister," Dan answered, and was about to lay the accusations down when Ira interrupted.

"Excuse me, Dan! You, sir, wouldn't you be Governor Stark?"

That individual jerked with a start and replied, "Why, yes I am, but how would you happen to know me, sir?" He was plainly agitated and nervous over the situation he had found himself in.

"I met you at a good friend's house several times over the last few years, Governor. We've talked of horses, Indians, and the state of Arizona with him many times. He happens to be the governor of that fine state."

"Oh yes, now I think I'm beginning to recognize you, you're.."

But Ira cut him off with, "You'd know me quicker without this week's worth of beard, Governor, but never mind that, I have a story to tell you that's rather incredible, if I may share it now?

"You see, I had intended to allow this young man here, Dan, to explain the situation to you, but I see that I know something more about this than he does.

"This man here, with whom these others have been scheming, is not to be trusted. How he purchased this fine ranch, I'll never know, but this I do know. Leeds, there, and his Captain are crooked, skimming money from the payments for Cavalry horses when possible. Oh, I don't have proof of that, but it's become plain as can be. You see, Chesterson, here, has tried to terrorize the local ranchers into selling to him. And these two men over there, with the railroad, have been supplying the backing, because they want to persuade the railroad to build through this valley. If they can do that, they stand to make a goodly profit from their own company!

"They even stooped so low as to kidnap my niece and steal her father's horses to force sale of their ranch, so you're dealing with a really bad bunch of vermin here, sir."

Jude Chesterson shook with rage as he challenged the old man, "You babble like some kind of idiot! You ride in here with no proof of anything with some crazy, made up story, and expect to discredit two fine businessmen, two respected Army officers, an honest rancher that you people have been trying to steal from, and you expect an intelligent man like Governor Starks to swallow it! Get out of here, rustlers! Twin Forks men, get out here, pronto!"

During this tirade, Leeds and Thanes had drifted purposefully further apart to get the men in front of them in more of a crossfire, but were unaware of Bear and Bud behind them. They also forgot to reckon with the old fox, Lane Glover, and his experience at this sort of stand off, for he slipped the hammer back on his rifle with a nearly silent click and picked Leeds as his first target, for Thanes was closer to Bear.

When no riders showed from the south section of the house, Chesterson bellowed out once again, only to receive the reply, "Boss, we cain't go nowhere, some hombre has a Winchester layin' 'crossed the windersill, an' he looks as though he's daid serious!"

Ira said to Dan quietly, "Son. I'm gonna open this ball up real soon, you be ready for anything." And to the governor he added, "Sir, I suggest you do two things. One, get down on the floor, and two, listen closely, for I'm about to back up my claims.

"First off, we have a rider back in Crosstown that overheard these men planning the kidnapping. He may not live, but he gave his story to the doctor there. Second, we didn't kill the leader of the kidnapping, one Harvey Croft, and he's been spilling his insides out begging for medical treatment. He'll testify, all right.

"But more important than all of that, this man that claims to be an honest rancher? See that missing arm? Well, if I were to shave, he'd sure recognize me, for I'm one of the men responsible for sending him off to prison for life! My name, sir," he went on, turning to Chesterson, "is Ira Nelson. And the man you've been trying to put down is my brother-in-law, Paul McCord."

By now Chesterson was trembling with rage, his hand shivering above the gun at his side and his face turning an ugly purple as he fought for control.

"But more important than all of that, your name isn't Jude Chesterson, it's Jules Chelsea!" Ira continued, his voice now ringing, "And this man here is Dan Kade, whose shotgun took your shoulder off down in Metsal!"

Dan went numb with a sense of shock that would have cost him his life had it not been for the old rancher's readiness. Chelsea screamed "Kade!" and pulled at his pistol, getting it nearly level before the horrible sound of a ten gauge Greener interrupted his life for the second time. He hurtled backwards against the wall of the house and sunk to the floor there, as Leeds pulled his service revolver level.

Lane Glover's loud "Hyar!" was only a split second ahead of the report of his rifle, and was followed by a scream of agony from Thanes. Leeds fell dead at the governors side from Glover's shot, and Thanes screamed again as Bear pulled a huge knife from the captain's shoulder.

"Ya shoulda knowed better'n to try thet, what with the odds like they wus," the big man admonished him. "Didn't they teach ya better'n thet in Army school?"

Horses were milling around in fright, and men were shouting at each other, and in the midst of the mayhem, Dan had a vivid picture of the mournful face of Jules Chelsea staring out at him from his place on the floor. His right arm was terribly mangled and totally useless. An ironic twist, to say the least, in the life of this ruthless individual.

As Dan stared at him, he realized that here was the man responsible for several lost years of happiness. Years that could never be replaced, and yet he couldn't help but feel sorry for him. He, Dan Kade, would start his life over again, but all that was ahead of this sorry excuse for a man was death at the gallows. And the hangman wouldn't even find hands to tie behind his back! This then, was the ironic justice to be served to the survivor who had sent Dan off into his lonely exodus.

The two old range riders had collared the play with quickness and precision, along with the big mountain man's skill with a throwing knife, but the real surprise was the two crooked railroad men. They stood very still, not moving a hair, and as the wranglers studied the two, it soon became obvious that they were held motionless by the threat of both Governor Starks and his railroad owner friend's small pistols.

When Starks saw Dan's questioning look he smiled and reminded him, "Remember son, we came out here to settle this area, and it wasn't nearly so peaceful then as now. I guess old horses like us just never got out of the habit of carrying a little insurance," and he chuckled as he ended his little speech.

Dan smiled a weak smile as he dismounted to join those who were tending to the two wounded men. Thanes was cursing Bear as he was bound up, for the big fellow was less than gentle in his doctoring, while Jules Chelsea appeared to be near tears of frustration at seeing his condition. His arm was so mangled there was no doubt that it would have to be removed, and the ribs on that side were bleeding profusely from the wounds.

Ira looked up at Dan as he approached and spoke, "He'll live to hang, Dan. It looks like your ride is over once and for all, son."

As he finished binding the wounds they heard the sound of many horses and looked across the river to see Marshall Haynes and the troopers charging through the water behind Joe. Their horses were lathered and looked as though they could drop at any time. When they pounded to a stop the general took immediate note that the situation was well in hand and ordered his troops to unsaddle and rub down their mounts. As soon as that order was given he then turned to the Governor to take care of the human end of things. Dan swelled with immediate respect for the old cavalry man, realizing that his first concern was that the men's mounts be cared for in order to maintain a readiness and to treat the animals with the respect they deserved for their efforts.

In a very short time, the circumstances were explained, the prisoners secured, and the Twin Forks men were herded out onto the front yard for questioning. Soon, the whole entourage was mounted and headed for Crosstown, with Dan driving the wagon that transported the guests and wounded. Blue followed along behind with no lead rope attached, a fact which brought no end of amusement to the governor.

During this ride, Dan had opportunity to question that individual concerning the Army contracts for the McCord ranch, and what was likely to happen to the Twin Forks spread. He arrived in town with a whole new perspective on his future. The only dark cloud remaining was the prospect that Reddy might not live out the day. That, indeed, was a very dark cloud.

TWENTY-SEVEN

Fall was busy announcing its arrival by tinting the leaves of the aspen and oak trees, declaring its superiority over summer as it did so and daring any to try and stop its march to envelope all of nature's being with the blanket of color it carried.

The McCord ranch was bustling with activity as all who were able worked feverishly to bring all the herds closer to the ranch in preparation for winter's eventual conquering of fall, much as fall was overtaking the summer. There was hay to store in strategic locations for the winter feedings, and wood to cut, and so many other chores that it seemed impossible to manage everything in time.

They were working short-handed as well, for Dan Kade had left to spend time with his parents as he and Ira returned to Metsal, and Red Elk could only set on the porch and gripe at the riders who showed what he thought to be too slow a pace. He continued this everyday until he would incur the wrath of either Rollins, Bud, who had stayed to help, or his cousin Five Ponies. Then one or the other of these worthies would calmly wheel him down to the stable, park his wheel-chair as close as possible to a manure pile, (facing it, of course,) block the wheels so it wouldn't move, and return to the tasks of the day thus leaving the hapless Reddy to stew until Allie would discover him missimg and go to his rescue. This usually subdued him for the rest of the day.

Farther south, in Arizona, Jules Chelsea lay three weeks in his grave, cold and lifeless from the hangman's rope. Justice had been swift and final this time around for the evil one.

The K-Bar-D was running normally once again, resplendant in a new coat of paint, compliments of Dan's efforts, and the Kades' were packed for a trip north to Idaho for a wedding. Dan had left three weeks previously, planning a stop over at the governor's office in Boise.

The end of this day was near, with the shadows of dusk just beginning to slip into the area. They found the Twin Forks ranch house as it unsucessfully tried to hide from them in the shade of the oaks that surrounded it. A huge beast roamed the front yard, quietly cropping grass with eager appetite, and a form of a man relaxed against one of the posts that held the porch roof up. He watched the big blue roan peacefully grazing, and smiled with affection as he noted the large ears lift from time to time as the animal stopped to search the air for danger. Habits of survival learned in the wilds never leave an intelligent being, and Blue was certainly that.

Dan Kade knew that it wouldn't be many minutes now before the mount would cease his meal as he found the scent and sound of an approaching rider. At least he hoped not. He had sent word to Allison by telegraph to meet him here on this night when he was leaving the state capital, and had ridden directly to the abandoned ranch without stopping in either Crosstown or at the McCord ranch.

It had been two months now since he had seen his bride-to-be, the last time being when he had proposed to her just before riding off towards Arizona. He hadn't even given her a ring! But that situation was soon to be remedied, for he carried in his trouser pocket the diamond he hoped would grace her finger for many decades. And he carried in his heart information calculated to astound her with his plans for their future together.

Finally, an eternity later and amidst the ever deepening shadows, the big roan snapped to attention, searching the east with eyes and nostrils alerted to an approach of strangers. A flash of brilliant red color showed briefly across the river, then the horse and rider emerged from the underbrush to disclose Flame entering the water at a mild gallop. As soon as Allie saw him, she raised a gauntleted hand in excited greeting and spurred the stallion to a run. The water fairly flew beneath the swift hooves and within seconds she was leaping from the saddle to become completely engulfed in his arms.

"Oh Dan! I've missed you so much!" she exclaimed.

He confessed the same to her, then drew her to the porch steps where he bid her set down. When she had done so, he knelt before her and said, "I didn't really do this right the last time, so I'll try and do better now. Allison McCord, will you be my wife?"

And with that, he produced the large diamond and slipped it onto her finger. She squealed with delight at the sight, then admonished him for spending money he didn't have.

"Now you just wait a minute here, young lady," he replied, "We didn't discuss finances before, so you don't really know what you're getting into.

"You probably figure you're marrying some poor puncher who's down on his luck, just like all the many suitors you've had before, right?"

"Now you look here, Dan Kade, to start with, I never had any suitors before, and being down on your luck has nothing to do with being frugal."

"Oh, so now I'm a spend-thrift! I think we need to discuss this a little further."

She put a frustrated hand on his mouth and scolded, "You stop teasing me, Mister, you know darned well what I meant!"

He laughed and took her hand in his. "OK, Sweetheart, but you do have a right to know where we start as far as money is concerned. First, there was a reward out for Chelsea, and they insisted I take it because of the years of wandering I did as a result of his crimes. That more than paid for the ring.

"Then, you forget that we partners have been wrangling wild horses for four years together, and we've saved our money to buy a spread together. Plus, I've saved in other ways as well. So, my love, we are far from destitute!"

She smiled demurely and lightly scolded him, "So, you paid for my ring with blood money, huh?" and before he could reply she went on, "And where do you plan to look for a ranch? Just how far do you plan to displace me from my folks' home, Sir Galahad?"

He laughed, enjoying the byplay immensely, and then sprung his surprise.

"Well, why don't we just settle down here on the Twin Forks spread? It's beautiful here, and we could build a little frame house over there in that little grove to the north. I think that would be very nice, don't you?"

She pushed him playfully and asked, "Seriously, Dan Kade, where are we going to live? You set a wedding date without even asking me, and we have absolutely no place to go!"

He reached into his pocket and withdrew a packet. These he spread out at their feet and lit a match so she could read the topmost sheet. It was a deed to twin Forks.

"Dan! How can this be?" she cried out, "Dad said this ranch wouldn't see an owner for years because of the courts."

"Well, he should have talked to Governor Sparks before he said that," he returned, "I did, and he pulled some strings for us. I wired the fellows for a decision, and we voted unanomously to buy. It was a great price, too. So, young bride-to-be, now what do you say?"

"I say that you're making me the happiest woman in the world, Sir Galahad!" she exclaimed. "Now if only the frame house were possible soon. Too bad we're broke now, after buying this wonderful place."

"Oh yes, the house. Well, I sorta went in debt just a little bit, and there'll be a freighter pulling in here with three wagon-loads of lumber in a couple of days. I think we can manage quite well within a few weeks.

"Come on back to the house with me Allie, it's getting too dark to see where we're stepping, and I'd like to set on the porch and just listen to the sounds of OUR ranch at night!"

As the night was thinking seriously of turning into morning, two large figures lay in the grass in front of the house, one of them much larger than the other, and both with bellies full of the rich, green grass of the Twin Forks lawn.

Two lesser figures could be just made out on the porch steps, the larger of those two reclining back against the post with the other seated beside him and leaning back against his chest with her head on his shoulder. They sat there in the rapture that only true love can produce, and they talked endlessly of their love for each other and of their plans for the future. For a surety, dawn would find them still engrossed in their conversation, and loneliness would no longer be able to find Dan and Allison Kade. They were home.

Coming in 2009 !

Read the exciting second episode in the ongoing
Rocky Mountain Odyssey adventure series:

Mountain Odyssey

Order your copy now from:

www.whitefeatherpress.com

www.amazon.com

For a signed copy, order from:

www.authorwillhinton.com

Will Riley Hinton was born and raised in the foothills of the Appalachians in southeast Ohio. He grew up on a farm with a grandfather who had made his living with horses and as a result, Will literally grew up on them. Having a mother who encouraged his active imagination along the lines of role playing and storytelling at a young age contributed greatly to his creative writing.

He was consumed by a love of horses, books, and airplanes. He served a hitch in the Navy and afterwards spent time as a part time flight instructor and crop duster. Will is married and has two grown children with five grandsons and two great grandchildren. Not surprisingly, his reading preferences are westerns and folklore.